BEYOND
CAROUSEL

Brendan Ritchie is a writer and filmmaker from Fremantle, Western Australia. In 2015 he published his Inky Award nominated debut novel, *Carousel*, and was awarded a PhD in Creative Writing. In addition to writing, Brendan spends his time lecturing across a range of creative disciplines. Find out more at www.brendanritchie.com.

Praise for *Carousel*
'This is a lively and imaginative novel about consumerism, youth, art, isolation, entrapment and survival, the sort of thing that might happen if Kafka wrote a script for *Big Brother*.' – *Sydney Morning Herald*

BEYOND CAROUSEL

BRENDAN RITCHIE

 FREMANTLE PRESS

To C

1

We've been holed up in a mansion in the hills for more than a month now.

Too scared to go back down into the suburbs. Too embarrassed to run further eastward. We spend our days bobbing about in the pool and eating mandarins from the orchard, and our nights on the balconies keeping Chess from barking while the four of us watch the strange and epic lightshows in the distant city.

The house isn't powered like Carousel. Pretty much nowhere is. But it has a line of solar panels on the roof and two summers worth of power stored in the batteries. Enough for showers, air conditioning, pool filters – anything we want. Except for lights. Never any lights.

At night we shuffle the long hallways with tiny reading lights tucked into our belts and pockets, our voices hushed and careful against the manic drone of insects outside.

Lights are an unwelcome beacon in a city full of shadow. We had been drawn to them ourselves. At night in the suburbs. Lost and lonely and desperately craving answers.

The first place was a high school. A broken pathway of fluoros led us to a wing of buildings housing workshops for art, jewellery and woodwork. Inside it was deserted and ramshackle. Furniture shifted around, rubbish on the floor. The adjoining cafeteria smashed open and decimated. Somebody had been sleeping and working in the art room by a cluster of spidery easels. All around were piles of striking yet discarded abstracts. We called out, searched the grounds, stayed there for the night and most of the next day. But nobody came.

Then there was the Chinese restaurant. Its red and yellow glow breaking through the darkness as we trudged northward to the airport. The dining area was clean. Just one table used out of the thirty or so on offer. On it were some pens, a pot of mouldy green tea and a waning stack of waiter dockets. Again, the kitchen had been emptied. All that remained were two giant sacks of rice, one labelled Nov–Dec, the other Jan–Feb. No mention of a year.

At a mini-mart we ran into the dogs. Pit bulls bred in the suburbs by pot dealers and revheads. Feral now, if they weren't before. Hammering along in silent, terrifying packs. Drawn to light and smell and anything that moved. Lizzy locked eyes with two of them at the front of the store. Not knowing any better, she was just about to kneel down and call them over when a third one came bombing out of the shadows, straight for her. She flinched and it knocked her sideways before thundering into the wall. Luckily it was dazed and Taylor and I could pull her inside before the other two arrived.

For two days we bunkered in the store while the Bulls, as Taylor called them, paced around outside. They didn't really bark, which made them creepy as hell. If you listened closely you could hear them grunt and wheeze as they ran. Otherwise it was just the scrape of their claws on concrete or the sudden smack and gurgle of dog on dog as a fight broke out and the hierarchy shifted.

Perth's missing bogans had a lot to answer for.

Eventually we left and kept moving towards the airport. It had been early morning when the Disappearance happened. It seemed like most of Perth had still been in their homes. Asleep or shuffling through bedrooms and kitchens in weekday morning stupor. We found flooded bathrooms, clothes laid out on beds, garage doors halfway open, coffee turned from black to white, then evaporated into grey sludge.

A scattering of shiftworkers and early risers had been caught outside. Their legacy was dappled across the city. From cars strewn wildly across highways and suburban streets – some gently awaiting traffic signals, others crunched into lampposts and bus stops – to sunrise bootcamp sessions where medicine balls lay suspended in shrine-like circles at parks and ovals. A rank of late-night taxis covered in bird shit like rocks blipping from a giant concrete ocean. A tradie's ute still waiting to order at a McDonald's drive-through. Kickboards drifting the sagging lanes of an outdoor pool.

It was Pompeii 2.0, sans the plaster casts.

The eastern suburbs were browned over and ticking hot with the first months of summer. We had tried to push-start a couple of cars but the batteries were too far gone and the petrol spoiled. A Corolla almost turned over with Lizzy behind the wheel. Taylor and I screamed in excitement as she rolled away from us, only to stall, hop forward, then crash into the neighbour's fence. We felt guilty and rode bikes after that.

Eventually we hit scrubland and what I hoped was the edge of the airport buffer zone. It may well have been, but the bush was swarming with the Bulls. Initially we thought we might be able to go around them. They seemed distracted, fighting over something. One of them stopped to look at us. Then another. When the third Bull turned we saw what it was on the ground beneath them. The shreds of denim. The dirty All Stars. The fleck of white and deep red.

They chased us relentlessly and would have caught us if not for the highway. It was wide and smooth and not covered in crap like the smaller roads. We geared up and it took us eastward. Eventually the Bulls dropped away. Their hulking frames turned to dots on the horizon. When the highway began an incline and trees started to appear, we realised we were headed into the hills.

'Is this where your parents live?' Lizzy had asked, carefully.

I had shaken my head, relieved that they were still a long way to the south.

Still we didn't stop. The airport gone from our thoughts. The safety and monotony of Carousel a million miles away. When the highway turned too steep we disembarked and pushed the bikes upward on foot. The bush closed in around us and we calmed a little. Sprawling mansions began to pop up on private driveways and alcoves. They hung on the hillside and peered westward to the city and ocean as Perth did its best impression of LA. We passed dozens of them before Taylor spotted solar panels on a roof and we found ourselves a new place to hide.

That night we had collapsed on the plush poolside furniture and woke to a cool westerly and clusters of mosquito bites at our ankles. The three of us froze when a shaggy patchwork border collie surfaced from behind the trees at our yawning. This time Lizzy did crouch down. The dog dipped his head and carefully considered the thinning indie rock star. Satisfied, he trotted over for the greatest pat of his life and has been by Lizzy's side ever since.

So there we were. Sheepish and ashamed at how quickly the outside world had sent us packing. We felt like spoilt teenagers, lasting just weeks in the real world before whimpering back to our cushy suburban lives. If we had grown up during our time in Carousel, it sure didn't feel like it anymore.

I dangled my legs in the pool we had spent days cleaning and watched the Finns in their latest routines. Lizzy on a deckchair, reading some Hemingway from the mansion's slimline bookshelves. Jeans folded carefully at her ankles. A man-size pale-blue business shirt swallowing her waist and torso. Ray-Bans hiding her eyes as she flicked pages, often looking back on something she just read while she traced the squares on Chessboard's coat. The world alters irrevocably, yet Lizzy Finn still looks ready for a photoshoot.

Taylor was a different story. Powering through laps of the pool before stretching, as she did now, for a good hour on the warming pavers. Always preparing, building, thinking. Devising elaborate plans before silently changing her mind and making some more. It had taken her just months to sum up the cavernous confines of Carousel. Now she was trying to do the same for an entire city. Lizzy and I would catch her staring down at the sprawling, empty suburbs. Not looking, assessing. Tracing roads and highways. Tiny paths that looked safe and empty from a distance. Houses and buildings. Maybe some with food. Most probably without. Her gaze would often end looking north. Past the houses and the factories. Through the bushland and the roaming Bulls. To the dormant grey of the airport.

Less than a year ago we had seen an Air Canada plane coming in to land there. Its link to Taylor and Lizzy still felt tangible and strong. All of us wanted to survive whatever was happening. Maybe even escape it somehow. But more than that – we wanted to know what it was.

In a way there were answers all around us. In the buildings that stood upright. Tired and empty, but otherwise unaffected. In the lack of bodies. The pockets of power still fuelling random places like Carousel and the mini-mart, but nowhere else. The fading signs of their inhabitants. The lightshow that swept out of the city every night. Beams and waves of beautiful light. Constructed, timed and simulated in a manner that could be considered art and nothing else.

And our time in Carousel. Rocky. Rachel. Peter. The doors. The album. They weren't things we were ready to talk about. But they were bound up in everything we had seen since our escape. We took in all of these factors, added them together, and landed at a single theory. Something that had sparked in Taylor Finn long ago. An idea that filled me with a nausea so intense that at times it would keel me over. Something that made no sense, but also the only sense. That somebody, somehow, had sheltered artists from the apocalypse.

2

'I think he was an architect and she was a florist. Maybe with her own little store nearby,' said Lizzy.

'They sound like characters from *Lost*,' replied Taylor.

I laughed and the Finns looked at me. We were seated on the balcony, waiting for the sun to go down and the lights to start.

'God. Imagine if this whole thing was some bullshit *Lost* type deal,' I said.

'What happened in *Lost*?' asked Lizzy.

'Weren't they all dead the whole time or something?' I replied.

'I'll be so mad if I find out I was dead this whole time,' said Lizzy.

Taylor smiled at her twin and looked back out at the sunset. They were pretty killer from up in the hills. The horizon full of gleaming Indian Ocean. The city hazy and golden in the foreground.

Chess shuffled about next to Lizzy, standing up and trotting in a half circle before sitting again. He had been doing that a lot lately. Hearing things that we couldn't.

Lizzy gave him a ruffle and he settled. Taylor pulled open a can of baked beans and sniffed them carefully. The house had an amazing wine cellar, but not much in the way of unperishables.

'How come there aren't any foods that get better with age?' I asked.

'Cheese, sausage, kimchi,' said Lizzy.

'I wouldn't be hitting up any of the cheese that I've seen lately,' I replied.

'Do you think we could poison the Bulls with bad food?' asked Taylor.

'Holy shit, Taylor,' said Lizzy.

'We can't hide away from them forever,' she replied.

She and Lizzy shared a glance. I looked northward to the airport. The land was dim and blurry in the fading light, but I could still make out a flat stretch of grey signalling the runways.

'We could stick to the hills, go around and enter from the other side,' I suggested.

'Where there are no Bulls?' said Lizzy.

I shrugged. We still didn't totally get the animal thing. They were out there, but seemingly just in random clusters. A scattering of dogs. The odd house cat. A flock of shrieking waterbirds. We could only assume that the animals of Perth hadn't disappeared alongside the humans. What we were seeing now, almost two years on, wasn't a pet store madhouse but a thinning array of struggling urban survivors. Unsurprisingly, there were far more pit bulls than pomeranians.

'Maybe there aren't. It looks less suburban out there,' said Taylor.

Lizzy was silent. I wondered how much Chess factored into these type of discussions now. Taylor looked at me for an answer.

'It might be. Sorry, I haven't really been out that way much,' I said.

Taylor nodded and turned back to the horizon. This was how most of our serious discussions had gone lately. Never really getting off the ground. Everyone seemingly happy to let the conversation slide toward something less pressing.

The sun dropped into the ocean and a thin spike of red shot up abruptly out of the city. It swept dramatically north–south, then east–west.

We watched as the colour changed to blue and pulsed in a slow, rhythmic pattern. I traced the beams back to the ground and tried to work out where in the city they might be coming from. My memory of the city grid was vague, but the source was in there somewhere.

'Wow,' said Taylor, drifting out to the railing.

I still wasn't sure if I understood this kind of industrial art like Taylor and Lizzy and others seemed to. The way it took forever to orchestrate, then sometimes only existed for a moment. The way you couldn't compare it to another book or film or painting. How it didn't help you escape the world, but thrust you into it.

But since we had been up in the hills I had started to crave the lightshows. Nights without them felt shallow and insignificant. Like nobody had spoken to us. Or *for* us.

There was a final strobe of green before it stopped and the city returned to grey. We hesitated for a moment, then shuffled back inside. Closing the door on a bush that buzzed and ticked with life all around us.

The following morning Taylor and I ran an inventory of our supplies. We had left Carousel with nothing but a demo album, a couple of walkie-talkies and my mishmash book of short stories, and had been getting by on whatever we could find since then. Because the population had disappeared with their pantries full and houses intact we had survived okay. But we weren't living in a shopping centre anymore. We had to plan ahead.

We were low on food and also needed things like clothes, batteries and sunscreen. Although large, the house didn't have a lot to offer. No camping gear or outdoors stuff. No backpacks, torches or batteries. Just a giant wine cellar and stacks of beautifully folded linen.

'I'm trying not to think of your stash in Army Depot,' said Taylor.

She sighed and closed another cupboard. I shook off a rush of guilt.

'We'll have to check out the neighbours. This place is like some minimalist nineties shrine,' she said.

'Through the trees or back out to the highway?' I asked.

'I don't know. What do you think?' said Taylor.

'I prefer the trees,' I replied.

Taylor looked at me and nodded.

'Let's take a couple of these,' said Taylor.

She slid two expensive looking golf clubs out of a kit by the door.

'For the Bulls,' she added.

I took one, switched on my radio and we headed off into the trees.

The house was perched on the lower half of the scarp with hundreds of other mansions pocketed across the hills above. We trudged upward through the thin, leafy forest, checking them off as we went. From a distance the Perth hills could look dense and green, even alpine. But within them the towering eucalypts held just a spindly canopy above a floor of grass trees, banksias and ancient rock.

After just two houses we already had more food than we could carry. The hills weren't exactly rural, but the locals seemed to stock their pantries pretty liberally. Each place had the token rotted-out fridge and freezer. Generally the top shelves of the pantries were useless also. But on the lower levels, or at the back, we found cans, nuts and dried food. Never exciting, but edible and reassuring none the less.

I hated snooping through people's kitchens. They were always so full of past life and emotion. Photos and kids' drawings on the fridges. Lunchboxes half packed on the benches. Notes about dentist appointments and holiday accommodation scrawled down beside phones. I was training myself to look past this stuff. To stay objective and focused. Or numb, as Lizzy would say. But it was never easy. People's homes were nothing like the soulless shops to which we had become accustomed.

We left small stockpiles of supplies on driveways to collect on our way back and kept moving upward. Taylor chirped away to Lizzy on the radio, making sure we stayed in range. We had planned for all of us to go, but Lizzy was worried about how Chess might react to being out in the open like this. He didn't spook too easily, but we had no idea where he had come from or what he had been through. There was no evidence that the mansion was his home previously, so we assumed Chess had travelled from somewhere else before finding us. I think Lizzy was worried he might decide to take off back there.

By midmorning the heat had risen up out of the suburbs where it would cloak the bush until dusk. We would welcome this by the poolside, but not out here. The forest floor seemed to stay cool by bouncing the sunlight back upwards. Taylor and I had the uncomfortable sensation of being shaded from the sky, but slowly burned from the floor. Thankfully most of the properties stored water in huge tanks beside the houses in case of bushfires. We unclipped hoses and pumps to take cool blasts of rainwater in the face and neck.

Hydrated and more than halfway up the ridge, we kept moving, still taking the odd food item, but quietly more interested in seeing what lay east of the hills.

The final house on the ridge was a modest brick and tile place that looked older than the others. We stopped in the driveway and looked down at the bush speckled with roofs below. In another section of the hills one of them could easily be my parents' place. I felt a rumble of emotion and set off again, ignoring the final house and leaving Taylor to follow for once.

The ground rose sharply for fifty metres before levelling off. I moved out into full sunlight, the bush thinning in anticipation of the scrubland and desert to the east. Like explorers arriving a hundred years too late we took our final steps to the edge of the ridge and gazed out eastward.

'Wow,' whispered Taylor.

For a moment I thought she was being sarcastic. Then I realised she and Lizzy probably hadn't seen farmland like this before. A barren patchwork of paddocks broken only by the snake of bitumen or branches of a eucalypt. The farmland was serviced by a highway sweeping down from somewhere to the right of us. There was a petrol station and a cluster of stores a few kilometres along this road, and at least one homestead that we could make out. Otherwise it was the lifeless summer palette of rural Australia.

'That's it then,' said Taylor.

I looked at her. 'What do you mean?'

'It happened everywhere,' she replied.

'I'm pretty sure that the view from here would look like this a lot of the time. Irrespective of any global catastrophe,' I said.

Taylor wasn't convinced.

'See that truck down there?' she asked.

I turned back and traced the highway as it headed east into the distance. At the point where my eyes started to struggle, I saw something. A roadtrain. It was strewn about the road. The back half lying sideways. The front half off to the left. Shrubs had begun to grow up around the cab. The driver had disappeared with the rest of them.

Taylor turned and headed back to the house, writing off the rest of the country with a shrug, like only she could. I lingered for a while, trying to figure out how I felt about the world now that I could finally look at it. It seemed weird that our only view from Carousel for all of those months was of the hills. And now we were out of there, this is where we found ourselves.

When I arrived back down at the last house, Taylor was in the driveway, empty-handed.

'Should we check inside?' I asked.

'I did. It's empty,' she replied.

Her brain was ticking over.

'What, totally?' I asked.

'Yep. All the cans, packets, batteries. As if we had

already been there,' she replied.

I looked at the house with new caution.

'That's weird, right?' said Taylor.

'Yeah,' I replied. 'The final house.'

'Do you think somebody stopped here to load up before heading east?' asked Taylor.

'Maybe. Probably,' I replied.

'How far is the nearest city?' she asked.

'City? A long way,' I replied. 'There are small towns though. Maybe every fifty kilometres or so. Until the desert.'

'Do you think we should head that way, too?' she asked, carefully.

'I don't know,' I replied. 'It seems pretty definite.'

Taylor nodded, but was quiet.

'Plus the airport is west,' I said.

Taylor looked at me and smiled. She dropped her head onto my shoulder and kept it there for a moment. Taylor had been carrying around a stack of disappointment at what we had found since leaving Carousel. It could be blurred by the mansion and the pool and the sunshine, but days like this brought it hurtling back, front and centre.

She straightened. 'Let's get all this stuff back to the house before it gets any hotter. I need a swim and some breakfast.'

We set off back down to the house.

3

Days were long and dreamlike in the hills. We spoke
of leaving in general terms, but without any real sense
of urgency. In truth, the house had a rhythm that we
slipped into and were reluctant to disturb. I think a lot
of it had to do with sunlight. We were starved of this
in Carousel and our bodies had a thirst for it that ran
deep. But it wasn't only the sun. It was the pitch-dark of
night, the haziness of dusk, the spiking clear of morning.
The hills had a clock that told us what to do so that we
didn't have to decide for ourselves. Wake up and eat
something. Go outside and breathe the morning air.
Cool off in the pool. Sleep in the shade. Warm up before
dark. Eat, then sleep some more. Life felt simple and
comforting, yet strangely full.

If Tommy hadn't arrived we might have stayed there
forever.

We heard his footsteps on the driveway around
lunchtime on a hot, blustery Saturday. The three of us
had just been swimming and were drying off on the

pavers when Chess stood up and looked at the side gate. A few moments later we heard it too. We stared at each other in dopey holiday stupor, none of us with a suitable reaction.

'Hello,' called Tommy.

It had the tone of somebody expecting an answer. Somebody that knew the house was inhabited.

'Hello,' he said again.

He was at the gate now.

'Yeah,' said Taylor.

She rose and Lizzy and I followed.

'My name is Tommy. I'm not a Loot. I was just wondering if I could charge some batteries,' he said.

He had a slight accent. German, maybe. He waved both his hands above the tall side gate to show that they were empty. Taylor glanced at me. I kept silent.

'Just a second, Tommy,' said Lizzy.

She walked over to the gate with Chess on her heels. Taylor and I followed.

'This gate is tricky,' said Lizzy, fiddling with the latch.

After a moment it slipped and she stepped back to let it swing open.

Tommy was a young guy, maybe just in his twenties. Blond, skinny and sunburned. He was wearing a backpack and carrying a couple of camera bags and a small tripod.

'Oh hi,' he said, with a big, earnest smile.

The three of us beamed back at him like idiots.

'Come in, come in,' said Lizzy. 'I'm Lizzy. This is Taylor and Nox. And Chess.'

Tommy shook our hands and gave Chess a long, friendly pat.

'Taylor & Lizzy,' he said, knowingly.

'Yep,' replied Lizzy, beaming.

'Cool,' replied Tommy. 'Thank you for letting me in. It's going to be a real hot one I think.'

'No problem,' said Lizzy.

'Where have you come from?' asked Taylor.

Tommy put down his cameras and stretched.

'I've been tracking along the scarp for a few weeks now. I saw some lights over this way one night and really hoped I might find somebody,' he replied.

The three of us nodded, still dumbstruck by how relaxed he was.

'Or did you mean before that?' he asked.

Taylor nodded, pensively.

'Oh sure. I'm a film student from Denmark. I've been interviewing people since the Disappearance. For a documentary,' he added.

'Wow,' said Lizzy.

'What do you mean, Disappearance?' asked Taylor.

'Nobody knows really. People have a lot of theories, but mostly I just ask them about their lives now. What they miss, how they spend their time. That sort of thing. Most people have been really cool. I've been getting some great footage,' he replied.

Lizzy laughed.

'Sorry,' said Tommy with another big smile.

This made me laugh too. Tommy joined us. Taylor looked at me and Lizzy like we were idiots. Lizzy put a hand on Tommy's shoulder to apologise.

'You're breaking our brains a little, Tommy,' said Lizzy. 'Do you want a drink?'

'Oh yeah. Great,' he replied.

The four of us shuffled over to the poolside bar and poured some iced teas. Tommy hammered down two of them and started on a third.

'Thanks. This is great. Really great,' he said.

'How many people have you interviewed, Tommy?' asked Taylor.

'Gee. A lot now,' he replied. 'Maybe fifty or sixty.'

'In the whole of Perth?' I asked.

'Yeah,' he reflected. 'It's pretty empty I guess.'

'Have you been on your own this whole time?' asked Lizzy.

'No. No. I stay with people for a few weeks here and there,' he replied. 'And Genna and I stayed on campus together for a while after it happened.'

'Genna?' asked Taylor.

'She's a dance student. Really talented. We shot a film together in the library,' he replied.

'Is that where you were when it happened?' I asked.

'I think so, yeah,' he replied. 'It took us a whole day to notice anything.'

'Seriously?' asked Lizzy.

'Yeah. It's a bit weird but sometimes I hang out at the library for a while. They have some really cool old movies that you can only watch in the building. You're not really allowed, but sometimes I take a bunch of snacks into the downstairs viewing rooms and stay there all night,' said Tommy.

'So you guys were in there watching movies when everybody disappeared?' asked Taylor.

'Yeah I think so. I got back to campus pretty late at night from a film shoot in Fremantle. I had four macchiatos on set so I was way too wired to go back to the dorms,' said Tommy. 'You have to be pretty quiet over there or some students will complain to the RA.'

We nodded. The three of us were fixated on him.

'Anyway as a student you get a twenty-four-hour swipe card for the library. It's pretty great. So I grabbed a bunch of stuff from the vending machines and went straight downstairs to watch some films. After a couple of them I must have gotten tired because I fell asleep until Genna found me in there the next day,' he continued.

'How long were you guys in there for?' asked Taylor.

'The library? Just for the day,' replied Tommy.

'Oh come on,' said Lizzy to herself.

Tommy smiled at her with a flicker of sympathy and hesitated.

'What happened next, Tommy?' asked Taylor.

'Genna woke me up and we joked around. She's found me asleep in there twice now. She had *Flashdance* on Blu-ray so we watched that and talked about the choreography for a while. Then I had my camera and there was nobody around so we decided to shoot a film right then and there,' said Tommy.

His eyes were full of enthusiasm.

'It was really simple. Just Genna dancing in a stairwell down on level two. She really nailed the performance though. I ended up shooting it all in one take.'

'When did you realise something had happened outside?' asked Taylor.

'We finished filming and left out of the night exit. Campus was dead, but it was almost dark and break week, so we didn't really think about it. We went back to our dorms and were going to catch up later to watch the film properly. When I got to my dorm the power was out or something. I went to borrow some noodles from Mindy next door and ask her what the fuck was happening. But she wasn't in her room. Mindy is always in her room. Always. So I knew something was wrong,' said Tommy.

We were silent. Tommy downed another glass of iced tea.

'Did you see Genna again?' asked Lizzy.

'Oh yeah. She was pretty upset when she couldn't find anybody. We actually went back to the library after a while. For some reason it was the only place with power,' replied Tommy.

'Where is she now?' I asked.

'Oh. She's good I think. She left with Brian and Paula. An Aussie couple we met in the refectory,' he said.

'You didn't go with them?' I asked.

'No. They were great. But they were heading south. Getting out of the city,' he replied.

Taylor and Lizzy shared a glance.

'Did they say why?' I asked.

'No. They were kind of hippy. So maybe they just like the forests more,' replied Tommy. 'They wanted me to come. Especially Genna. She was upset, again. But I wanted to find out what was happening. After they left I broke into the tech room and took some sweet lenses and sound gear.'

His face brightened.

'I've been shooting the documentary pretty much every day since,' he finished and smiled at us.

The three of us tried to process some of the awe we felt for this guy. He had been out in the world, on his own, with those Bulls and who knows what else, for almost two years now. Not just surviving, but documenting. No sense of the existential crises we had draped ourselves in.

'What about you guys?' asked Tommy.

The question caught us out. I looked at Taylor to speak for us but she clammed up.

'We met in a mall and were stuck in there until just now,' said Lizzy. 'Taylor and I were on tour, killing time before we flew out to Asia. Nox was taking a cab to work but the driver wigged out and dropped him at the mall instead. We met another guy who worked there, but he caught something from the shitty aircon and died.'

Said out loud to a stranger, our story sounded vacant and separate from us.

'That's terrible. I'm really sorry,' said Tommy.

His demeanour altered and we got a hint of his maturity. I felt like Tommy had probably heard a lot of horrible stuff since he left the university.

'Wow. You were stuck in there for a while hey,' said Tommy, thinking it over.

'Longer than the other people you've met?' asked Taylor.

'Oh yeah,' replied Tommy.

Lizzy sighed, ruefully.

'Did you come straight to the hills when you got out?' asked Tommy.

'No. We were headed for the airport but ran into some trouble,' I replied.

'The dogs?' asked Tommy.

I nodded. Chess repositioned himself beneath Lizzy and eyed the gate.

'Tommy. The people in your documentary,' said Taylor carefully. 'Are they all artists?'

The three of us looked at him. He shuffled, a spike of

excitement dancing behind his eyes.

'You've heard of the Curator, too?' he asked.

'Who is the Curator?' asked Taylor.

'It's who I'm looking for,' replied Tommy.

4

Tommy was more tired than he let on. We talked for a while longer before he sat down on a lounge. Then lay back. Then fell asleep altogether. We let him sleep there for most of the day, before waking him up for some food. The four of us ate and talked and watched the lightshow across the city. Tommy looked on with interest, but no real excitement. The lights had been a fixture in his life for much longer than they had in ours.

We found out that he had two sisters back in Denmark, one older, one younger. He had been due to go back and visit them, and his parents, for Christmas a few months after the Disappearance. So when Christmas came around this year it would be his third without them. He also fessed up and told us that Genna and he were more than just friends during their time in the library. But he had still decided not to go south with Brian and Paula, because if he did he would never find out what was happening. Tommy's story broke our hearts, but was totally defiant and inspiring at the same time.

He slept through the night and most of the following day while the three of us flitted around the house trying to process all that he had told us. Not everyone Tommy had met and interviewed was an artist, but a stack of them were. Way too many to be normal, in his opinion. Normal wasn't much of a useful word these days, but we got what he was saying. He had met painters, writers, musicians, a sculptor, a bunch of actors and even other filmmakers. Some of them were established and famous, others were just starting out like him.

None of these artists knew for certain what was going on, nor why they were a part of it. Tommy said a lot of them had stopped thinking about it altogether, instead setting up studios wherever they chose and filling days and nights with work and whatever else constituted a regular life for them.

But others spoke of an orchestrator. Somebody that was somehow responsible for their survival amid this weird phenomenon. Put in this way it sounded like a religious figure or cult leader, but I don't think that was what Tommy believed. He seemed to think there was some kind of synthesis about those who remained in Perth after the Disappearance.

He was super excited to hear that Taylor and Lizzy had recorded an album in Carousel. As if this information somehow validated his theory. I know the Finns didn't feel arbitrary about the music they created during our time in Carousel. Recording the album had

33

brought them back together after Rocky's death and made a bold and defining addition to their catalogue. But Tommy's theory weighed it down – weighed everything down – with a stack of significance.

Tommy also didn't seem to have an issue pooling amateur artists in with the established ones. For me, watching Taylor and Lizzy record their album had proven that several significant and intangible traits separated artists like them from the rest of the world. Tommy's theory about the Curator was interesting, and, within the bizarre new circumstances of the world, maybe even plausible. If nothing else I would totally watch a documentary about it. But it fell down on one major level. Why would a curator shelter an arts grad working part-time at a stationery store from the apocalypse?

All of this stuff aside, it was great to have somebody else around. Without doubt the Finns and I needed some female company pretty desperately, but in Tommy we found a friend and a lightness that none of us had felt in a long time. Tommy's smile was automatic and infectious. With Taylor he swam laps of the pool and took long hikes where she would pepper him with questions about the city and return full of both hope and doubt. He sat through the new album with Lizzy, giving her a long-awaited second listener and a burst of something that seemed to start her thinking about music again.

With me Tommy just sat around doing not much. It sounds stupid but I didn't realise how much I needed this simple human interaction. It was like every relationship in the world had so much weight now. Before Carousel the people in my life would ebb and flow at a safe and casual distance. There was nothing major riding on these relationships. With Taylor and Lizzy, and with Rocky, the stakes were automatically high. We had to get along. Buy in. Be awesome. The microscope felt constant.

For some reason I didn't feel that way with Tommy. We just hung out and talked about anything but the state of the world.

'You two are such boys,' said Lizzy, stopping to look at us as we hunched over Tommy's Game Boy, surrounded by fun-size packets of stale Cheezels and Twisties.

We grunted in unison. Taylor sighed and left us alone.

'You got to use the grenade launcher on that dude,' I said.

Tommy was focusing hard on the small screen.

'I'm going to waste him with this pistol,' he replied.

He tried and failed. We laughed and he passed me the console.

'I can't believe you guys had PS4 and Xbox in Carousel,' he said.

'We had everything, man,' I replied. 'Arcade stuff too.'

Tommy sighed. I resumed the game where he left off.

'The library was so boring,' said Tommy.

'Do you think there were other people in there when it happened?' I asked.

'Oh yeah, I think so. People who work at the help desk. Maybe some students that were sleeping in the common room. We heard some noises while we were filming, but I didn't see anyone. The library is pretty huge,' said Tommy.

I nodded and blew up the remainder of a compound.

'Cool,' said Tommy, watching.

'Did you guys find any good food?' I asked.

'Not really. The cafe in the library is pretty bad,' he replied. 'I smashed up a vending machine though.'

'Serious? Weren't there heaps of coins in the cafe?' I asked.

'Oh yeah, but I thought fuck it. I'm going to smash that thing,' said Tommy.

I looked at him and laughed. My guy started getting shot-up on screen.

'Man. You're really getting pounded,' said Tommy, concerned.

I lost it and shoved the console at Tommy who took over.

'Watch this,' said Tommy.

He swapped weapons and started firing all over the place.

'Dude, you shoot like a maniac,' I said.

'Oh yeah,' said Tommy, proudly. 'How many batteries do we have left?'

I fished through one of the many bags of random supplies Taylor and I had collected.

'Loads,' I replied.

I opened another packet of chips and watched Tommy's avatar going mental on screen. Taylor was right. As much as anything Tommy and I were messy, apathetic, overstimulated Gen Y boys. It wasn't our fault that the world needed us to be something different. Tommy had been abiding from day one. Me too, for the most part. A brief return to sloth and apathy was as close to a holiday as was on offer these days.

Two weeks after Tommy's arrival Lizzy and I rose to find him checking over his gear in the living room.

'Hello,' he said, with his usual grin.

'Hey,' I replied. 'What's happening?'

'Just making sure everything is ready before I head off,' he replied.

For a moment Lizzy and I didn't have a reply.

'About time you stopped mooching,' said Lizzy eventually, and took up a seat on the couch.

Tommy laughed. 'It has been great here. Really great.'

'Where are you going?' I asked, trying hard not to sound affected.

'I'm just going to keep trekking along the ranges. It's cooler up here and there are still a lot of houses to check,' he replied.

Taylor entered from her wing of the house, glancing

at Tommy for just a moment before heading through to the kitchen.

'You're not leaving without proper supplies, Tommy,' she said.

'Oh thanks. Yeah, supplies would be great,' he replied.

We watched as he carefully cleaned a camera lens.

'You really think this Curator is living in the hills?' I asked.

'Oh yeah, maybe. Some people I have interviewed have said that,' he replied.

'What did they say exactly?' asked Taylor.

Tommy packed the lens away and started on another.

'I met a band living in a small shopping centre in a suburb called Gosnells. It's kind of at the bottom of the hills I think. They told me about this guy who used to visit them in a ute sometimes. He would turn up every month or so with fresh fruit and vegetables from the hills and ask them to play him some music in return. They said he could come and go from the centre whenever he wanted, but that they were trapped inside. Like you guys were,' said Tommy, eyes wide like a kid with a ghost story.

I looked across at Taylor. She was pensive.

'After a few visits the singer went kind of crazy and asked this guy why the fuck they couldn't leave the shopping centre. The guy said he didn't know and that he couldn't help them. All he suggested was that they write some new songs. They were pretty pissed I think. The guy never showed up again and they were stuck there for a while,' said Tommy.

'Until they wrote the songs?' said Taylor.

Tommy beamed and nodded. Lizzy groaned. My stomach contracted.

'Who else?' asked Taylor.

'There was a dude I met near the uni. He was pretty young and into graffiti art and that kind of thing. He had been sleeping in the top floor apartment of this sweet building near the river for a few weeks. He said that every few nights he would see headlights up in the hills somewhere. This guy moved around a lot, like me I guess, but he had never seen a car anywhere that was still working. Except up in the hills,' said Tommy.

Tommy finished with the lenses. We watched him, waiting to see if there were more stories to come.

'Plus I met a crazy lady who just kept screaming "bitch" up at the hills,' he added.

Lizzy laughed.

'Probably Rachel,' said Taylor.

'Have you met a trashy single mum with bottle-blonde hair and a gutter mouth?' asked Lizzy.

Tommy laughed. 'I don't think so.'

'She could leave when we couldn't,' Taylor said to herself.

Suddenly I felt flushed and guilty. My thoughts raced to the roller door in Carousel. It had shuddered its way open for me, but hadn't moved for the Finns. What did this mean? Was it connected to my writing? Or was I somehow the same as Rachel?

'Hmm. She sounds like a Patron maybe,' said Tommy.

'What the hell is a Patron?' asked Taylor.

'It's what people call some of the others that didn't disappear. The ones that aren't Artists,' he replied.

'Like the people in the library?' asked Taylor.

Tommy nodded. My head started spinning.

'So what is this Curator dude planning on doing with all this new art?' asked Lizzy.

'That's what I want to ask him in my interview,' said Tommy.

Taylor nodded and looked across at me curiously.

'When are our interviews?' asked Lizzy.

'I was hoping tonight,' he replied, smiling.

I stood up and got the hell out of there. I was acting like a weirdo and felt all of their eyes on my back. Outside it was bright and sunny, but the air was still cool from the night. I ignored the cold, pulled off my shirt and plunged deep into the choppy pool. I kicked down to the bottom and sat there in the watery abyss, not wanting to surface until the world had its shit together.

But when I came back up it was all still there waiting for me. The sky, cleaner and bluer than it had ever been. Lizzy and Chess playing fetch on a burnt-out lawn. Taylor pressing Tommy for more details inside our mansion. All of us surrounded by the deep, oppressing silence of a city in suspended hibernation.

5

With Tommy about to resume his search for the Curator, the issue of what the hell the Finns and I were doing finally came to a head. Since our escape from the Bulls we had sheltered away with no serious talk of resuming our journey to the airport or otherwise. Meeting Tommy, with his steadfast agenda and dedication to his documentary, had made us suddenly restless. We hadn't spent all that time stuck in a shopping complex to hibernate our lives away in a mansion in the hills.

I rose from a futile nap to find Taylor and Lizzy in deep discussion by the pool. They looked up at me as I wandered over. Lizzy offered a slight smile.

'Hey,' she said.

'Hey,' I replied. 'Where's Tommy?'

'Sleeping,' said Taylor. 'Says he won't get much once he's moving again.'

I rubbed Chess on the side with my foot.

'What do you think we should do, Nox?' asked Lizzy.

She caught me out.

'Ah, right. I thought you guys looked serious,' I replied.

Taylor stared hard at the floor, her mind ticking over.

'Are you guys still keen on the airport?' I asked.

'Tommy didn't see the plane,' said Taylor, avoiding Lizzy's gaze.

Tommy had dropped a bombshell when he revealed he hadn't seen or heard a plane since the Disappearance. Lizzy pressed him for anything about planes or airports, but Tommy had nothing to tell her. Somehow he had missed the thundering Air Canada plane completely. I guess it was possible. Tommy hadn't been living right on top of the airport like us.

'It was at night though,' I offered.

'Exactly,' said Lizzy.

I looked at them both, trying to establish the dynamic. Taylor took a breath.

'I think he might be right about the Curator,' said Taylor.

Lizzy rubbed an ache out of her forehead and looked at her sister.

'Even if he is, what does it mean?' she asked.

'I don't know. That we're here for something. Because of something,' Taylor replied.

Her tone caught both of us out.

'So what do you want to do?' asked Lizzy.

'Go to the city. See who's there. Figure out what the hell is happening for ourselves,' she replied.

Taylor's eyes were glistening and Lizzy's quickly followed. She was asking her sister to forget about the plane, Canada, their mother, everything that was behind them.

Lizzy sniffed and turned away to the horizon.

'God,' she said, exhaling shakily.

It was easy to think that Lizzy didn't care about much these days. She had a way of looking at peace that probably wasn't reflective of how she really felt.

'Are you okay with this, Nox?' asked Lizzy.

'The city? Sure, why not,' I replied.

Taylor looked at me carefully.

'No bullshit, Nox,' she said.

'What does that mean?' I replied.

'If you think this is crazy, you need to say so,' she replied.

'It's all crazy, Taylor. Tommy is making a film about a bunch of artists that survived the apocalypse thanks to some Jim Jarmusch type curator. And it's a fucking documentary,' I replied.

I stood up and stretched my neck. Chess peered up at me restlessly.

'We just want you to be in on whatever we do, together,' said Lizzy.

She looked at me. There was a softness in her gaze. I had kept a lot of stuff to myself in Carousel and it had gotten us into trouble more than once. Taylor and Lizzy talked the hell out of everything. Now that we were out in the world I could see how it was important to be up-front.

'I think the city idea is dangerous,' I replied. 'If there's Bulls in the suburbs and the airport, there's a good chance they'll be in the city too.'

Taylor nodded. Lizzy ruffled Chess reassuringly.

'Plus, remember what Tommy said about the Loots,' I added.

Tommy had only ever seen the Loots from a distance, but they sounded full on. Patrons and Artists turned cracky and desperate. Smashing into shops and houses to stockpile food and supplies, but also just to break shit. And their fight wasn't only against the city, but other survivors too. Tommy had heard stories from Artists who had been beaten and ransacked when they had next to nothing to begin with.

Taylor and Lizzy were quiet for a moment. I sat back down.

'Do you think it would be safer to go to the airport?' asked Taylor.

I thought about it. Not the question, but Tommy's theory. About the idea of meeting more Artists in the city. People with talent and status like Taylor and Lizzy. People that felt a million miles removed from me.

'No,' I replied. 'I think it will be just the same. And if we are going to go anywhere it might as well be the city.'

Taylor smiled at me and a few more tears dripped from her eyes. Lizzy nestled into her sister's lap and stayed there, staring across the silky blue surface of the pool. I took a breath and tried to make my brief flicker of courage sink down to somewhere deeper.

The three of us made a wordless decision to leave the next morning.

We spent the rest of the afternoon away from each other, packing our things and saying our goodbyes to the house. Tommy was excited to hear of our plan, but may have felt similar to hear we were staying in the house to work on some art.

I piled my things together quickly and spent the remainder of the daylight hours desperately trying to write something. It was pretty futile. The prose felt forced and overly descriptive. Plus I didn't really have any ideas that I was into. Tommy's mythical Curator hovered over me like some disappointed English teacher. I cursed myself for lazing around the whole time we had been up there instead of building on my work from Carousel. Tomorrow we would be on the road with a thousand other things to deal with.

Taylor and I had laid out all of the supplies we had collected in the garage. Late in the afternoon I met her and Tommy down there to put together some travel packs. We would be riding out of the hills on the bikes we had arrived on. We figured this gave us the best chance of escaping any future Bulls, but made carrying supplies difficult. Lizzy's bike was a red fixie with a delicate looking basket attached to the front. It slumped hopelessly as soon as we loaded anything decent inside so Tommy and I took it off and replaced it with an old milk crate, drilled to the handlebars. Taylor refused to be a part of this, knowing Lizzy would be mad.

We did the same to our bikes and eventually were able to store a small amount of supplies onboard. It was mostly cans and noodles, but we also took a bunch of under-ripe fruit from the trees bordering the house. Taylor figured it would ripen in the heat and keep us in vitamin C for at least a week or two.

For the Bulls, Loots and whatever else happened to be out in the world we strapped a golf club to each bike, along with a can of insect spray. Tommy had discovered that this messed with the Bulls' breathing – if you could spray it in their face before they started chewing on your neck, that is.

Tommy travelled light. He took a couple of cans and some fruit, but didn't seem overly worried about going hungry. It was easy to feel reassured by Tommy. Nothing in the new world seemed to faze him much. You could be mistaken to think he'd had a cushy time of it, but then he would casually drop a story about not having water for a day and a half, or fending off a pair of Bulls with a school ruler and some bug spray, and you quickly realised it wasn't the case at all.

At dusk the four of us wandered up to the balcony to watch the lightshow and drink some wine from the cellar. It was delicious and probably crazy-expensive, but I would have killed for something cold like a gin and tonic or a beer. Summer had cloaked the city in a heavy blanket of heat. The only respite came with the early-morning easterly that blew in from the night-cooled deserts. By ten this wind was stick-dry and ominous. By one it was deadly.

Taylor and I observed the lightshow carefully, trying to get a final gauge on the source before we headed down from the hills toward it. Lizzy slipped away with Chess before the show had ended. We stayed on for a while without her until we heard music from beside the pool below. The three of us drifted across to find Lizzy at a keyboard she had found in the guest linen cupboard a few weeks back.

'Oh cool,' said Tommy.

Lizzy keyed away, aware of us watching, but also kind of oblivious. She was experimenting with some new progressions and melodies. They were raw, but still sounded poppy and interesting.

I glanced at Taylor to catch her reaction. She seemed preoccupied.

Tommy ventured inside and returned with a camera. He waited for Lizzy to give him a small nod before filming her for his documentary.

Taylor and I moved over to the pool to finish our wines. Our legs dangled and disappeared into the cool black void of water.

'We didn't ask you if you wanted to go to your parents' place,' said Taylor, a little ashamed.

'It's fine,' I replied.

'We totally can if you want to,' she said.

'I don't know really. I've thought about it. But I figure it won't change anything,' I replied. 'Plus my mum is obsessed with cheese, so the place is probably rancid by now.'

Taylor smiled and looked down at the dancing surface of the pool.

'I think this is harder for you than it is for us,' she said.

'How come?' I asked.

'Because this is where you live. For Lizzy and me, home still looks the same in our heads. It's still out there waiting for us,' she replied.

I looked out at the dark spread of Perth. There was half a moon somewhere above us. Enough to outline the snake of the river and wide edge of the Indian Ocean. It was weird to think of how many lives had existed between where we sat in the hills and the start of that ocean. It just seemed like geography now. Water. Soil. Undulations of earth. But for the people that used to be down there it was a whole universe and more. I felt numb and sick at the same time.

'I don't live in this place,' I said, softly.

Taylor looked at me.

'I hover above it. Looking around and freaking out like one of those ghost dudes in *Super Mario Bros*,' I said.

'Boos,' said Taylor.

'What?' I replied.

'The ghost dudes. They're called Boos,' said Taylor.

'Right,' I said.

'You know they cover their eyes when you look at them,' said Taylor.

'Sounds about right,' I replied.

She laughed and shoved my shoulder. Lizzy's music wafted down past us and was swallowed by the bush.

'What's it like being an artist?' I asked.

Taylor looked confused.

'I mean, like a famous artist,' I said.

'What do you mean? Having money and playing festivals?' she asked.

I shook my head. 'Just being part of somebody's life that you have never met. Maybe will never meet,' I asked.

Taylor thought about it for a moment. 'It's the best thing in the world,' she replied, deadly serious.

I nodded.

'Do you think you and Lizzy will still be able to work on music once we're on the road again?' I asked.

Taylor shrugged. I swirled some water around with my legs.

'Pack some writing pads in your bag tomorrow. You'll figure something out,' said Taylor. 'There will be time.'

She kissed me on the head and left.

6

Tommy's interviews were weird.

By the time they happened we were all a little drunk, Tommy included. I guess it might have taken our inhibitions and left us more honest and open, but for me I just felt vague and dopey. Plus we had to do them in the garage so we could hide the lights. Our bikes and gear were already in there, packed up and ready to go. Sitting down next to it all felt like hovering in limbo between one world and the next.

Lizzy went first, taking a good hour before returning to the pool and immediately resuming her position at the keyboard, where Chess had been waiting. I sat alone and listened to her play as Taylor went down next. She wasn't gone for as long as Lizzy. A half-hour or so later she returned, said a quick goodnight and headed straight to bed. I finished my drink and wandered down a few moments later.

Tommy had a half-empty bottle of water with him and seemed to have sobered up since I had seen him last.

I took a seat in the chair he had set up and tried to talk some crap with him. It didn't really work. Tommy was focused from the last two interviews and it just felt like I was stalling.

Eventually he hit record and stopped me.

'You were sheltered in a shopping mall with Taylor and Lizzy Finn, is that correct, Nox?' he asked.

I took a breath and steadied myself.

'No,' I replied.

Tommy raised his gaze from the viewfinder.

'You didn't live in Carousel?' he asked.

'I did. But I was dropped there by accident,' I replied.

The words bounced around the concrete, sounding like they had come from somebody else.

'Why do you say that?' he asked.

'I was waiting at a bus stop when a taxi pulled up and the driver asked me if my name was Stuart,' I replied.

Tommy stared at me. His lens drinking up my every word.

'I lied. Told him it was. Figured it was better than waiting for the bus,' I continued. 'The driver believed me and we set off towards the city. He seemed kind of stressed – driving fast, watching the clock. About halfway there he swung into Carousel and said he couldn't take me any further.'

I exhaled, finally laying bare the truth of my existence. It had happened suddenly, without any planning. I looked up at Tommy, wondering whether he might stop the interview then and there, saving his gigabytes for a real Artist.

'Can you tell me about the art you created during your time in Carousel?' he asked.

I looked up, surprised.

'You were in there for a long time. What did you write?' he asked.

I hesitated. 'Short stories, mostly,' I replied.

'Is there a common theme or are they all individual works?' he asked.

'Fate, I guess,' I replied, not having really thought about this before.

Tommy continued to coax me until eventually I was able to talk about the writing I had done in Carousel with at least some detail. He asked about how being in the shopping centre influenced the work. Whether being isolated from society was a help or a hindrance. What kind of hours I kept. All kinds of stuff. Rather than feel like a fraud, in a way it made me feel more legitimate. Answering questions about the work proved that it existed, and that in creating it I had invented, made decisions and done whatever else an Artist was required to do. Once I got talking I forgot about my arrival and focused on what I had done since.

After half an hour Tommy said he had enough footage. I felt flat, but tried not to let on. We packed up his equipment and put the batteries back on charge. Tommy looked tired. It was well into the night and the morning loomed like an unwelcome relative. We hovered above the chargers, waiting for the lights to turn green.

'You haven't told that to anyone before?' asked Tommy.

I shook my head. 'Sorry. It just came out,' I replied.

'It's the camera lens,' said Tommy. 'People think it will keep them from talking, but it does the opposite I think.'

I nodded and took a breath.

'Have you spoken to anyone else that was taken to a shelter without being a real Artist?' I asked.

Tommy looked at me squarely and shook his head.

'Have you met a guy named Stuart anywhere?' I asked.

'No. Sorry, Nox,' he replied.

I looked away, feeling about ten years his junior.

'Maybe it is just about the timing,' said Tommy.

'What?' I replied.

'Maybe everything,' said Tommy.

I rubbed my tired, stinging eyes and tried to think this over. A hangover was doing its best to check-in early.

'Have Taylor and Lizzy gone to bed?' asked Tommy.

'I think so,' I replied.

Tommy nodded, looking suddenly pensive.

'If you are going to the city to find the painter, there is something you should know I think,' said Tommy.

'The painter?' I asked.

'The girl who came to Carousel on Boxing Day. Taylor asked me about her. At first I didn't remember anyone like that. But the other day I was doing some editing and something triggered my memory. I was in the city for a while, just hanging out and interviewing some people. Just before I left, a painter arrived. She said she had come from the suburbs in the east. I was going to interview her but there were rumours of some Loots around. I was stressed out for my cameras so I got out of there.'

'But you think it's the same painter that came to Carousel?' I asked.

'Oh yeah, I think so,' he replied. 'Taylor gave me a pretty good description.'

Wow, I thought. That's why she wants to go to the city so bad.

'Anyway,' said Tommy. 'The city is cool. There are some great Artists there. But you need to be careful.'

'Why?' I asked.

'The place has been without maintenance for a long time now. Parts of it are starting to break down. When I was there last winter a storm blew over a huge crane and it smashed up a bunch of buildings and roads pretty bad I think. Some people say that it took out gas lines, too,' said Tommy. 'I don't really know how this stuff works but some people say it's a matter of time before there is an explosion. And when it happens there'll be no firefighters to put it out.'

I looked at him. It was as serious as Tommy got.

'Just before we got out of Carousel we started hearing these noises. Kind of like thunder, but from the ground, not the sky,' I said.

'Pockets of gas going off,' said Tommy.

'You heard them, too?' I asked.

'Oh yeah. Everyone did, I think. Sometimes you could see them, too. Little flashes of light,' he replied.

'Did you see many of these in the city?' I asked.

Tommy shook his head. I thought this over.

'Maybe that's a good sign,' I said.

'Yeah, maybe. Or maybe there will just be one big one,' he replied.

The two of us stood in silence.

'Maybe it's not such a great idea to only save Artists,' I said.

Tommy smiled and nodded. He looked young again. Like the student he was. I patted him on the shoulder and tried my best to be reassuring. The battery lights turned from red to green.

7

Tommy had left before we woke in the morning. For some reason none of us were surprised. Maybe he had said his goodbyes to the Finns after their interviews. I guess my talk with him was also a goodbye of sorts. We had said a lot of stuff, and there were other things that probably didn't need to be said. I think each of us felt a void somewhere deep and important upon Tommy's departure. We were alone in the world again. And we couldn't hide out any longer.

After breakfast we spent a few hours cleaning the house. It was an odd and excessive place, but it had been good to us, and our only home since Carousel. We didn't feel right about leaving it ransacked and messy. The three of us worked away, carefully returning the place to its sparse and minimalist self. The only real difference was the empty pantry and sparkling-clean pool. I had a feeling we would miss that pool severely.

We loaded up the bikes with the last of our stuff. Taylor and I couldn't help but smile at Lizzy's reaction to the alterations on her fixie. Chess hovered anxiously at her feet as she tested the new load. Somehow he knew completely that this was no daytrip.

It reminded me of when I was a kid and Mum, Dad, Danni and I would sometimes head out for a walk through the hills at night. It was rare for us to carry out such a structured, all-in family outing. But sometimes, amid the slow drag of summer holidays, on a night when the four of us might linger at the dinner table rather than slip away to our own corners of the house, Dad would suggest that Herb, our scruffy old Jack Russell, might like a walk. So the five of us would head out into the quiet hum of the patchy forests surrounding our place. The lights of the city blipping into view as we crossed streets and passed neighbouring houses and properties. Herb sniffing his way along, more vibrant than on his morning walks, which had become something to tick off before school, work and – for him – a day shuffling about the deck, following the sun, then the shade. What Danni and I loved was that our cat Ezra also came along. His senses triggered by the irregularity of an event that saw all five of us leaving the house together. He would slink along behind us. Watching out for signs that our journey might be something permanent like when we shifted to the hills from Bull Creek.

There had been no discussion over bringing Chess. He was in this with us now. A Patron in dog form. Poor guy, I thought. Lives through the apocalypse and the only people left are a straggle of wounded and aimless Artists. What he would do for a simple life with a farmer or fisherman.

I propped up Taylor's bike as she hit the controller on the garage door and dashed out as it angled slowly to the floor. Lizzy circled the driveway in slow, distracted loops. Taylor clipped on her helmet and tested her tyres. I looked westward through the trees at the murky spread of Perth below.

'Sayonara, you weird, awesome house,' said Lizzy.

She shot me a mischievous grin.

'Sorry about the cellar,' I added.

'You guys up for the highway?' asked Taylor.

'Totally,' I replied.

'Just don't leave me and Chessboard behind,' said Lizzy as she swung out of her loop and down the driveway.

'Hold up,' said Taylor.

We stopped and looked at her. She was fiddling with something that was taped to her handlebars.

'What?' asked Lizzy.

A song licked out into the morning air. Taylor had strapped an iPod and speaker to her bike.

'A bit of Cold War Kids,' she replied. 'For the journey.'

'Nice,' said Lizzy.

The two of them shared a smile before Lizzy and Chess took off again. Taylor ramped the volume and shot off after her sister with a spark I hadn't seen in her for a long time. Maybe it was the thought of the painter she had almost met in Carousel. The girl she was secretly heading toward. Maybe she was just excited to be moving again.

I felt something too. Coasting down that long concrete driveway. Bush, sunlight and wind washing across my senses. In my mind I dressed it up as fearlessness. The four of us hurtling downhill into battle. But I think it was more about something Tommy had said. The possibility that down there, ahead of us, was the chance to make something of my sheltering. To become what this Curator had intended. To somehow morph an accident into fate.

As it turned out, it was Taylor and I that had trouble keeping up with Lizzy and Chessboard. Given the delicacy of her bike, the two of us had taken on the majority of the supplies, leaving us heavy and unstable. We sat back on our brakes, careful not to shift our weight too far and scatter our cargo into the trees. Lizzy rolled freely and with Chess a born runner, they set a cracking pace. We caught them on the straights, but lost them around each bend as the bush closed in and the highway snaked back into the outer suburbs.

When we began to level off and slow down I started looking around for signs of life. It was still pretty green on the lower slopes. There were patches of brown and yellow where lawns and gardens had been starved of irrigation, but in many places the natives had survived and started to spread. We passed a big Italian house with pillars and a double-door entrance being rapidly engulfed by a runaway creeper. A cluster of kit homes, part of an estate for young families, pushed to the very edge of the city by a booming property market. An accompanying primary school looking lifeless and sombre in the morning sun. Whenever I saw play equipment now I got a flash of Sarah Connor in *T2* watching kids on swings being blown to pieces by the robot apocalypse.

If there were other Artists up there, we didn't see them. Maybe it would be easier at night when a light might give them away. Or maybe they would try to stay dark and quiet like we had. By venturing into the city we were assuming that people there would be out in the open rather than hidden away. Tommy had made it sound like this. For the most part I hoped he was right.

By lunchtime our legs were already starting to tire. Taylor was the only one of us in any shape, and even she seemed to be flagging without the help of the slopes. We ambled along at pedestrian pace as the road started to radiate heat like some giant, never-ending pizza stone. Shade became sparse and I noticed Chess seemed reluctant to remain stationary on the bitumen for more than a moment.

We had all but left the hills and reached what looked like a series of market gardens when Lizzy slowed on the road ahead of us. Chess peered up and circled her curiously. My hand dropped down to my golf club. Taylor stopped and glanced sideways at her sister.

'Do you think there's any food here?' asked Lizzy.

Taylor had become a bit of a plant expert during our last year in Carousel, growing all kinds of things under the dome without much to work with. She looked around at the messy, browning pockets of land.

'Could be some tomatoes. Maybe citrus. If the birds haven't got to it all,' said Taylor.

'God, that would be awesome. I have hella scurvy right now,' said Lizzy.

'We can't really carry anything else on these bikes,' I said.

'But we could have a fresh lunch for once,' said Lizzy.

Taylor looked around and thought it over.

'Okay. We gotta head this way anyhow. Let's check it out,' said Taylor.

She turned us down the remnants of a dirt road, eyes scanning the passing foliage as she went. One in four of the large, rectangular planting areas had some hint of life. Here Taylor found several patches of tomatoes and capsicum. They were clustered from self-seeding and stunted badly from the lack of water. But even so there were countless pockets of fruit and vegetables tucked under leaves and spread out across the cooler dirt. We put the bikes aside and trudged our way through, eating as we went. At first we took anything that was half ripe and bug free. But as we realised how much was on offer we quickly became fussy, taking only premium produce to eat or stash for later.

Lizzy was excited and hopped about at each new discovery. She jammed tomato after tomato into her mouth, before holding her stomach and forcing down some more. Taylor blissed-out in the peaceful, sprawling gardens. This was probably what she had dreamed about for all those days stuck in Carousel. I could see her here, making a life for herself. Bringing the gardens back to life. Collecting water and cooking by the fire in winter. Harvesting and preserving in the baking-hot summers. It seemed as good an existence as any these days. If it wasn't for her painter I wondered if she would have stopped dead ahead of me and announced that she was staying.

The gardens gave me another flicker of home. I thought of messing about in Dad's veggie garden with Danni after school. Sprinklers tossing fat droplets of water in circles across the rows of green. Dad with his pants rolled up to the top of his calves. The three of us thumbing seeds into soft warm soil while Mum looked down on us with a white wine in one hand and the phone in the other. I meandered in the warmth of this for a while, getting a small pang of sadness on the way back out.

All of the fresh fruit and vegetables rocketed through our unsuspecting stomachs and left us bailed up in a rusty outdoor toilet for the rest of the day. The toilet was beside a machinery shed on the border of a few acres of soil and wilting citrus. We felt stupid and hoped that the vitamin hit would be worth it. Night seemed to close in much quicker now that we were off the hills. Tired and edgy, we took our final visits to the toilet, then locked ourselves in a four-wheel drive parked in the shed. It was musty and cramped and smelt like canine. The sprawling king beds and fresh linen of our previous home were a million miles away now.

At first light we staggered from the car and set off again. We weaved our way along the grid of roads servicing the market gardens until a sweep of tiled roofs appeared and we surfaced into a subdivision. The drone of insects disappeared and an unnerving silence took its place. Lizzy hummed and chatted away to a skittish Chessboard. The more blasé she acted, the more I knew she was worried sick about him. We rolled quietly past the dormant houses. Some of them had paved frontages instead of gardens and looked no different to how they might if inhabited. I cooked up ridiculous fantasies of the cute uni students that could be inside. Killing time on Facebook and sunbaking in the backyard. Home alone until their mum brought their brothers and sisters back from school. Flirting with me on text about how they were bored out of their mind.

It had clouded over during the night but the heat had remained. Now the air felt sticky and we heard the distant echo of thunder somewhere to the north. At the outer edge of the houses was a long, high wall blocking them in from whatever lay to the west. We traced along this wall for a while without any luck. Eventually Lizzy stopped and looked back behind us.

'Does this thing ever end?' said Lizzy.

'What is it even for?' said Taylor.

'I think it's like a sound barrier to the highway on the other side,' I replied.

'There's a highway over there?' asked Lizzy, looking up at the wall.

'Does it go to the city?' asked Taylor.

I shrugged. 'Sorry,' I said.

'You're the worst, Nox,' said Taylor, deadpan.

'Let's just keep heading north. Otherwise we have to backtrack and who knows how long it goes southwards,' I said.

I pedalled off without waiting for a reply.

Following the wall was slow going. There wasn't always a street that ran parallel, so we had to work in semicircles, keeping it on our left shoulder until finally it was gone.

I was right about the highway. It sat on top of the subdivision, stretching away to the north and south like a runway. Six lanes of vastness broken only by the occasional overpass and hulk of an abandoned car. We climbed down a steep, sandy slope onto the nearest lanes. These were separated from the other side by a tubular concrete island. The section we were in felt low and enclosed. It would be almost impossible to get back up the slope with our bikes and supplies.

Taylor and Lizzy looked at me for an opinion on which direction we should take. The highway wasn't familiar, but I knew that the city was still closer to our north than it was to the south. So we pedalled northward with hopes that it might magically deliver us to the city.

The riding was good on the highway, but none of us felt at ease. There were long stretches without an exit where the road seemed to close in around us like a concrete riverbed. It amplified the noises we made. Our voices, the squeak of our wheels, the rattle of tins in our baskets. At one point Chess let out a solitary bark that was shrill and piercing and sent a chill rippling across my arms. There were also more abandoned cars out here than we had seen anywhere else. We weaved around their creepy, silent frames and tried not to think of *The Walking Dead*. I tried to work out why this highway had more early risers than anywhere else we had seen. The only explanation I could think of was that it was heading towards the airport.

Ironically it was Lizzy who wanted out of there first. The thunder we had heard in the morning sounded closer now and the sky took on a slightly purple tinge. The highway had maintained its trajectory with no indication of swinging westward. There was a good chance the city would be south of us now.

Subconsciously our pace had quickened and more than once Chess stopped and rubbernecked to look back at the empty road behind us. It was seriously creepy.

'Okay, we're getting off at the next exit,' said Lizzy in the wake of more muffled thunder.

There was no argument from the rest of us.

Twenty minutes later we spotted an overpass. We cycled up the entrance ramp, then swung west and crossed the bridge down into the welcome mess of houses.

The suburbs that used to mark the fringes of Perth were old and tired. Bricks changed to dark browns or morphed into weatherboard. Yards were large and rambling, filled with rusted-out cars and spindly shrubs. The silence of the highway and newer subdivisions was broken here by creaking shed doors and jittery wooden windows. Chess's ears were rigid with these noises and others. He knew, as did we, that these were prime suburbs for the Bulls.

We picked out one of the nicer houses and sheltered for the evening as the thunderstorms drifted closer. It was a loud and unsettling night. Storms seemed to shift all around us, filling the house with pops and rumbles and flickers of light that outlined the lumps of our bodies huddled together on the living room floor. And there were other noises. Doors banging shut. The rev of an engine or generator. Music, murmured and vague, as if on the edge of a dream, but never quite within it.

Suddenly we were in the same world as these sounds. Not listening from the safety of a shopping centre or mansion.

None of us mentioned these things in the morning. But they were written on each of our faces. These suburbs were alive. With what, we would find out soon.

8

For the best part of two days we worked our way westward. The older suburbs were sprawling and full of cul-de-sacs and dead-end streets that had us backtracking and winding north or south to creep our way forward. We stopped into a few houses for food and to use toilets that still had water in the cisterns. But generally we stayed away. They had a feel about them. As if they belonged to somebody. Not the vanished owners or renters. Somebody that was still around. Up until now nothing we had done in Carousel or elsewhere had felt like trespassing. But I couldn't shake the feeling that this was exactly what we were doing.

I was writing at every opportunity. On breaks in drought-stricken parks. On the dusty kitchen tables of strangers. At night beneath a harsh circle of torchlight. The work wasn't singular or focused. I was just filling pages. Writing to convince myself that I could. Racing towards some hidden moment when I might become the same as Taylor and Lizzy and the rest of the living world.

The distant city felt like a ticking clock running faster and faster as we closed in towards it.

The Finns watched me with a mixture of bemusement and encouragement. I hadn't told them what I had Tommy. But then, the two of them knew me better than anybody now. They knew that the writing wasn't just about what was on the page. Their silence and space was solidarity in its simplest form.

Lizzy seemed busy with her music anyway. She had brought a laptop along and would occasionally allow herself an hour to fiddle around with mixes before quickly shutting it back down and hoping the battery might last until we found more power. Meeting Tommy had made the album real again. It actually existed. And so did she. The poppy half of Canadian indie pillars Taylor & Lizzy. A fixture on any alternative radio station or hip summer festival. If what Tommy and Taylor said was true and we were now in a city, or a world, full of Artists, Lizzy wanted to be on her game.

Taylor seemed edgy for other reasons entirely. Things I knew about that maybe even Lizzy did not. I had underestimated the connection she had felt with the Boxing Day painter. Sold it off as loneliness. The thought of human contact after years without it. But Taylor felt a real connection to this mystery girl. Enough to convince Lizzy to forget the airport and its fractured link to Canada and their mother. Enough to have us leave the security of our cushy hillside life. To risk running into Bulls and Loots and whatever the hell else lay in the abandoned sprawl of future Perth. Leaving the hills was about much more than Taylor finding her painter crush. Yet once again Taylor was leading, and Lizzy and I following. Like the doors in Carousel, it was Taylor's goal that defined us the most.

We started passing the occasional shop and warehouse. Really niche places like a repair centre for remote controllers or a ride-on lawnmower reseller. They filled the gaps between a depressing series of houses. Small box-like fibro places set back on quarter-acre blocks, sold off in the seventies in a city sprawling outward wherever it pleased. We were relieved to be emerging out of endless suburbia, but what lay ahead didn't feel overly welcoming.

We came across a couple of blackened buildings and street corners where it seemed like a gas pipe might have blown and burnt out the surrounding area. Chess sniffed cautiously and I thought again of Tommy's warning about the city.

'I need a bathroom and some lunch,' said Lizzy.

She had stopped cycling and was assessing the options.

'Which one of these palaces would you like to make a home?' asked Taylor.

The three of us looked around. One side of the street had a series of water-stained fibro houses. The other had a warehouse with an ambitiously large car park neighbouring some kind of fenced-off power grid.

Lizzy rolled forward.

'Number twelve has roses in the garden. Let's run with that,' she replied.

The laundry door was open at the back. Taylor let herself in and walked through to the front.

'Soup anyone?' she asked as she let us in.

'Wow,' I replied.

A wave of *old-lady-at-the-stove* smacked us in the face as Lizzy bombed through to find the toilet.

'I swear that smell is immune to the apocalypse,' I said.

Taylor smirked and wandered through the neat shrine of a living room. It was dated and dusty, but neat as a pin. Patterned wallpaper. A cabinet housing glassware and football memorabilia. An orange couch with wooden veneer. I stayed away from people's photos, but Taylor drank them up like some wacky anthropologist. She nosed around while I distracted myself with an ancient TV guide.

'This place is empty,' said Lizzy from the kitchen.

'Let's go next door,' I said, replacing the guide.

'You'd think there would be some minestrone at least,' said Taylor.

We went next door but found the kitchen empty there also. As were the following four houses. Doors unlocked. Cupboards ajar and empty.

'Popular street,' said Lizzy at the sixth house.

Taylor and I glanced at her. It was unnerving to see

such obvious signs of someone else in the area.

'Let's get out of this weirdo suburb,' said Taylor.

We cycled through a series of similar streets as the sun dipped and spread giant eucalypt-shaped shadows across the bitumen. I checked a couple of houses and a deli as we went. Each place told a replica story. No sign of habitation, but the cupboards and shelves were stripped bare. We stewed quietly over our lack of supplies and kept moving. Eventually it was dark and we bunked down in a brick-and-tile place to eat some dry noodles from the hills. Taylor got caught out in the toilet and Lizzy and I had to ransack the place for tissues. It was like somebody was going from house to house, taking everything but the furniture.

The place was hot and musty and before long the three of us gravitated to join Chess on the porch. Taylor and Lizzy scrolled through the iTunes library on somebody's laptop. Between them they had a couple of hard drives and a plan to collect some decent music as we journeyed to the city. So far the bounty had been small. Most laptops were out of charge, having lay dormant for so long. Others, like this one, did have charge, but the library was full of *Idol* winners and top forty.

Chess shuffled about and whimpered. I watched as his ears shifted about with the sounds of the night.

Abruptly they stopped.

There were footsteps coming from somewhere

down the street. The three of us froze and stared out into the blackness. The footsteps shifted from the road to concrete or something smoother. A door opened somewhere, then there was silence. We shared a glance and strained our ears. After a few moments we heard the door reopen and the footsteps resumed across the concrete, then back out onto the street. This time they were getting louder. Moving toward us.

Lizzy took a hold of Chess's collar. Out of the darkness came the tiny red glow of a cigarette. Then the thin silhouette of a young guy carrying a can of food and some toilet paper. He shuffled along, smoking and humming a silent tune in his head. He was right alongside us when he stopped and looked up.

Chess let out a bark.

'Hey,' he said.

'Hey,' said Lizzy.

'Just getting some beans,' he said.

We nodded. He finished his cigarette and looked up at the sky for a while as if he had almost forgotten we were there. He looked like your regular everyday hipster. Beard. Boots. Oversized flannelette.

'You live near here?' asked Taylor.

The guy looked confused. As if the idea of having a home was somehow strange.

'We jam at a warehouse on Henry Street,' he replied.

9

The warehouse was a slum. In a previous world it had been a food wholesaler with a converted rehearsal space for bands built into the back corner. Now it looked like the set from *Trainspotting*. There were mattresses scattered around the floor. Rubbish kicked into corners and stacked in overflowing boxes. The charred remains of haphazard fires made during winter. A layer of dirt on the floor so thick that it felt springy to walk on. And, slumped on couches beneath a bank of jittery fluoros, four anaemic looking members of local five-piece Kink & Kink.

Joseph, the guy from the street, didn't introduce us. He just took his beans over to a sink area and started looking through a stack of grimy pots and plates. The people on the couch, a girl and three guys, had glanced at us upon entry, but appeared totally underwhelmed at our presence in their warehouse. A Smiths record was droning away under a dusty needle in the corner.

Taylor glanced over at Joseph and shifted uncomfortably.

'How are you guys doing?' asked Lizzy and strolled over with Chess at her heels. Taylor and I trailed behind her.

The band looked our way, a little surprised.

'Where did you find an Australian shepherd?' another bearded guy asked.

'Oh, he's a border collie I think. He kinda found us,' replied Lizzy.

'It's an Australian shepherd. The colouring is darker,' said the guy.

Lizzy mouthed *okay* and looked like she might walk out then and there.

'I'm Taylor, this is Nox and my sister Lizzy. Our dog's name is Chessboard,' said Taylor, trying to salvage the situation.

The girl looked up and flashed a big smile as if she had just noticed there were other people in the room. I got a weird feeling in my feet and clammed up.

'Do you have a Residency in Kewdale, too?' she asked.

'How do you mean, Residency?' asked Taylor.

Lizzy had tired of waiting for any kind of hospitality and slumped down onto a couch. Taylor and I sat down next to her.

'An Artist Residency. Somewhere you can work on your art without distraction,' she replied.

'Oh. No. We're just passing through,' said Taylor.

Joseph walked over, eating the beans straight from a

pot. The others watched him hungrily. Adjacent to the couches was a semi-enclosed room with an impressive array of instruments, amplifiers and mixing desks.

'What do you guys play?' asked Lizzy.

The band looked at Lizzy like she was some boring auntie or writing for a community newspaper.

'Anti-folk,' replied a guy wearing what I'm pretty sure was a ladies' leather jacket.

'Oh yeah. Like The Racketballs?' asked Lizzy.

'Who?' replied Joseph, mouth full of beans.

'They're small. You probably haven't heard of them,' said Lizzy.

A couple of the band members nodded. Taylor looked at Lizzy, slightly agitated.

'Anyway. Joseph said you guys have been here since the Disappearance?' asked Taylor.

'I didn't say Disappearance,' said Joseph.

'It's a time vortex,' muttered a scrawny dude from behind a book titled *A Detailed History of the Nautical Knot*.

The girl looked at him and pondered this earnestly. She looked dirty, with matted brown hair and jeans that seemed pasted to her legs. But her face was animated and pretty. I tried my hardest not to stare.

'Have you met a lot of other Artists?' asked Taylor, moving on.

'A Japanese manga Artist. His work is amazing,' said the bearded guy.

'Right,' said Taylor. 'Anyone else?'

They shrugged, uninterested. I took a trail bar out of my pocket. All five band members turned my way.

'Do you guys want a trail bar?' I asked.

They nodded, but none of them got up. I walked over and handed them a box of six. They sat eating quietly, like mesmerised schoolkids. Taylor and Lizzy glanced at each other. Neither of them seemed to have a handle on these guys.

Taylor sipped on some water and looked around.

'Is that spring water?' asked the girl.

Taylor looked at her. 'You don't have any water?'

'There's something wrong with the plumbing here,' she replied, sheepishly.

Taylor sighed and passed her the bottle. The five of them huddled around and hydrated their sickly hipster bodies.

'This is amazing. Thank you,' said the girl earnestly.

Taylor forced a tiny smile.

'You don't have any blues records, do you?' asked the bearded guy.

Taylor stared at him. Lizzy held in a laugh.

'No. Just food and water,' replied Taylor.

'Are you guys Patrons?' asked the ladies' leather guy.

Lizzy groaned. Taylor shook her head. These idiots had no idea who they were talking to. Lizzy walked over to the guitars, plugged in a Gibson and ripped through a couple of riffs that shut everyone the hell up.

Taylor turned to me in between riffs. 'These guys are amazing, right?' she whispered.

'I don't get how they're still alive,' I replied.

'They cleaned this place out, then just started going from house to house whenever they remembered to eat lunch,' said Taylor.

I couldn't help but laugh. Taylor looked at me for a moment, then started laughing too. Thankfully Lizzy's guitar drowned us out.

'It's getting late. We might as well crash here and see if we can find out anything useful,' said Taylor.

I nodded but felt uncomfortable in our abruptly social surrounds.

'You should talk to that girl,' said Taylor.

My face burned like a fool. Taylor smiled and ruffled my hair. 'There's whisky in my bag,' she added and walked over to join Lizzy at the guitars.

Chess hung by my side looking overwhelmed by all of the smells in the place. I knelt down and hugged him under my arm while I rummaged for the whisky. I necked some and looked up to see Kink & Kink staring right at me. I held up the bottle and they shuffled over.

The bearded guy, Yoshi, insisted that we drink it three-to-one with some room-temperature water. Even though there weren't enough glasses, and the ones they had were stained with who knows what. At one stage Lizzy walked over and took a swig straight from the bottle, just to spite the guy I think. He just started on about Polish vodkas.

I found out the girl's name was Molly. She was friendly and smiled a lot, but talking to her was weird. It was like she really thought about and assessed everything I said. Which in turn made me do the same and question whether I even had opinions or stories or anything. She also looked right into my eyes, like *right* into them, the whole time we spoke. I had no idea what this was about, except that it probably wasn't a come-on in any traditional Hollywood sense. If Molly was with one of the other band members it wasn't obvious to me.

Meanwhile Taylor and Lizzy were putting on a belting live rendition of their new album. The instruments and amplifiers here were way better than anything they had in Carousel and the songs sounded dense and awesome. Even Kink & Kink seemed to be into it, albeit in their apathetic, underwhelmed way. It was cool to see Taylor and Lizzy back as themselves for a while, but the music brought with it a heavy wave of emotions and memories from our time in Carousel. Together with the whisky and the heat and the strange girl wedged into the couch next to me, the whole thing felt a bit like a dream.

After a while Yoshi got on a drum kit and started tinkering away on a series of snares. Taylor and Lizzy stopped playing their songs and tried to jam along with him, but it didn't really mesh. Sweaty and buzzing, they took a break and left him to it. I joined them to look for a bathroom and we found some pretty disturbing stuff. The toilet looked as though it had been blocked for a long time now. Instead of this, a door stood ajar to an alleyway full of buckets and a smell that was insane. The warehouse still had power, but, from what we could gather, no running water or plumbing. There were also no plants, food or medical supplies. Nothing you might associate with extended survival. These guys had somehow survived living day to day from the very start. It was as impressive as it was sad.

A silky, wavering voice pulled us back into the warehouse. All of the band were at their instruments now. Yoshi at the drum kit with a mic hovering to the side of his face. The ladies' leather guy and his thinner version on guitars. Joseph taking himself way too seriously on the bass. And Molly, hovering waiflike below a mic stand, magically transformed, like a thousand singers before her, from nobody to somebody within the space of a note. Their stuff was raw and messy, but then Molly came in over the top and gave it an ethereal quality. Like some winding, backroad trip to a tropical paradise.

What the hell was happening in the world, I thought. These guys were stranded in the suburbs, the least equipped people to survive in the regular world, let alone one without Centrelink or parents or drive-through takeaway. Yet here they were, almost two years on, still alive, still cooking up kooky, beautiful music for nobody to hear.

Taylor and Lizzy poured themselves a whisky and sat

down to discover Kink & Kink like they might have in a club back in Toronto or Vancouver, or out on tour, or on any night in their pre-Carousel lives. I was happy for them, but felt like the last regular person on the planet. I left my drink unfinished and took a notepad and torch outside.

There were some milk crates grouped in a small circle by one of the side exits. I sat on one and pulled another over for a desk, then propped the torch on a drainpipe running down the wall. I had written in worse places since we left the hills. Music and light spilled out of the leaky warehouse into the silent black suburb. I wrote about Molly and the band and how they were nothing like the cardboard cut-outs I had envisioned in Tommy's stories.

At some stage the vocals dropped from the music inside and a door opened, beaming light and noise into the alley. Molly surfaced with a cigarette and tiptoed over to where I was sitting. There was no time to put away the torch or notepad.

'Hey,' I said.

Molly hovered, somehow unsure of where to sit even though there were milk crates all around her. I pulled one across to the wall beside me. She looked at it for a moment, then sat.

'You guys are good,' I said.

Molly smiled, but seemed to have forgotten the music playing inside.

'I love the stars in our new city,' she said, looking up at the strip of sky above us. The nights were heavy with stars these days. As if somebody had selected them all and hit *bold*.

'Yeah. I feel like I hadn't really seen stars before the Disappearance. Except for in a planetarium or something,' I replied.

A breeze trickled past us from the east and we both shivered.

'Are you guys okay here?' I asked.

'Oh yeah. We're great. Thank you for the whisky,' she replied.

It felt like we still hadn't really looked at each other when she slipped off her seat and propped herself on my legs. Her hair flickered around my face as we made out without saying anything else. She tasted of smoke and whisky and the house parties of my youth. We touched each other and wrapped legs around each other and did everything that might normally lead to sex. Then we stopped and Molly dropped her head into my chest and kind of tucked up into a ball. This caught me out a little. I looked down at her, then put my arms around her. She burrowed deeper. Her voice and her music felt a million miles away now. Across from us my notepad blew open. The empty pages flickered mockingly in the wind.

10

The morning was blustery hot with the faint smell
of bushfire. The Finns and I had been up for hours.
Carrying out our routines of stretching, eating and
washing the best that we could. The warehouse looked
even more dismal in daylight. Like the worst sharehouse
you can imagine, without any walls to shelter the mess.
Molly, Joseph and co lay comatose throughout the
space. I looked over at Molly's small, mousey face and
wondered what filled her dreams. Her parents' inner-city
townhouse. A full fridge and endless wi-fi. The basics of
life sorted so that she was free to simply exist and be the
artist she wanted to be. Or maybe I was wrong. Maybe
she had arrived in the place she had always dreamt of.
A society where anarchy reigns and self-expression is
regarded above all else.

Still, I couldn't shake the feeling that Molly needed
rescuing. It didn't seem possible that someone could
be so unaffected by such a monumental shift in the
world. And Molly wasn't in denial. In a way, she and

the band were more accepting of what was happening than anyone we had met. I felt a weird desire to be there when she finally succumbed. To offer her a shoulder and shelter from the inevitable floodlight of reality. To ignore myself because she was pretty and in a band and somehow these things made it justifiable. But the more I thought about it, the more it seemed to be about me, rather than Molly or anybody else.

When she and the others still hadn't risen by midmorning, the Finns and I gathered out the front to debrief.

'There's no point in waiting around,' said Taylor.

Lizzy and I looked at her.

'You think they will be okay?' asked Lizzy.

'They have up until now,' replied Taylor.

We stood in some weighty silence. None of us felt great about the situation.

'Look, they need to get their shit together, but I don't see how we can really help with that,' said Taylor.

'We could clean the place up. Try to fix the plumbing. Put in a garden or something,' said Lizzy.

She didn't sound overly keen.

'It would be back looking like this in a week,' said Taylor.

'Did they mention the Curator?' I asked. 'Maybe he checks in on them.'

Taylor shook her head.

Lizzy sighed. 'So what do we do?'

'We can't take them with us. They wouldn't last a day in this weather,' said Taylor. 'Plus we don't even really know if where we're going will be any better.'

'It couldn't be much worse, could it?' said Lizzy in a mini stand-off.

I looked out at the dusty, barren street.

'I don't think they want to come with us anyway,' I said.

The Finns looked at me.

'What did she say to you?' asked Taylor.

'Nothing really,' I replied. 'I just don't think they care about growing a garden or living somewhere better. They want other things. Cred or status or something.'

'To be famous, but still stay unknown,' said Lizzy.

Taylor and I nodded. It was true. They were hipster kids trapped in a bizarre ideology where success held a delicate line on the scale of popularity. You had to creep up on it, but never tip over into the mainstream. To be known was to be labelled, and to them to be labelled was to die.

Taylor and Lizzy hovered in silence and waited, Chess restless by Lizzy's side. It seemed to be up to me to make the decision.

'Let's get out of here,' I said.

The Finns nodded and Lizzy put a hand on my shoulder.

'We'll leave our food for them,' said Taylor. 'It will keep them off the streets for a while.'

Lizzy and I agreed and the three of us emptied our bags and left a pile of supplies inside the door for them. Before we left I tore out the pages I had written about the band – actually more so about Molly – the night before, and left them with the food. They read like a review of her and her music and I thought there was at least a chance that it would offer the kind of validation she could stomach. At the top I wrote, *On Molly – of Kink & Kink.*

The suburbs changed not long after we left. As if the Kink & Kink warehouse was the final marker on Perth's outer suburbs. Cautiously we shifted ahead into new ground. There was a swampy nature reserve to the north of us. The bush looked thick and uninhabited. Probably full of Bulls. We skirted around it and got a glimpse of some towers that looked like they might have been part of the airport. Lizzy ignored them and kept on without a fuss. It was hard to tell how much she was putting her sister first in this venture to the city. For Lizzy the airport, operational or not, had always held the strongest link to home. Now we were bypassing it for the second time with no real plan to return.

By lunchtime we hit another highway, this one bordered by airport hotels and rental car outlets. It was ghostly and exposed. Rather than walk along it we crossed over to some small streets that ran parallel and followed the dirty green signs that now pointed us back southward to the city.

'Is that like the main river?' asked Taylor.

'Yeah,' I replied, and followed her gaze toward the Swan.

Pockets of shimmering water broke through the trees and houses to the west of us.

'Are there many bridges?' asked Taylor.

I hadn't really thought about bridges.

'I know there are some closer to the city,' I replied.

Taylor looked at me for a moment, then nodded.

We kept onward between the river and the highway and at dusk we came across a racetrack. We walked our bikes through the patchy, overgrown grass of the track, past a series of windblown marquees and an ageing grandstand. The whole place felt sad and not part of a world just gone, but something of another age entirely. Where people rode horses in great circles so that others could dress up, drink and trade money.

'Old World,' said Lizzy.

I nodded. It was the term we had started using for places like this that seemed totally normal just years ago, but now felt somehow ancient and strange.

No breeze had come that afternoon and the night felt as hot as the day. We slept out under a skewered marquee and woke with mosquito bites spread dangerously across our arms and legs. We were inadvertently playing a numbers game where the more bites meant the more chance of a virus. No big deal in our previous lives, but out here things might be different.

Taylor hovered restlessly as Lizzy and I yawned and fumbled about with breakfast. She was eager to keep moving. As if every minute that passed lessened her chances of finding her painter. Maybe the heat was slowing us down. Maybe Perth was bigger and more sprawling than I remembered. Either way, our progress was slow. We trudged our way forward, then spent the night in a soulless, box-like motel shouting *Free Foxtel* on every surface. I didn't feel so bad kicking our way into one of these places. Not like somebody's house or business. But it was quiet and eerie as hell. We were desperate for our own space, but too scared to spread out into separate rooms. The beds were still made but covered with dust, so we stripped them back and started over with sheets from a housekeeping trolley. Not that we needed any. It was muggy and unsettled outside, and breathless in.

We hadn't found anywhere with power or running water since the warehouse. Lizzy and I had climbed to the top of the motel to see if there were any pockets of light in the surrounding suburbs. The view wasn't exactly panoramic, and we found nothing. An Artist-free zone.

Still the highway kept on southward. Occasionally we would get a glimpse across the river to the city. At the conclusion of each lightshow, it had remained black and mysterious. No towers of light or giant mining logos. But now, during daylight, it seemed grey and steadfast, and no different to any other day.

The only stores we passed were service stations, where cars were still attached to bowsers. We pillaged tepid water, Gatorade and whatever else we could stomach without cramping too badly.

As the sun finally dipped into a murky bank of storm clouds we settled on a narrow high-rise of self-contained apartments peering east or west, depending on your budget. I volunteered for the sofa, hoping that the Finns would crash out early in the bedrooms and I could sit up and write. Taylor stayed up for a while and the two of us played Bullshit by torchlight with a deck of cards from the bedside table. At first it felt forced but after a few hands we got into it and had a couple of laughs.

Taylor gathered the cards for one final hand. She started working away on her longwinded shuffling routine.

'How was it hooking up with a girl again after all this time?' she asked.

I hadn't spoken to either of the Finns about making out with Molly, but somehow, as always, they seemed to know everything about me.

'It was weird, mostly,' I replied.

Taylor nodded. 'It's been almost two years. That makes sense,' she replied.

'Actually a little while before that,' I replied, for some fucking reason.

'Oh really? How come?' she asked.

'I don't know. Bad timing, maybe,' I replied. 'I guess I

was kind of in a rut before Carousel.'

'Not writing much?' she asked.

I shrugged. I hadn't been writing at all.

'I finished uni and was just working. Not going out much,' I replied.

'Because of that Heather girl?' she asked.

'Maybe. I haven't really thought about it.'

Taylor rolled her eyes.

'What?' I asked.

'Come on. We were stuck in a mall with nothing to do for like forever. Don't tell me you didn't rehash every single tiny event in your life a thousand times over,' said Taylor.

'Nope. That must just be you I guess,' I replied.

'Fuck off, Nox.'

We both smiled and Taylor was finally ready to deal the cards.

'What about you and this painter girl?' I asked, without thinking.

Taylor looked at me carefully.

'Do you think we might run into her somewhere out here?' I backtracked.

'I don't know,' replied Taylor, casually. 'Tommy said the more time that passes, the less people he sees,' said Taylor.

'What do you think is happening to everyone?' I asked, slightly alarmed.

Taylor shrugged.

'It took us so long to get out of Carousel,' said Taylor. 'For a while people were probably looking around, trying to figure out what the hell happened. But eventually people start to accept things. They settle down and find a place in the world. Whatever the hell it looks like.'

I looked at her. Taylor was a realist and right on the mark with most things. Probably this, too.

'Do you think we'll have to do that one day?' I asked.

'Probably,' she sighed.

'Where would you want to live?' I asked.

Taylor looked through her cards and thought about it.

'The beaches here are pretty awesome, yeah?' she asked.

'I guess,' I said.

'So we'll find a house right out front of the best one. Wire up some solar panels. Grow a garden. Teach ourselves how to surf,' said Taylor.

I felt like crying and had no idea why. Taylor looked at me curiously.

'Yeah?' she asked.

'Yeah. Totally,' I replied.

We finished the game and Taylor left for bed.

I had willed myself awake and wrote steadily for an hour or two about some of the things we had seen. The real Stuart hovered at my shoulder with a steady critique of every line. Was he even a writer? I hoped he was a weirdo puppeteer or something as opposed to some world-famous novelist that I had cheated out of his place on the ark.

At some point I had stopped writing and fallen asleep. I woke to Chess nuzzling his wet nose in at the base of my neck.

'Chess!' whispered Lizzy harshly.

I opened my eyes to find her huddled by the glass door to the balcony. Lightning licked across the hills in the distance. Chess dipped his head and padded back over to join her.

I sat up and rubbed my eyes. The room was pitch-dark. Lizzy and Chess were silhouetted by a weird purple glow somewhere to the east. It could have been the rising sun, but it felt too early for that. I pulled on a hoodie and joined them on the floor. Lizzy gave me a brief smile and turned back to catch the flickers of lightning. The thunder was soft, but constant. Storms seemed to run the entire length of the hills.

It was hard not to think of Rocky. He and Lizzy used to love watching lightning. A storm in the hills had been the last thing he saw in Carousel. Now that we were out in the world we had discovered that there was a name for people like me and Rocky. Patrons. Sheltered not by intention, but by fate. The old world had been cruel to Rocky, and the new one not much better. I felt an anger rising that for once I didn't feel like swallowing.

'Rocky would have loved this one,' whispered Lizzy.

Lightning pulsed across her delicate, elven face.

'I fucking hate the Curator,' I replied.

Lizzy looked at me, surprised.

'Don't you?' I asked.

Lizzy shrugged. 'He's probably just a regular dude.'

'That can make the population of the world disappear?' I replied.

She shrugged again.

'I just mean that people project a lot of shit onto famous people. In their minds they twist them from what they are, into what they need them to be. The answer to why life is so hard or weird or random,' said Lizzy.

I turned back out to the lightning, unconvinced.

'You know why bands never reply to fan mail?' she asked.

'Because there's so much of it?' I replied.

'Well, yeah. But also, reading too much of that stuff will make you crazy,' said Lizzy. 'Everyone has their take on who you are. What your songs are about. How you performed. You start to second-guess yourself. *Maybe I am like that. Maybe that song is about something else.* It's a fucking identity crisis waiting to happen.'

'You think the Curator has an identity crisis?' I asked.

'I would, if I were him,' said Lizzy.

'I still say *fuck him*,' I said. 'For Rocky.'

Lizzy smiled. 'Sure. For Rocky,' she said.

Chess stood up, shuffled, and sat back where he was. He wasn't enjoying the storm like Lizzy.

'What do you want to do when we get to the city?'
I asked.

'Look around. Meet some people. Not die,' she
shrugged.

'Totally,' I said.

'Honestly,' she added. 'The only thing I'm excited
about is gigging the album.'

I looked at her and smiled.

'Does that sound messed up?' she asked.

'Nah. It sounds awesome,' I replied. 'Put me on the
door?'

Lizzy feigned reluctance. I shoved her.

'What do you want to do when we get there?' she
asked.

'I don't know. Just fit in,' I said.

'Nox, come on. That Patron thing is bullshit, man,'
said Lizzy.

I looked at her. Wondering if she somehow knew
about Stuart and the taxi.

'All of this is bullshit,' said Lizzy, nodding out at the
blackness and lightning. 'Plus you're with us now.'

'I don't know. Are you guys still cool?' I joked.

'Well, that's a point,' said Lizzy. 'Maybe not, according
to Kink & Kink.'

'Or The Racketballs?' I asked.

Lizzy let out a laugh and turned to check that she
hadn't woken Taylor.

'I knew you made them up,' I said.

'Those guys totally bought it. Kids your age are screwed without the internet,' said Lizzy.

'You sound like a hundred,' I replied.

'Shut up, Nox. God. Way to ruin my storm,' said Lizzy.

I smiled and we stayed there until dawn really arrived. And we could see that the hills were on fire.

11

A swampy red glow engulfed the hills for as far as we could see. The scarp seemed bigger than normal. As if it were trying to rise up and run away from itself. Within the mass of black and red were the ripple and snap of great flames. The Perth hills were dry and overgrown and now they burnt with a fire to end all fires.

Immediately our thoughts went to Tommy. He was up there somewhere. Most likely alone. Most likely without a car or a bike. Tommy probably didn't know this, but those hills were bushfire central during Perth's summer months. Every year houses were lost and people evacuated. Now, without fire trucks and water bombers, a fire could tear its way through the bush as it pleased.

The three of us stared at it in horror for a while, trying to reassure ourselves that Tommy would be fine. Eventually we left the apartment and resumed our way south, glancing sideways to the hills as we went. We left behind the motels and hire-car rentals, moving into an area where the highway widened and buildings shrunk back, making way for exit ramps, bus stops and token parkland.

At eight the wind turned to the east, blowing giant mountains of smoke across the outer suburbs. It took a half-hour to reach us. By eight-thirty the whole of the east was blanketed. By nine we lost sight of the highway in front of us.

'Okay. So do we have a plan or something?' asked Lizzy.

Taylor and I stopped and squinted into the distance. The smoke wasn't choking thick just yet. More like a cloud wrapping itself around a mountain.

'Do you think we're far from a bridge, Nox?' asked Taylor.

'I don't think so. But we could walk straight past in this,' I replied.

'Do we really want to be on a bridge when we can't see properly?' asked Lizzy.

Taylor sighed and coughed.

'We should keep moving south towards the city. Even if we miss a bridge there are others, right?' said Taylor.

'Yeah, eventually,' I replied.

'Alright,' said Taylor, and set off without waiting.

Taylor seemed kind of frantic. As if our path to the city was somehow closing. Lizzy and I shared a glance. She put a leash on Chess and grudgingly we followed.

We kept on. Walking our bikes like trolleys. Wayfarers covering our eyes and t-shirts pulled up over our noses. Ill-equipped hipsters coughing our way through the apocalypse. What I could see through my tinted lenses looked surreal. The world had turned the plastic cheese yellow of a fast-food chain. Smoke shifted, slow and ominous like a giant squid on some secret current. Two dirty pairs of Chuck Taylors scraped their way along the footpath ahead of me. I got a flash of reality. This was our world now. This is what it looked like at the end of things. I was terrified but at the same time tuned into the world like never before.

The easterly was heating up and getting stronger. None of us could see anything now, let alone breathe properly. Chess stopped and looked around as if to say *Okay. This is getting stupid.*

'We need to stop somewhere,' said Lizzy.

'There is nowhere,' replied Taylor.

Stupidly we had waited until the smoke had swallowed everything around us. I felt the Finns' eyes on me, waiting.

'There were more buildings back the way we came,' I said.

'We're not going backwards,' said Taylor bluntly.

'She's not going anywhere, Taylor,' I snapped.

'What? Who's not going anywhere?' asked Lizzy.

'Nobody,' said Taylor sharply. 'Come on. This is ridiculous.'

'Taylor. What the fuck is going on?' asked Lizzy.

'Nothing, Lizzy,' said Taylor.

'Fine then. Let's go back and find shelter,' said Lizzy stubbornly.

'Oh my god. Seriously. This is so fucking stupid,' said Taylor.

Lizzy stood firm. I cursed myself for letting the painter slip.

'Okay. Alright. He's talking about the Boxing Day painter. Tommy said she might be in the city. So what?' said Taylor.

'Wow,' said Lizzy.

Chess started barking. A triggered smoke alarm was wailing away in a distant building.

'Lizzy. Come on. Do you really want to do this out here? Let's find somewhere to shelter before we all choke and die,' said Taylor.

Lizzy was silent. I could feel her fuming away beside me. My mind was racing, trying to dig us all a way out of this.

'There's a casino on the river,' I blurted out. 'We should be right beside it now. If we head west I'm sure we'll run into it.'

Taylor was silent.

'Alright. Leave the bikes. We'll come back for them later,' said Lizzy.

She and Chess hovered impatiently beside me and we set out away from the highway toward what I hoped would be the river and casino. At first there was grass beneath our shoes. Then road. Then grass again. Alarms were triggering all over now and the smoke was thicker than ever. We should have tied ourselves together or something. Not that Taylor and Lizzy would go for that right now. I stopped, suddenly freaking out that I had lost the others. Taylor bumped into me.

'Are we there?' she yelled, above the alarms.

Lizzy and Chess emerged from the smoke behind her.

'Almost, I think,' I replied, without confidence.

We kept moving. The grass started sloping upwards. Climbing felt hard. Like we were on a mountain, not some small, sculptured hill. I was breathless and straining but every step we took upward made the smoke even worse. I began to feel a giant pressure on my shoulders. Like the casino had disappeared or was someplace else entirely.

I screamed as my shin rammed flush into steel.

'Are you okay?' yelled Taylor.

'Yeah,' I replied.

'What is it?' asked Taylor.

'I don't know. A fence or something maybe,' I replied.

I heard the zip of Taylor's backpack and saw the dull beam of torchlight. She leant in close to the steel.

'It's a billboard,' said Taylor.

'What does it say?' I asked.

'Guess,' said Taylor.

'Seriously?' I replied.

'Pink,' said Taylor, laughing and coughing at the same time.

'What do you mean?' I asked.

'She was supposed to play here. At the casino. You found it, Nox,' said Taylor.

I slumped down against the billboard and held my leg.

'Thank fuck for that,' I muttered.

'Lizzy, check this out,' said Taylor.

There was just alarms and smoke. Taylor looked up and waited.

'Lizzy!' yelled Taylor.

No reply. Lizzy and Chess were gone.

12

The Burswood resort and casino had been towering over the river to the east of the city for as long as I could remember. There had been name changes and expansions, but the chunky pyramid design and murky white walls had remained. It was Perth's sole casino. Home to a mix of haggard old pokey fiends, FIFO workers just back from shift, bank accounts brimming and body clocks all out of whack, and wealthy tourists from Asia sold on glossy brochures and partner deals with casinos on the east coast.

I had been there a few times. A birthday dinner for Dad in the fancy Chinese restaurant. With some German mates from uni to watch European soccer in the sports bar. Once with Heather for a one-night stay on our anniversary.

For a while there was a giant pressurised dome next door housing tennis tournaments and big touring artists like Katy Perry and Coldplay. Now it was all car bays and sprawling construction, like the rest of Perth.

Taylor and I hit the east side of the building and traced it around to a taxi rank and some restaurants. These places were locked, but further along was a foyer area where the doors were open and an information desk with flyers, luggage and trolleys stood unattended. I sat there alone on an empty trolley. My head numb and swirling. My eyes gone past stinging to some other sensation. Taylor had spent just a minute inside breathing the semi-fresh air before racing back into the chaos to find her sister. I was to stay by the taxi rank in case Lizzy and Chess found their way to the building.

My mouth felt dry and I realised that I was probably super dehydrated. I took the final bottle of water from my bag and forced myself to drink it despite feeling like I could throw up at any minute. Time felt fractured and uncertain. Like I had just watched Taylor run back out into the smoke, but also like I had been sitting there for hours. I felt a sharp spike of panic and ran outside to yell after them. My voice was hoarse and weak. I pushed through the smoke to the edge of the building and yelled some more. Nothing came back to me.

Suddenly I remembered the radios.

I raced back inside and rifled through my bag to find my walkie-talkie. It was tucked away at the bottom. I pulled it out and switched it on, but the battery was dead. We had charged them before we left the hills, but not since. A lot of the time the three of us still acted like we were inside Carousel or our mansion; not stressing about things like batteries or drinking water. We were idiots and the world had quickly found us out.

I sat back down and lent against the wall. Visions of my parents' place swamped through my thumping head. It was probably gone now. The big, awkward deck that Dad had designed and built. The mishmash floorboards that Mum was constantly sweeping. Our bedrooms. Empty, but with the smells and sounds of our childhood. All of it burning or burnt already. I never loved our house in the hills, but I couldn't stand the idea of it burning down with nobody around to fight for it.

The smoke outside had started to finger its way into the foyer. I swore at it, kicked the doors shut and felt about as alone as I ever had.

Taylor would find them.

Taylor would find them.

Taylor would find them.

I twirled downward into a horrible, empty sleep.

The daylight was fading when I awoke. I pulled myself up and looked around. I was alone in the foyer. The smoke outside in the taxi rank was thick and seemed no different to before. I tied a shirt around my face, put on my sunglasses and pushed open the door. It was quieter out there now. A lonely smoke alarm sang in the distance. The wind blew, but had softened from the howling version of the morning. Somewhere to the east I could hear a low rumbling. Dull, like the idling of heavy machinery. It was the sound of the hills still burning.

I shuffled out to the edge of the building and braced myself.

'Taylor?' I yelled, meekly.

I wheezed and coughed like a chain smoker. My voice had all but gone. The Finns would struggle to hear me across a table, let alone a suburb. I cursed myself and ventured out further from the building to assess the surrounds. It was futile. The smoke had swallowed everything and it looked like the sun would be gone soon too. I turned around and felt a ripple of panic as I couldn't see the casino. I stumbled back towards it, arms stretched like a zombie.

I tried the headlights on a couple of the taxis parked in the rank to see if I could send a beacon out that way. The batteries were long gone. I went inside and rummaged through my backpack for some tape and the second torch. I stuck this to the bonnet of the furthest taxi and pointed the light out into the smoke and distance. Maybe once it was dark the beam would be strong enough for Taylor or Lizzy to see and trace back to the building.

My throat started to itch with dryness. I had no water left and the foyer had nothing to offer. I took my torch and headed through a door into a larger lobby area. It was brighter in there. Walls of glass rose on two sides to a decorative atrium above. Smoke blocked any view outward but the remaining daylight seeped through to illuminate the space. There was a bank of elevators to my left and a couple of function rooms to the right. I looked around for a map of the place but found only ads for meal deals and loyalty clubs. It felt weird being back inside a cavernous building like Carousel. I wasn't keen to stick around.

There was a dual staircase wrapping away decoratively behind the elevators with a sign reading *Bars & Gaming*. I pointed the torch up there reluctantly. It was dim and uninviting. I set off before I had a chance to chicken out. The stairways took a long sweep and then converged on an ornate double door and a chasm of blackness. I swiped my torch around the space ahead. Blackjack tables. Money wheels. The glint and sparkle of pokey machines. The room seemed to fan out sideways and stretch on forever. It was impressively dark. Not a hint of natural light. A place designed to swallow time and people with it.

But there were bars in there. Lots of them, if I remembered correctly. I just had to find the closest one, load up with waters and get back out to the foyer.

I weaved my way slowly forward into the darkness. The tables were abandoned mid-game. Half-empty bourbon-and-Cokes festering away on sponsored coasters. Chips and cards spread in careful clusters on the felt. I looked in on a blackjack game. One player had loaded up on a King Queen. Another was clinging to their final chips on sixteen, hoping to hell the dealer would bust. There were chips set out across the numbers and colours of a roulette table. Cups of coins resting on the holders of pokey machines. A wheel set to spin full of cherries, gold bars and lemons. Nothing moved a whisker. It was as if fate itself hung in limbo all around me. Nowhere else we had seen had spoken of the Disappearance like the casino. But then casinos didn't sleep.

The room seemed to be getting larger the further I ventured in. My torch couldn't reach the side walls anymore. I turned around and shone it back towards the entrance. I had to squint, but it was still there.

I rounded a big enclosure where plush seating circled a decadent poker table. At the other side I finally caught a glimpse of a bar to my right. It was a small, freestanding island at the junction of some walkways heading off to different gaming areas. I headed over and stepped inside. The knee-high fridges were fully stocked with imported beers and colourful pre-mix. I fished around and found two lonely rows of water amid the alcohol. They still had a hint of cool and I skulled one, then the best part of another, and sat down to catch my breath.

The room was deathly quiet.

Conscious of the time I had spent away from the foyer, I packed the remaining waters into a garbage bag I found in the bar and set off back to the staircase. I found the enclosed poker table without a problem, turned and kept moving toward the exit. I still had a long way to go when my torch dropped out.

I froze. The darkness around me felt immense. I put down the waters and gave the torch a gentle shake. There was a half-second of light, then nothing. The battery was dead and my spare was outside beaming away into nothingness.

I took a breath and tried to stay calm. Maybe I could rotate the batteries and get a bit longer out of them. I sat down on the floor and carefully worked my way through the process. Again the torch flickered back on. This time for a long, teasing second, before dropping out once again. Now for good.

My eyes still hadn't adjusted to the dark. Long moments passed but nothing seemed to change. I thought of the cave Dad and I had visited down south. The guide had told us that you could experience *total darkness* in there; meaning that there was insufficient light for the human eye to adjust. Could that be the same in a casino? Surely I could pick out something to guide me back to the staircase.

For a while I stood, craning my head around the space, trying desperately to make something out within the blackness. It was impossible. I quietly swallowed down my panic and edged my way forward. Tables emerged like icebergs out of the dark to turn me left, then right, then right again in a mishmash and ridiculous fashion. I knew that I was no longer heading in the direction of the staircase. That felt impossible in this kind of darkness. But I figured if I kept walking until I hit a wall, then maybe I could follow it around to the exit.

It was slow going. The empty spaces were the worst. When I could run my hand on a table or some stools it felt okay. Like I had some sense of forward trajectory. But in the spaces between these objects I felt dizzy and disorientated. Twice I stumbled forward too quickly and crunched my foot into the thick wooden leg of a chair. Other times I felt for sure that I had turned a one-eighty and returned to a table I had only just passed.

After a while my hand found a railing and I felt the floor taking a slight incline beneath me. I shuffled forward until it levelled again into a bank of pokey machines running in rows away from me. I followed the length of one of these rows, then found myself being turned at a right angle as another row of machines began. At the end of these there were more again.

It felt like *Labyrinth* without Bowie and the puppets.

I started to smell something ahead of me. It was sweet and citrusy. I slowed down and tried to figure out what it was. It was different to the fresher smell of the lobby. As I rounded out of the final row of pokeys, a wave of it hit me flush in the face.

Rotting food.

I was on a walkway with a buffet ahead of me somewhere. I covered my nose and veered right. The way was clear and had a railing so I moved quickly until the smell had drifted away behind me. It was hard to imagine that nobody left in Perth had been in here yet. My decision to enter the casino felt like a giant mistake.

The railing stopped and the walkway met a junction or something. I felt my way around, trying to work out the options. My hands met a bench or table. It was higher than the others. I moved closer and found some fridges. One of the doors was open.

Shit.

I was back at the bar.

I dropped the bag of water and slumped down to the floor. The place felt so oppressive. Not just the darkness, but the air or the energy or something. I felt lower than I had for ages and didn't have the Finns around for company. They could be in the foyer right now wondering what the hell had happened to me. I closed my stinging eyes and, alone under a gaming room bar, sank into a dreamless sleep.

13

For three days I was stuck in that hellhole place, surviving on stale peanuts and warm OJ. Eating, sleeping, then clearing my head, shuffling around anxiously, and eating and sleeping some more. The casino was swiftly swallowing me into a dark and permanent void.

Clocks weren't allowed in a gaming room, but I found a barman's watch stashed away under the counter. It had a tiny blue light that showed me the hours that were passing. This reminded me that a world existed outside of the room. There was daylight out there, and, somewhere beneath this, Taylor and Lizzy. I gathered myself and strapped the watch tightly to my wrist. With the tiny blue light I searched the surrounding tables where, eventually, I found a cigarette lighter.

The flame was too dim to guide me so I lit a coaster on fire. It crackled away and I waved the extra light around excitedly for three or four seconds before it burnt my fingers and I dropped it on the floor. Fuelled by this I made a stack of coasters on the bar and splashed it with some one-hundred-proof whisky. The stack lit up with a whoosh and I stepped back and looked around.

Flickering light radiated out from the bar. I could see walkways, some gaming tables and what looked to be the edge of the poker area. Beyond this it was still dark. I took a pile of fresh coasters from the bar, along with the whisky, and set out to the edge of the light. When I could no longer see I made another fire on a blackjack table. More light spat out into the room. Gaming tables. Money wheels. Another bar. I pushed on with the fires. Moving to the edge of darkness before lining myself up with the smouldering lumps behind me and lighting another. I had six fires going but there was still no sign of a wall or door.

Then something smashed behind me.

I turned and saw flames spreading across the bar where I had started. There was another smash and a whoosh of light. The spirits were on fire. An evil, plasticy smell started to fill the room. It felt chemical and dangerous, but at least now there was some light. I had played a hand. Not a great one, but maybe the only one available. Now I had no choice but to find an exit.

I dashed forward and something flickered to my right. I stopped and stared at it hard. It flickered again. It was a fake gold sign reading *Cashiers*.

Fucking bingo.

I stumbled over to it. Thick smoke was filling the room and stinging my eyes. I found the sign, and the wall it was stuck to. I swung left and traced it along.

My lungs burned from exhaustion and smoke. The wall continued, uninterrupted.

Abruptly the room was wet and screaming with sirens. The smoke alarms and sprinklers had triggered.

Immediately it got darker.

Shit. The fires were going out.

A wall jutted out in front of me. I smacked into it and almost knocked myself out completely. I dragged myself up and followed it. My head was swampy and vague from the fumes and noise.

I couldn't see anymore. All the fires were out but for the bar that hissed away angrily in the distance. I kicked into chairs and signs and other things that I couldn't see. Still my hands found nothing but the smooth of a never-ending wall.

Then ahead of me I saw a light. Not a tiny reflection this time, but a big wash of light coming from a doorway. Somebody was holding a lantern and propping the door open. I ran for it like a drunken kid who had started a whole bunch of stuff he shouldn't have. The light rose up in front of me. I felt a tingle on my neck and suddenly worried who it was in the doorway. I squinted hard and looked up.

In a wash of warm light and smoke, straight out of some crappy eighties music video, stood a woman wrapped in a plush casino robe, holding, of all things, a cigarette, and a look of mild annoyance. It was an expression I had seen before. On a shopping centre cleaning lady. On Rachel.

14

Of course Rachel was living at Burswood. She was a battling single mother, paroled for who knows what, cleaning toilets in the largest shopping centre in the city while bickering over her kids with her slobby council-worker ex. That is, until fate sheltered her from the weirdest apocalypse on record and left her footloose in a world without rules, only Artists. Taking up residence in the swankiest room in the state of WA was a great big *fuck you* to the world. Life had kicked Rachel around from day one. If this felt like she was getting her own back, then good luck to her.

I had followed her upstairs through a careful pathway of stairs and halls, sucking in the stale but smoke-free air, still unsure if she recognised me from Carousel. It grew lighter as we moved upward. My eyes cowered away from windows full of sunlight and sweeping river views. Ornate pots with evergreen plastic plants rested in corners and beside elevators. Door tags hung on handles, their owners asking not to be disturbed and getting their wish a thousandfold. By the time we reached the penthouse level the smoke alarms had stopped. It was serene and spacious and hard to tell that anything had happened.

There were four doors spread out across a wide marble hall. Each of them was propped open with a pot plant. Rachel headed inside the closest one. I hesitated, then trailed after her. She fished a Diet Coke out of a fridge and turned to look me over.

'You trying to burn this place down with the rest of the city?' she snapped.

'No. Sorry,' I replied. My voice was weak and croaky. 'I got stuck in there.'

I coughed. Rachel handed me a Diet Coke of my own. I wasn't normally a fan but skulled it down thirstily. It was icy cold.

'Does this place have power?' I asked.

'A bit,' she replied, defensively. 'There's gennies downstairs. Can't have Taylor Swift stuck up here in a blackout.'

I looked past her. The room was giant. A wall of glass peered westward past the river to a smoke-shrouded city. Daylight filtered in across ottomans and lazyboys, funnelling into bedrooms and spa-filled ensuites.

'Do you live here?' I asked.

'Across the hall,' nodded Rachel. 'Where are your friends? The skater kid and those twins?' she added.

'Have you seen Taylor and Lizzy?' I asked, rapidly.

Rachel shook her head, uninterested.

'We lost each other in the fire. Were supposed to meet downstairs but I got stuck in that fucking gaming room,' I said. 'You definitely haven't seen anyone else outside or anything?'

'I don't go downstairs,' she replied. 'Unless there's a fire.'

She glared at me, still a little pissed that I had put her new home at risk. She looked the same, from what I could remember. Thin, with a wiry, kind of boyish figure. Overtanned like she had taken one too many trips to Bali. A round, symmetrical face that was pretty in a burnt-out British pop star sort of way. Her hair was a disaster though. Half grown out of a bad self-dye job. Hacked up at the back where she couldn't see. A telltale sign of the local apocalyptic survivor.

'Is there anyone else here?' I asked.

'Doubt it,' she replied. 'Were some hippy kids on level five for a while. They took off to get food and didn't come back.'

Rachel finished her drink and put the can in the sink.

'Anyway, I'm going back to bed,' she said. 'Show you how the place works later.'

She pushed through the door back out into the hall.

'Wait,' I said. 'How do I get to the taxi rank?'

'You want to go back downstairs?' she asked.

'My friends might be down there,' I replied.

Rachel sighed and looked like she actually regretted saving me.

'Remember that staircase at the end of the hall on level twenty?' she asked.

I nodded.

'It's a fire escape. Take it all the way down to the last floor and push the door open. You'll be outside. The taxis will be out there somewhere,' said Rachel.

'Thanks,' I replied.

'Don't lock yourself out,' she said. 'I'm not trudging up those stairs twice in one fucking day.'

She turned and walked away from me down the big, lonely hall.

'Did you find your kids?' I asked.

She paused and turned back around. Her eyes were stony and fierce.

'They're sporty. Not arty,' she replied, and disappeared back into her room.

I bolted down the fire escape for what seemed like forever before exiting onto a concrete landing on the south side of the building. Lawn and trees stretched away peacefully into the distance. Most of the smoke had cleared, replaced by a bright and breezy Perth morning. I took a gulp of the freshest air I had ever tasted and took off around the building.

The taxi rank was static and empty. I jogged past the cars and back into the foyer where I had meant to be waiting. There was nobody in there. I looked around for signs that Taylor and Lizzy had been back. Everything seemed the same. My backpack on the floor. The empty bottle of water beside it. A heaviness was already growing in my chest when I saw the note.

It was central on the help desk. A faded yellow post-it that should have said something like *Cereal* or *Pilates*. Instead – *Where are you Nox? I have to go back out there. T.*

I read it once and turned away.

Taylor hadn't found them. She had come back for help, but I wasn't around. Now both of the Finns were gone.

I dashed back outside and down onto the grassy embankment at the front of the building. It was wide and barren. I called out for Taylor, then Lizzy, then Chess. My voice sounded loud and shrill, but somehow disconnected from reality. The grounds and suburbs swallowed it easily and offered nothing in return. I passed the Pink billboard and kept on until I reached the highway and found the lonely frames of our abandoned bikes. They were there where we had left them. Where Taylor and Lizzy had bickered before I led us blindly towards the casino. I looked around and yelled some more, then felt dizzy and got a bizzaro flash of Luke Skywalker dangling alone from the edge of Cloud City.

It hit me then. Taylor and Lizzy were gone.

Back in the foyer I sat on the floor and cried noiselessly. Month upon month of balled-up emotion finally reached a precipice, then crashed down with numbing force. The taxi. Stuart. Peter. The gnomes. Rachel. Rocky. The dome. The writing. My family. Their house. The fires. Tommy. And now, Taylor and Lizzy. The weight of it all felt like it might crush me then and there.

For a long time I lay foetal beside my backpack. Getting up and going on felt like something I might do in another world or life, but not this one. Eventually I reached over to the backpack and pulled out the contents. I looked past the clothes and shoes until I found my iPod. It still had a whisker of charge. I put in the earphones and played the Taylor & Lizzy album.

At the end of this I sat up, then stood and moved back to Taylor's note. I found a pen and wrote beneath it. *I'm upstairs. Will check in here every day at 7 and 7 until you're back. Nox.* Then I gathered my things and made my way back up to the penthouses.

15

The following day Rachel woke me up to run through the hefty list of conditions to staying on her penthouse level. The backup generators that kept the top floor powered during a blackout had run out of diesel some time ago. However, Rachel had an undisclosed store of diesel that she used to top them up. She didn't tell me where this was nor how much she had, just that it would run out quick if I started screwing around. She only used power for four hours a day. Once when she got up in the morning – which, for Rachel, was almost midday – and once at night. This routine was designed to eke out the diesel and also to keep her fridges cool. When the power kicked in she ran them at full blast for the two hours. They would frost over, chilling the hell out of everything inside, before cutting out and slowly thawing until the next blast.

The toilets still drained, but had to be flushed manually with a bucket. For water Rachel carted up fifteen-litre bottles of artisanal drinking water from a storeroom on the lower levels. With this she bathed, flushed toilets, washed clothes and made ice for her rum-and-Cokes. If I wanted to do the same I would have to cart it up myself.

Rachel was less forthcoming about her food stores. There were obviously mini-bars full of snacks and drinks all over the place. And Rachel directed me to a kitchen a few levels down where she said I might find some stuff. But I had a feeling that there was somewhere else she wasn't letting me in on. I guess I couldn't really blame her.

Otherwise she told me to keep my noise down and curtains drawn at night. Rachel wasn't stupid. The penthouse level was visible to most of Perth. Lighting it up at night would be a welcome sign to the rest of the city. Loots, Artists or otherwise, Rachel wasn't keen on visitors.

That was about it. A list of rules was as close to an invitation as you got from Rachel, and I took it gratefully. The weeks on the road had left me thin and sickly. I boiled kettles for a bath in my room. By the time I rose out of it the water had turned deep brown with dirt, smoke and who knows what else. I wrapped myself in a bathrobe and trudged downstairs to the kitchen Rachel had suggested. I brought back cans of tuna and asparagus and ate them with water crackers. At the first hint of night I drew the curtains and watched the city lightshow sneaking in through gaps to bounce around my giant bedroom. But mostly I slept. And I dreamt.

Of Taylor and Lizzy in some beautiful city warehouse, where artists, press and PAs flitted about them as they chatted about their album and all they had endured to bring it to fruition. Talk of moving on and future projects. Nothing about the young guy they had spent the last two years with.

I dreamt of taking my family to see my new girlfriend Molly's band play. The four of us standing up the back of a dingy pub like awkward second cousins. Mum and Dad's concern as Molly avoided us at the end of their set. Danni pretending not to notice and feigning hunger so that we could leave and she could shield me from further embarrassment.

I dreamt of being back in Carousel. Sheltered by its comfort and familiarity. An old man now. With giant plants and notepad after notepad full of ramblings. Settling down to write some more when abruptly the doors opened and hundreds of shoppers converged on my settlement.

The dreaming was intense and draining, but waking was far worse. I had been fastened to the Finns for so long that being alone felt foreign and disorientating. Before Carousel I was a borderline loner and happy to keep it that way. Now it suddenly felt like I had full-blown separation anxiety.

I set alarms on the barman's watch and kept up my promise to check the foyer twice daily. It was a long walk down and an even tougher one back up. I charged my walkie-talkie and took to scanning the channels while I waited. Outside, the smoke had cleared from the city for as far as I could see, but still the Finns didn't come. Again I searched the casino grounds. But Burswood was quiet and deserted. Just how Rachel liked it.

On my fourth day in the suites Rachel banged on my door and told me to come over that night for a barbeque. She left before I could answer but I was lonely as hell and all out of tuna, so it was a pretty good offer.

After my seven pm visit to the foyer I took another bath and dressed myself in a tacky casino club shirt and a pair of shorts I had found in somebody's luggage. I left my suite, then stopped as I realised I didn't have anything to bring with me. Do people still bring stuff to barbeques after the apocalypse? It was the type of question Lizzy and I could normally bullshit about for hours. But now I was alone and lingering weirdly in the hall. I returned to my room and took a bottle of sav blanc from the fridge. I felt stupid but thought whatever.

Rachel didn't answer the door so eventually I just let myself in. She was out on the balcony and held her drink up slightly in greeting when she saw me by the door. I made my way over.

Rachel's pride in her penthouse was obvious. The space was giant but clean and dust-free. She had brought up an array of plastic plants from other floors and polished the leaves back to a high gloss. They stood in jungle-like clusters above lounges and rugs. There was a framed picture of Pink in one of the TV areas that looked like a recent addition. Out on the balcony was an exercise area with a bunch of fluorescent aerobic equipment and a stereo. There were also lounges, spa baths, a fully stocked bar and, in the corner, a giant gourmet barbeque with actual seafood sizzling on top. The smell of it made me dizzy with hunger.

This wasn't somewhere flash Rachel was crashing before moving onto the next place. This was her home now.

'Do you want to drink that?' asked Rachel from the hotplate.

'Not really,' I replied, looking at the wine.

'There's beer in the bar,' said Rachel.

'Cool. Thanks,' I replied.

I put the wine aside and took a beer from one of the many fridges in the outdoor bar. It was cold and sharp and tasted amazing. I shuffled back over and stood awkwardly by the barbeque.

'Is this fish from the kitchen downstairs?' I asked.

Rachel shook her head and looked at me cagily.

'You guys didn't take any food with you when you left Carousel?' she asked.

'No. We left kind of suddenly,' I replied.

'Is that skater kid still stuck in there?' she asked.

I nodded and took another swig. My eyes filled with fizz.

'He died last year,' I replied.

Rachel looked at me.

'Fucking shithole place,' she said.

I nodded and stared silently at the fish. Rachel took a long pull on her rum-and-Coke.

'How long have you been living here?' I asked.

'Ten months,' she replied. 'Best room in the city.'

Rachel looked at me, fishing for an argument.

'Did you meet many people on the way here?' I asked.

'Enough,' she said.

'Were they all Artists?' I asked.

Rachel shrugged. 'Probably. They were all pretty useless,' she replied.

She flipped the fish. It was charred to high hell and getting worse by the second.

'Plates behind the bar,' she said.

'Sorry?' I asked.

'To eat off, Nox. Go get us a couple,' replied Rachel.

I hesitated for a moment, surprised that she actually remembered my name.

'Right. Sure,' I said.

Under the bar I found a thinning stockpile of plastic dinnerware. I took enough for the two of us and made up one of the tables.

As the sun finally dropped, Rachel and I sat for an awkward, but kind of lovely, barbeque dinner. It reminded me of Sunday lunch at my aunty Linda's, with her drab salads and droning chitchat. Danni and

I used to hate those visits. Dad too, probably. But lately I would kill for that type of thing. To be stuck talking crap with my family on the weekend, cocooned deep down in sleepy suburbia, daydreaming of something big happening one day.

Few things have tasted better to me than Rachel's overcooked fish and weird gherkin and sweet corn salad. I stuffed my skinny, anaemic body with protein and buzzed off icy bottles of imported beer. Rachel tipped, inevitably, into slushy territory and told me some more about her kids, Kelly and Chad, and her ex, Steve. It seemed as though her bitterness towards Steve had faded. She still thought he was a 'useless loser' but she said this with a flicker of nostalgia and sounded proud of his ability to do nothing at his job with the council, yet still get paid.

The sun set and I realised that Rachel had all of the tables positioned to face the city lightshow. We talked throughout the display but twice I caught her gaze wandering up to the lights as if they were the nightly news or something. When they finished we were basically in darkness. Rachel disappeared inside while I stared across at the blocky and pensive city. Giant grey towers etched out of the dark. I traced their shapes and tried to remember which was which.

Rachel returned with a bucket of Ferrero Rocher. I had been gorging on chocolate for days but didn't let on. Instead I thanked her and forced down a couple more.

It was quiet but for a soft sea breeze and the hum of insects by the river.

'How long are you staying for?' asked Rachel.

'I guess until Taylor and Lizzy come back,' I replied.

'What if they don't?' she asked.

I shivered and didn't answer.

'What are your plans?' I asked, changing the subject.

'Plans?' cackled Rachel. 'Nothing. Live here. Relax. That Curator can fuck himself.'

I sat up.

'You've heard about the Curator?' I asked.

'Who hasn't,' replied Rachel.

'Have you seen him anywhere?' I asked.

'Ha,' she snorted. 'He wouldn't want to run into me.'

I smiled, but Rachel looked deadly serious. Fair enough, I thought. Here she was, no kids, no ex. Alone in the world but for the odd encounter with some Artist she probably couldn't stand. Why should she feel anything but animosity towards the Curator. Why should anyone.

I stayed there late, drinking and bitching and trying my best to offer some common-people solidarity as Rachel and I hovered between decadence and poverty in the post-apocalyptic wonderland that was Perth.

16

I kept up my visits to the foyer as the summer meandered on. In the mornings I dressed in exercise gear and used my time waiting there to stretch, before heading back up to work out in a gym on level five. At night I took down a beer and a magazine and hung around until one or the other was finished. The same thing, day after day. My note still central on the desk. The colour fading and the corners curling up.

My routine ignored a reality that I wasn't yet ready to face. With each day that passed it became less and less likely that Taylor and Lizzy would return. I ran through different trajectories of events in my mind. The start made sense to me: Chess is spooked by the alarms and runs. Lizzy chases after him, her calls are lost in the wailing. They become disorientated, can't hear us yelling after them and take shelter. Taylor fails to find them and returns to discover the foyer is empty. She looks for me. She waits. She feels a deep guilt for the loss of her twin. She has to leave.

But then what? She finds Lizzy and Chess. They come back and see my note. She doesn't find Lizzy and Chess. She comes back and sees my note. Lizzy and Chess surface without her. They head to the casino and find my note. In none of my projections was I left alone in the casino with Rachel. When I lingered on this thought I felt great rumbles of emotion. Guilt. Anger. Grief. A vast and profound loneliness. Things that were dark and enveloping.

So I held fast to routine and to numbness. I worked out. I sunbaked. I went room to room and built a wardrobe and a library. I watched the lightshow and barbequed with Rachel. My writing petered, then stopped completely. I settled back into the life of a Patron. No rules. No pressure. Just the day and the night and whatever it took to fill them.

Every second Tuesday Rachel took a battery-powered golf cart to a shopping centre in Victoria Park for underwear, batteries and whatever else she couldn't find in the resort. I sat out the first couple, worried about the Finns returning while I was away. But eventually I grew bored and restless and asked her if I could come along.

We set off around one pm. This was effectively midmorning for Rachel and she seemed tired and grumpy. The golf cart was one of hundreds housed on the adjacent country club. Rachel kept it tucked away by a taxi rank on the east side of the building with a stack of spare batteries. We slid aboard and she rolled us out through the sweeping casino gardens and onto the highway.

'Are there pit bulls in Vic Park?' I ask her.

'Yeah. A few,' said Rachel.

I glanced at her. She didn't seem concerned.

We turned from the highway and climbed through some streets to the east. Before long the hills came dramatically into view. Great swathes of barren, grey hillside spread out as far as I could see. Within the mass of dotted tree stumps were small patches of bare earth where a house or shed had once stood. It was bushfire on a scale I had never seen. Like a giant firefront had charged across the deserts from the cities of the east and crashed like a wave into the hills.

Rachel ripped through side streets, parks and stationary traffic as if she was running late to pick her kids up from school. I held on for my life and couldn't help but smile at the sight of her. Blinged-up designer sunnies. Cigarette wedged between chunky diamonds on her fingers. Head to toe in Nike gear, ready for a workout that rarely eventuated. Before long she screeched to a stop outside the local IGA.

'My rule is ten minutes and two bags,' she said. 'Any longer and people start sniffing around.'

'People?' I asked.

'Loots,' she replied.

I looked around warily. It was quiet and suburban. Trolleys had drifted like leaves to all corners of the car park. There was a long delivery truck backed up to a loading bay at the side. Rachel stepped out of the cart and headed in that direction. I followed her as she tracked alongside the vehicle. It had been frozen mid-delivery. The boxes and crates that were still aboard had been ransacked and scattered. A small forklift held up another stack of boxes. These were emptied too. Just a lonely crate of Chum dog food remained untouched.

Inside was pretty ghetto. It was shadowy and dank and the floor felt crunchy with dirt beneath our shoes. Fat insects circled about the roof space above. Rachel grabbed a couple of shopping bags from behind a register and headed off alone into the aisles. I took some bags of my own and looked around snobbishly. This wasn't the type of shopping to which I had become accustomed. People had gone to town on the shelves. Spilling and grabbing greedily as if the earth was about to be struck by a meteor. I picked my way through and eventually found some of the razors I liked. Also some sports socks, Minties and Vitamin C tablets. Otherwise the selection was dismal. It wasn't the biggest store, but I was still surprised at the extent to which it had been cleared out.

When I finished Rachel was already waiting impatiently at the front of the store. Her bags were stuffed full of who knows what.

'Did you get paper plates?' she asked.

'No. Sorry,' I replied.

Rachel sighed. 'Aisle six,' she said.

I turned back obediently to get the plates. Arguing with Rachel was never really an option. The stocks of plates were diminishing but I grabbed a few packets and jammed them into my bag. Abruptly Rachel's voice boomed out through the aisles.

'Don't fucking touch me, arsehole.'

I stood up.

'Get a move on, Nox,' she yelled.

I freaked out, but ran back to her regardless.

Rachel was in stand-off with a filthy looking bearded guy by the checkouts. He glanced at me. Then back to Rachel. He looked super cracky and reminded me of a dexie fiend we had to fire from work.

'What's going on?' I asked.

'Give me the keys, hag,' said the guy.

'Get your own fucking car,' replied Rachel.

The guy stepped forward. Rachel pulled a can of something out of her pocket.

'Do you want to get sprayed in the face again?' she asked.

'I need a car,' he replied.

'Why?' I asked.

The guy turned and looked at me closely.

'He's in the hills,' he whispered.

'Who? The Curator?' I asked.

Before he could answer Rachel sent a shower of spray into his eyes. He shrieked and keeled over. She turned to me and nodded to the door. The guy started groaning.

'It's just Impulse, you big baby,' said Rachel.

We circled around him to the exit.

'I need a car!' cried the guy.

'It's a golf cart, idiot! You won't get past Cannington,' said Rachel.

She swung back outside without waiting for a reply. I glanced back at the crumpled, jittery dude on the floor, then followed. We threw our bags in the back and Rachel ripped a savage turn back out onto the street.

'I told you. Ten minutes. Two bags,' she said.

'Who was that dude?' I asked.

'A poet or some crap,' she replied.

'Do you know his name?' I asked.

'His name?' asked Rachel. 'His name is loser poet guy. Friend of skanky dancer girl and pervert photographer.'

I didn't know whether to laugh or cry.

17

For a week in autumn I hooked up with an actress
named Georgia from Ohio. She was sitting in the foyer
one night, waiting to see if anyone would make good on
the note that was still stuck to the counter. I wandered
inside in my track pants and froze.

Georgia kind of looked me up and down.

'Sorry. I'm not T,' she said.

'What?' I asked.

'T. From the note. It's not me,' she said.

'Oh, okay,' I said.

'But you're Nox, right?' she asked.

'Yeah,' I replied.

She stood up and moved over to shake my hand.

'Georgia,' she said.

'Hi,' I replied.

Georgia was pretty. She had a classic look. Her face
was lightly tanned, proportionate and highlighted
by magnetic green eyes and ringlets of dark-blonde
hair that bounced around her shoulders like she'd just

teleported in from a Hitchcock film.

'Is T your girlfriend?' she asked.

'No. She's Taylor. And Lizzy. They're sisters. Twins,' I replied, confusingly.

'Oh cool, Taylor & Lizzy,' said Georgia.

I nodded and tried to loosen the dorky white t-shirt that was swallowing my neck.

'Have they been gone long?' asked Georgia.

'Since the fire,' I replied.

She eyed me cautiously as if to weigh up whether I had lost my mind like the rest of the city.

'Well, that sucks,' she said. 'Are you a musician too?'

'No. A writer, I guess,' I replied. 'You?'

'I'm an actress. I'm trying to be an actress. I *was* trying to be an actress. Before all this,' she replied and swung an arm out theatrically.

'You're from the States?' I asked.

'Ohio. Go Buckeyes,' replied Georgia.

I nodded as Georgia wandered the space.

'Sorry. How come you're in Perth?' I asked, confused.

'Acting school,' she replied.

'You're at WAAPA?' I asked.

'The one and only,' said Georgia.

WAAPA was the performing arts school famous for ex-student Hugh Jackman. I had met a couple of WAAPA students before. Friends of my old housemate. They were chatty and brash twenty-four-seven.

'So you're living here in the casino?' asked Georgia.

'Yeah, at the moment,' I replied.

'That's cool. Are you here on your own?' she asked.

'There's a lady in one of the penthouses. Rachel. She's been here for a while,' I replied.

Georgia nodded. She seemed restless.

'Well, I need a place to crash for a few nights. Do you wanna show me around?' she asked.

'Yeah. Sure. What kind of room do you want?' I asked.

'Just something small and humble,' replied Georgia.

She stared at me for a second, wide-eyed, then shoved me like I was an idiot.

'I want a palace, Nox. I haven't slept for like a week.'

I didn't want to piss off Rachel so I stopped a few levels short of the penthouses and ushered Georgia into a corner suite with a view of the river. She unpacked some of her stuff while I brought her up some food, water and candles from the kitchen below. I also grabbed a pot and one of the portable gas burners that Rachel and I used for hot water. Georgia thanked me and asked if I could come back later when she wasn't so 'gross'.

I went back upstairs, changed out of my track pants and paced around like a teenager wondering what this meant.

When I eventually went back down Georgia was yawny and doe-eyed at the door.

'Were you sleeping?' I asked.

'No. No. Come in,' she replied.

I moved past her into the dim, candlelit space inside.

'I just thought you might come back sooner,' said Georgia.

'Sorry,' I replied.

'You're fine. How much does it suck without Facebook or a phone?' she replied. 'I'm constantly like *cool I'll see you around* and then realising I will probably never see that person again.'

'Yeah. Totally,' I replied.

'Oh my god. Sorry. I'm such a dick. I'm sure you will see Taylor and Lizzy again. I just mean like, random people,' said Georgia.

'It's cool,' I replied.

The darkness made things awkward. Georgia moved around when she spoke and her face was slipping in and out of the candlelight. She looked at me and smiled, then yawned again.

'God. Sorry,' she said.

We stood quietly for a moment and I considered leaving her to sleep.

'Oh hey, the mini-bar is loaded. Do you want to take a shot with me?' asked Georgia.

'Yeah. Definitely,' I replied.

She grabbed a handful of single-serve bottles from the fridge and scattered them across the counter. We picked out a couple of vodkas, clinked them and drank.

'Wow,' said Georgia with a hand on her chest. 'I'm so lightweight these days.'

I smiled, feeling the exact opposite.

'Should we try a gin?' she said.

'Sure,' I replied.

We looked through the bottles and found some Bombay Sapphire. The drinking felt mechanical. A high school regression. The necessary precursor to making out with somebody where you could avoid mentioning what you both wanted to do before somebody plunged in and it was suddenly, thankfully already happening.

We coughed and laughed and Georgia's arm brushed mine as we looked through the other bottles. Our eyes met and held for a second or two, then we started making out. With Molly this had felt foreign, part of the fabric of the strange new world. Kissing with Georgia was different. It was how I remembered it before the Disappearance. Where the world would blur out to just smell, texture and a sudden abyss of thoughts and feelings.

Georgia was kind of frantic. Her hands wrapping around my neck, then working off my clothes, then stopping to wrap around my neck again. We kept going until we were almost naked and Georgia pulled away and crouched down in the darkness.

'Georgia?' I asked.

'Sorry. You're fine. I have condoms in here somewhere,' she replied, rummaging through her stuff.

We had sex twice on the giant, dusty ensemble. Georgia's face dipped in and out of the blackness.

Looking down at me, her brow tight and focused. Underneath me, whispering *Nox Nox Nox* over and over as if she might forget who I was or everything that had happened to us.

Afterwards she slept and I sat up looking out a gap in the curtains to the dim outline of the river. I had forgotten the spike of clarity that would sometimes come with sex. Lying there I realised that I had settled into a life without the Finns. I was checking the foyer out of obligation to them, but now knew they weren't coming back. Worst of all, I felt safer without them. Like I could get on with a life that I could deal with. I didn't know who I was or what I was doing, but I also wasn't asking myself every other second.

Being away from them felt good and I hated myself for it.

Georgia was too chatty for the next morning to be awkward. She snacked on juice and biscuits and peppered me with questions.

'What kind of stuff do you write?' she asked.

'Just fiction,' I replied, still sleepy.

She nodded and laughed at my lack of detail.

'Sorry. I'm not really writing at the moment,' I said.

'I totally get it. God. It's so hard to focus on work once you leave your Residency. This city is full on,' said Georgia.

'Where was your Residency?' I asked.

139

'WAAPA,' replied Georgia. 'I was there with a director named Claudia.'

'How long ago did you leave?' I asked.

'Bit over a year maybe,' she replied.

'What have you been doing for a year?' I asked.

'Mainly just trekking around, looking for work. I was shooting a film in Guildford over the summer. Hanging out in the Collective for a while before that,' she said.

'The Collective?' I asked.

Georgia stopped and looked at me, wide-eyed. 'Wait. Is this place your Residency?'

'The casino? No. We were in a shopping centre,' I replied.

'Okay cool. For a second I thought you hadn't been out of here yet,' she replied.

'No, we left last year. Then lived up in the hills for a while. Before here,' I replied.

'But you haven't been to the city?' asked Georgia.

I shook my head.

'Oh wow. It's amazing there. The Collective is intense,' she said.

'What is it?' I asked.

'Just a big community of Artists. People started gathering there when they finished their Residencies. You know, safety in numbers and all that. But now they collaborate on projects, hold forums and concerts – tons of stuff,' said Georgia. 'There are some totally famous Artists there.'

She was wistful and excited and, for some reason, I felt immediately sceptical.

'How many people live there?' I asked.

'Hard to say. People come and go. There aren't really any boundaries. Some people live in houses nearby. Others just crash in tents or wherever,' said Georgia.

'Is there food and power?' I asked.

'Oh yeah. There are vegetable gardens and fruit trees. I think it used to be a community garden or something,' she replied.

'City Farm,' I said.

'Right. That's it!' said Georgia.

I knew the place. It was just east of the CBD. A ramshackle place full of sheds, cafes and gardens set up through volunteers and community funding.

'Oh my god, Nox. You have to go there once Taylor and Lizzy get back. You can work on your writing. Meet heaps of cool people. Seriously,' said Georgia.

'How come you left?' I asked.

'Oh. I don't know. I can get pretty restless,' replied Georgia.

It seemed vague, but I left it alone. The whole discussion had been fairly overwhelming first thing in the morning. I also felt a ripple of panic about how I was going to broach Georgia's arrival with my landlord Rachel.

18

Rachel shrugged off the news of the casino's newest resident. Told me she didn't give a crap what happened on the lower levels and I wondered why I had bothered telling her. But I knew that if I didn't she would have been majorly pissed. So I let her be and went back down to Georgia's room with some more food. I waited at the door and hoped I wasn't being a massive freak by showing up again so soon. Georgia flung it open and asked me where the hell I had been.

We made out for what felt like the whole rest of the day. It was like we were teenagers renting a room on some tiny anniversary. Fixed to the bed to eat, drink and fool around like it was an island we couldn't leave. Our conversations were polite and friendly, but felt more like filler than anything.

I liked Georgia. She was a year or so younger than me, but super sharp and worldly. And she seemed so decisive and confident; from small things like what she wanted to eat, through to massive, weighty decisions like becoming an actress or travelling alone to the casino. In others these traits may have been rooted in naivety or recklessness. But with Georgia I got the feeling that she was aware of the stakes.

In spite of all of this I still wondered whether my want for her company was mainly driven by the fact that I had been living without it for so long. And whether this was the same for her. As if we were avatars with icons for *love* or *emotion* that had been run so low they would take days to replenish before we could consider setting off again.

So we hibernated in her room. Rolling around the bed in our clothes. Taking them off and remembering what we knew about sex. Waking up in the middle of the night to find ourselves clinging to each other. Skipping big and important relationship junctures because our bodies, and maybe our souls, didn't have time for first dates and dinners with friends. It was primal and simplified. Maybe that was how this stuff worked in the world now. Maybe it was the only way it could work.

The following day, when I missed the third scheduled trip to the foyer for the Finns, Georgia checked with me that I didn't need to go down there.

'It's fine,' I replied. 'I'll go down there a bit later. I'm sure they will leave a note or something if I'm not around.'

It was a lame response, but Georgia was happy to buy it, neither of us keen to disrupt whatever it was that was happening.

Gradually we found out some basic information about each other. Georgia's parents were both drama teachers, but divorced. She had a younger brother, Brad, and a stack of friends she missed 'like crazy' from high school and college. She had applied for WAAPA, along with a list of other high-ranking acting schools, having burnt the first year out of college making showreels and posting headshots to agencies in LA. Two of the applications came back with a Yes, and she chose WAAPA on a whim one night when she flicked a channel and found Wolverine on TV. The Disappearance happened in her second year at the course. She told me that if it had come a year earlier she would have probably curled into a ball and never left the campus. It was as good a testimonial to WAAPA as you could ask for.

She and Claudia had ventured straight into the city upon completing a one-woman play at their Residency. They had a brief run-in with some dogs that sounded like Bulls, but otherwise reached the city and Collective without issue. From here the stories turned hazy and took on a Hunter S Thompson vibe. Week-long parties. Iconic and obscure figures of the art world. Epic theatre productions in empty houses. Installation art merged with plumbing projects and windmills.

I didn't really delve for too many details.

They had eventually left with some filmmakers and actors to shoot a film on the grassy slopes of Guildford, north-east of the city. Georgia wrapped her scenes early and ventured back south with a few other actors. She hadn't bumped into Claudia again since, but seemed totally fine with this.

Then came a few intense months practising 'method' in a beach house at Trigg, a play in South Perth, and, eventually, a trip east that led to the casino.

My story seemed shorter and less adventurous. Still, Georgia dropped a tear at my account of Rocky's death, and shared my worry over Tommy and the fires. She had heard rumours of people being lost in them, but was quick to add that the city pretty much ran on rumours these days. The biggest of which was the Curator himself.

Georgia hadn't seen him. Nor had anyone else she had met with any real credibility. She told me that the stories originated from the sounds and noises of a solitary car driving the streets in the hours and days after the Disappearance. Some say they saw it from windows and doors. A regular white ute making its way calmly through the carnage. Lonely tail-lights traversing back into the hills at night. Others say they heard it pull up and idle outside Residencies, as if to check that everything was in order.

Then there were the stories of actual meetings. These varied wildly, each one contradicting the next. Georgia said that some people clung tight to the myth of the Curator for direction or purpose. Others resented it and refused to speak of him. But, more and more, he was becoming a forgotten figure. People were moving on with their lives. Grappling with the significant challenges of survival, here and now. Like a superhero or prophet, he was mostly myth and memory these days. My heart went out to Tommy when she told me this. Just a few months ago his resolution seemed so strong that even Taylor believed him. I hoped to hell that it hadn't cost him everything.

A thin blanket of drizzle blew in for an afternoon, shadowing the sun for the first time in months. Georgia and I snuck upstairs to my room for a proper bath and some movies. It took forever to fill the huge corner tub. We gave up halfway and slid down low so the water still covered us over. We watched Pixar Blu-rays on the wall-mounted TV while a westerly blew flurried waves of soft rain against the windows. It was the first time we had just hung out without sex, conversation or sleep, and it felt like something.

When we eventually got out we draped ourselves in towels and robes and tiptoed through the darkness to my bed. It was still early but we slept and whispered our way through to the morning.

I woke to find Georgia sitting on a couch with an old diary. I wandered over and took a seat beside her.

'How is your week looking?' I asked.

Georgia flashed a smile. 'Where do I even begin?'

'Is that thing current?' I asked, nodding at the diary.

'Nope. Last year's,' she replied. 'I still like to use it

though. Just to see where I've been.'

'So it's retrospective?'

'Yeah, I guess,' she replied. 'Hey, have you been to Fremantle much?'

'Not for ages. Obviously. But yeah, I used to hang out there sometimes,' I replied.

'I'm thinking of trekking down to spend the winter there,' said Georgia.

I nodded and tried not to panic.

'Apparently there are some Artists working in the western end in some of those big old buildings. It sounds pretty awesome,' she added, eyes dancing with energy.

'Cool,' I replied.

Georgia looked at me with a slight smile.

'Do you want to come with?' she asked.

I felt a wash of relief, but also something else.

'I don't know if I can right now,' I replied. 'Because of Taylor and Lizzy.'

Georgia tilted her head and studied me.

'But you know they're not coming back,' said Georgia.

I looked at her.

'Why would you say that?' I asked.

'Because it's true, Nox. You haven't even been down to the foyer since I arrived,' said Georgia.

I felt trapped and judged.

'I've been with you the whole time,' I replied, sharply.

'I know. It's been awesome. And you should come with me to Fremantle,' said Georgia.

'What are you going to do when you get there?' I asked.

Georgia shrugged. 'Meet people. Find somewhere cool to stay. Hopefully do some acting.'

'When do you want to go?' I asked.

She shrugged again. 'Later today.'

My head ached like I had been drinking.

'Sorry, Georgia. I can't leave here yet. I have to give them some more time,' I said.

We sat there in silence. The last night and week suddenly a million miles behind us. Eventually Georgia took a long breath, turned and gave me an amazing smile. It was warm and hopeful, but final.

I felt like it would haunt me forever.

19

Autumn drifted nervously across the pensive city. I wandered the halls of the casino cloaked in robes and sunglasses, brooding over the past and squinting away from the future. Georgia had left. The Finns were gone. Rachel tolerated me at best and bemoaned me at worst. If I were Conor Oberst or Ryan Adams this would be the perfect time to scrawl out my new album. But I wasn't a musician. Or an actor. Or even a writer. I was part-time stationery assistant Nox, and yes, winter was coming.

The foyer was cold and dim at seven in the morning, and much the same twelve hours later. But I didn't dare miss a day. Convincing myself that it was this dedication that had kept me from joining Georgia on her trip to Fremantle. That one night the Finns and Chess would stumble in, tired and dirty but so thrilled that I had waited. Their stories would be long and crazy, but the thought of abandoning me would form no part of them.

Rachel was the weird lady who lived next door. Somebody I would bump into in the hall for an awkward conversation. Or hear up late drinking on a Tuesday, alone and celebrating something tragic like the birthday of her long-lost son. Occasionally we would share a meal when some seafood was about to go bad. Sit out on her balcony and sip our favourite drinks while groaning about the resort like it was a regular apartment building. I left her to do the golf cart runs alone and she seemed to prefer it that way. She would take along my list of items while I stayed back and minded the place. 'No promises,' she would say, but always come through with the goods.

When the nights turned cold and Rachel was too stubborn to come in from the balcony, she caught herself a brutal head cold. It was right about the time we needed to do a golf cart run. Rachel put it off for a few days, but only got sicker. When I ventured in with my list and saw the state of her, I reluctantly decided to step in.

Rachel croaked through some directions and gave me a fairly random list of requests.

'No promises,' I joked.

She just coughed and glared at me.

'Is there a chemist near that IGA?' I asked.

'Why?' asked Rachel.

'I could get you some cold and flu tablets or something,' I replied.

'Just get me Nurofen like it says on the list,' she grumbled.

'Okay sure,' I replied.

I took the keys and turned to leave. Rachel said something I didn't hear.

'Sorry?' I said.

'Ten minutes. Two bags,' she repeated.

I gave her a nod and left for the golf cart.

It took me a while to find my way out of the overgrown gardens, but eventually I linked up with a path and followed it out until I bumped down onto the highway. It felt wild and expansive. A breeze blew across with a soft whistle, shifting sand and leaves from one side to the other. I edged out and carefully rounded a couple of lonely taxis until there was a break in the island where I could cross over.

Aside from the casino, the suburb of Burswood was predominantly made up of car yards and light industry. Rachel had given me a list of specific streets that would take me to the supermarket, but I quickly lost track of them. I wasn't too worried though. It was on a main road that I had sometimes used to get from my place to Heather's a few years back.

What was more on my mind was the cracky poet we had run into the last time I had joined Rachel in the cart. Confronting him, or others, with the ever-assured Rachel for company was one thing. Dealing with him on my own was another. Rather than Impulse deodorant I had brought along a small can of the super-strength bug spray that Tommy had suggested we use on the

Bulls. It rolled around on the dash as my eyes searched the streets for signs of movement. But Burswood was a sleeping graveyard of cars. Row upon row of filthy new Toyotas and Mitsubishis with signs barking *Finance Available* and *Free Auto*.

Eventually I reached the top of a rise and drove down into the sunken streets of Victoria Park.

At the supermarket I parked the golf cart, turned off the engine and listened. All was quiet in the car park and surrounds. I set a timer on my watch, took the cap off the bug spray and headed inside.

It seemed darker than last time. The weather was overcast and just a dim haze found its way into the supermarket. I paused briefly and listened some more. The ceiling shifted and creaked with the wind funnelling through the door. There was a drip of water from the freezer section. Otherwise it was quiet.

I gathered Rachel's items first. Nurofen. Nail polish remover. Tampons. I moved quickly, filling the first bag and starting on the second. Tinned asparagus. Noodle cups. M&M's. Four minutes down and her list was done.

My list was slightly longer. There were some things I hadn't wanted to ask Rachel for on previous runs. Just stuff like the valerian that I used to sleep better. And the after-dinner mints that reminded me of Mum and Dad.

Still, I had six minutes left. There should be time.

At eight minutes I was all but done. I just wanted to check out the small Blu-ray section to see if there was

anything worth taking. As I knelt down to take a look,
I heard a noise outside. Like a rumble or churning.

Like an engine.

I shot upright. Then bolted outside.

The poet was already moving when I got there.
Hunched over in the golf cart. A screwdriver wedged
into the ignition.

'Hey!' I yelled.

His head snapped in my direction. Eyes wide.
Shoulder twitching.

'What are you doing?' I shouted and ran after him.

He ignored me and crunched the cart up and over
a parking island. It slowed him down and I made some
ground. I had the bug spray held out in front of me like
I was chasing some giant insect. I closed to within ten
metres when he ploughed over another island.

'You're going to blow the tyres,' I yelled.

I was right behind him now but there was just the
kerb left between him and the street. He rammed up and
over it at full speed.

The front tyres popped in unison.

I got alongside him and tried to grab onto the cart.
He saw me and freaked, pulling the cart hard left onto
the sidewalk. It shuddered and slowed, but I was slowing
too. The sidewalk began a decline. He bumped down
onto the road and picked up some speed. I fell behind
and sprayed the can desperately. I was too far away and
most of it blew back into my face.

The rampaging poet sped onward as I hunched over, defeated. My breath was ragged and shallow. There was a popping noise ahead of me. Another of the tyres had gone. I watched as the guy chugged onwards ambitiously towards the distant charcoal hills. Off to find some dude that probably didn't even exist.

'Great,' I sighed.

I stood up and looked around. My skin rippled with panic. The streets had swiftly resumed their oppressive calm. I quickly set off back to the supermarket before it got any worse. It was a long walk back to the casino, but it wasn't like I had any other options.

I gathered our shopping and looked around for something to help me carry it all. I found some dusty laundry bags in the cleaning aisle. They were effectively just cotton sacks with a drawstring opening at the top. One of them was able to house all of our stuff. I pocketed the bug spray, swung the bag over my shoulder and took off westwards towards the river.

The sun dropped fast this time of the year and I cursed myself for leaving the casino so late in the day. I could see the resort from where I walked, and it seemed like I could make it back before dark, but I hadn't had to judge this kind of thing for ages. And I didn't think to take a torch.

This side of Victoria Park was mostly residential. I passed quickly through streets full of proud Federation homes. Cobwebs strung across their long verandas.

Volkswagens abandoned in the driveways. These gave way to small high-rises peering westward at the city lights. Shifting winds jittered balcony furniture and windows on the higher levels. I lost sight of the horizon and focused hard on the street names so as not to take a detour.

I started noticing street art on the sides of buildings and fences. It was complicated and dramatic. Big swathes of colour morphing their way into intricate typography. It covered walls, but also ran across windows, doors and down onto the sidewalk. It made me think of the graffiti Artist Tommy had mentioned. I wondered whether this might be his work. Whether he might be staying somewhere nearby. But there was something disconcerting about these apartment buildings. They weren't that old, but they felt like they could topple down on me at any minute. The whole suburb did. It creeped the hell out of me.

Finally I reached the top of the rise and started heading back downhill. I cut across a playground where a Transperth bus had ploughed through the waist-high fence and come to rest against a bordering townhouse. Grass had grown around its tyres, giving it the look of a giant forgotten campervan. The high-rises fell away and I relaxed a little. There were some shops and cafes ahead, before the car yards began. I swapped the laundry bag to my other arm and kept a lookout for a chemist. Rachel would be pissed about the golf cart. Maybe if I found her something for her cold it would soften the blow.

A lot of the shops looked like they had been smashed into some time ago. The glass was dirty and clustered into piles by wind and rain. I passed a Baskin-Robbins where the ice-cream had melted into a sludgy rainbow across the counter and floor. Gloria Jean's, where the chairs and tables had been pushed aside to form a path in and out of the ransacked kitchen. A lonely health insurance outlet with just a token rock thrown in through the window.

We had been late to the party on all of this stuff. Sheltered and oblivious inside the talcum-white walls of Carousel. Walking those streets I got the unnerving sensation that I had arrived at some kind of post-post-apocalypse. A place where a new civilisation had been trialled, and swiftly failed, with no obvious successor rising up to take its place. Perth drew a nervous breath and hung in limbo all around me.

I found a chemist and some supplies to take back to Rachel. Mostly vitamins. Most of them were out of code, but a few looked to be fine. As I exited the dank and dusty store something caught my eye.

A solitary white ute was parked across the street.

It was out the front of a neat Federation hotel. A posted timber balcony wrapped around the upper floor. A bar with decorative brickwork and brewery logos sat tucked away beneath.

I stopped and looked at the car. Something wasn't

right about it. Not with the vehicle itself, but where
it was. It was parked squarely inside the car bay. Not
abandoned and part of the old world. But somehow new
and foreign. As if it had only just arrived.

I crossed the road and looked it over. It was a
late-model trayback Toyota. Nothing fancy. There was
some dirt on the lower panels and windscreen. I peered
inside and saw the cab was empty but for a road map,
some food wrappers and a pair of sunglasses. I stood
and listened, but the quiet streets told me nothing. It was
dimming rapidly toward dusk and my instincts told me
to forget the car and get the hell back to the casino. But I
suddenly remembered something Rocky had done when
we found the Fiesta in Carousel, and placed my hand on
the bonnet.

It was warm.

Somebody was inside the hotel.

20

'So I guess you're the Curator?' I asked.

The guy sitting at the bar picked up his beer, finished the inch or so that remained in the bottle and placed it back down on the coaster.

'Can I buy you a beer?' he replied.

I hesitated, still just a step inside the door. The guy waited calmly on his stool. He was shortish and had the weathered, everyday face of a dad who coached the cricket team. I quickly recognised him as local folk singer Ed Carrington.

Ed was a bit of an icon in Australia. It felt like he had been around forever. He wrote the simple, melodic songs that soundtracked just about everybody's barbeques, Christmases and road trips. His music was nostalgic and truthful in a country without a lot of either. Everyone in Australia was supposed to like Ed Carrington. And there I was wanting to punch him in the face.

'It's not cold. But it's not warm either,' said Ed, looking

at the empty bottle like he was about to write a fucking song about it.

'What have you done with everyone?' I asked.

Ed exhaled and weighed up his answer.

'I can't answer that. But I can tell you a bit of what I know, and some more of what I think,' he said.

'Why not?' I asked. '*Are* you the Curator?'

I was still standing by the door with the bag strung over my shoulder. Ed slid off his stool and pushed out the one beside him as an invitation for me to sit. I placed my bag carefully by the door and edged my way over. Ed's eyes flashed a welcoming smile and he held out a hand. I took it and shook, despite myself.

'I prefer Ed,' he replied.

I sat on the stool while he circled the bar and disappeared beneath the counter, then emerged with two beers.

'Melbourne Bitter okay?' he asked, opening the bottles before I could answer.

I nodded. Ed placed them on the bar and made his way back to his stool.

'People drink a lot of fancy stuff these days. Now that it's free and everything,' he said. 'But you have to ask yourself, when the shit is hitting the fan, is that really your drink?'

We clinked bottles and I took a small sip.

'I didn't catch your name,' said Ed.

'Nox,' I replied.

'Where you from, Nox?' he asked.

'The hills,' I replied, bitingly.

Ed put down his beer. There was empathy in his gaze.

'North or south?' he asked.

'South,' I replied. 'Roleystone.'

Ed took a moment to think this over.

'I've spent some time in the hills. Was up there last weekend,' he replied. 'The fire took out a lot of land. Nearly all of the north and down into the valley. But I've heard that some pockets in the very south made it through okay. Maybe some of Roleystone.'

'My friend Tommy was up there,' I said. 'He was looking for you.'

'I hope he's okay, Nox,' replied Ed. 'We got a lot of people out before it really took off. But it's hard to know how many are about these days. People have scattered.'

'Not what you expected to happen?' I asked.

Ed looked at me, then took another swig.

'I got to level with you, Nox. I'm a regular guy. Just like anyone else left wandering around this city,' he replied.

I didn't buy it.

'How come you have a car when nobody else does?' I asked.

'I'm a mechanic by trade, so that helps. But these days it's mostly about the fuel. Petrol goes bad pretty quickly. Diesel is better, but there's not a lot of that around now either. I read somewhere that a country should have a three-month stockpile of fuel in case of a catastrophic weather event. How much do you reckon we have in Australia?' he asked.

I shrugged.

'Around three weeks worth,' said Ed.

He seemed staggered by this, but I felt like he was avoiding my question.

'So why do people call you the Curator?' I asked.

'There's a lot of grief in this city. People are lost. They need a lighthouse,' he replied.

'A lighthouse?' I asked.

Ed looked at me and waited.

'My family is gone. One of my friends died in a shopping centre. The others were lost in a fire. People need more than a fucking lighthouse,' I snapped.

I shoved my stool away and paced across the bar. My head was swimming with confusion and bitterness.

Ed remained seated, calm as ever. Eventually I stopped and glared over at the solitary figure seated at the bar. Shafts of late afternoon sun stretched in through the windows. Ed took a long draw on his beer, then turned to face me. It felt like we were standing off in some bizzaro western.

'I'm sorry, Nox,' said Ed.

He sounded genuine. Actually, Ed was kind of genuine personified.

I took a breath and thought about my conversation with Lizzy. About how we project stuff onto famous people depending on what we need from them. How we make them out to be something they're not.

'You said you could tell me what you know,' I replied.

Ed nodded. 'And what I think,' he replied. A showman's sparkle danced in his eyes.

I returned to my stool and necked my beer. Ed finished his off and settled comfortably against the bar. I watched him and waited.

'Have you ever heard of something the French call the Prix de Rome?'

In that shadowy abandoned pub, over a series of lukewarm Melbourne Bitters, Ed Carrington filled me in on the history of the Prix de Rome.

The Prix de Rome was an award for artists that dated all the way back to the seventeenth century. It was started in France by a king who decided that the country's best artists should get the opportunity to develop their art from the masters in Rome. Winners were given residencies in the city in order to study, develop their craft and create definitive artworks. These residencies often lasted several years before the artists returned home to continue their careers.

Ed was quick to add that it wasn't all 'beer and skittles'. Returning artists were often expected to use their new skills to glorify the relevant king to the public in future work – no pressure. The award was also adopted by other countries and became super competitive. In the Netherlands artists had to pass a series of exams just in order to qualify. The final of these tests involved being locked in a cubicle for months, where you were fed meals through a hatch while you tried to paint a masterpiece that justified your place in the residency.

Since then the award diversified from painting to include all kinds of art forms, and ebbed and flowed throughout history until France abandoned it in the sixties.

'What happened?' I asked.

Ed carefully returned his bottle to its coaster.

'A lot of stuff went down in France during the sixties. The government was conservative. Had been for a long time. But the people were headed in another direction. They wanted to be progressive; to feel represented. So they protested,' he replied. 'It started with the students. Protests. Rallies. Debates. And a lot of great artwork,' said Ed.

He paused for a moment. 'Nobody protests like the French.'

'Suddenly an award like the Prix de Rome seemed kind of bourgeois. It was restrictive and part of the establishment. Art was supposed to be challenging, not conformist. Gradually the people lost interest. The government abolished it in sixty-eight. But really, it was the people who decided.'

I took a breath and stared into space. I was wrapped

up in the story and the beer and had all but forgotten why he was telling me this.

'For the art world, sixty-eight was a line in the sand. The sixties in general I guess,' said Ed. 'But lately things have crept back into dangerous territory. Artists are being forced to chase fame harder than ever before. Fine art is all about winning awards and being represented by galleries. Cinema is full of sequels, prequels and remakes. Music has lost its gatekeepers, but also a lot of its soul.

'You see, Nox, residencies don't exist so that painters can practise painting kings. They exist so that artists can be challenged. So they can be transported a million miles from their reality. Away from the stuff that clouds things over and makes all art feel the same. Not just the famous artists, either. All kinds,' said Ed.

'But a while ago they stopped being able to do that,' said Ed. 'The world needed a new kind of residency.'

He stopped and let these words hang in the air.

I looked at him.

'You can't be serious?'

'Afraid so,' he replied, eyes all sparkly.

'So when is this *new kind of residency* supposed to finish?' I asked.

'September second,' he replied.

'This year?' I asked.

'This year,' he replied.

'Why?' I asked.

'Two years to the day it started. The minimum length

of the Prix de Rome,' said Ed.

I felt dizzy and pressed down on my temples.

'That's what I think. Not what I know,' said Ed.

'Say you're right. What do we do on September second?' I asked.

'Go back to your Residency. Take your art with you. It was customary for artists to present their work at the completion of their stay,' he replied.

'To who? And then what?' I asked.

'I don't know, Nox. But if I took a punt, I think that might be our ticket back home,' he replied.

'Does everybody know about this?' I asked.

Ed shook his head gravely.

'I tell who I can. But people have spread out. Bunkered down,' he replied. 'I can't get to all of them.'

'What month is it now?' I asked.

'It's the first of July,' he replied.

'Two months,' I whispered.

'Two months,' echoed Ed.

We sat in silence. The bar was all but dark now. Bottles glinted with moonlight bouncing in off the street. A dog yelped somewhere distant and suddenly my mind jolted.

'I have to find the Finns,' I said.

'Taylor and Lizzy Finn?' asked Ed.

My head shot up. 'You know them?'

'Sure I do,' replied Ed.

'Do you know where they are?' I asked.

'A photographer told me about some twins that were staying in the city. It sounded like the Finns,' he replied.

'When was this?' I asked.

'A while ago now,' he replied.

I stood up and swayed backwards. There was a long line of empty bottles on the bar.

'Steady there, Nox,' said Ed.

'I need to get moving,' I replied, looking around for my bag.

'It's dark out now. No place to be walking. Let's break some bread and we'll make our way to the city in the morning,' he suggested.

Ed didn't wait for me to reply. Instead he disappeared outside and returned with an esky and a small portable barbeque. I watched as he moved about the bar. He was a diminutive looking guy, but he had a serious aura. It made everything he said seem somehow grandiose and resonant. Talking to Ed was like hearing fables unfold. Things that sounded simple and obvious, but then when you thought about them they made sense of the world in a way that didn't seem possible.

No wonder people here called him the Curator.

I sat by as he fried eggs and salami by the light of an old gas lantern. We ate at a proper table and talked of football and politics like they were things that were still in our lives. Ed opened some wine and downed a couple of glasses while I sipped on mine carefully. The guy just didn't get drunk.

My head started to droop badly after dinner. Ed cleared the plates and tossed me a mat and blanket from his ute. I stretched them out on the floor, and spiralled rapidly into blankness as Ed took up his stool back at the bar.

21

The morning was bright and spiking cold. I woke and
tried to shake off a hangover while I helped Ed load up
his ute. He had said good morning, but otherwise been
silent. There were clearly things on his mind that he had
taken leave from the night before. When everything was
packed into the ute Ed took a jerry can from the tray and
started refuelling.

'I can take you to the city, but then I have to head
south,' he said. 'There are Artists down that way that I
need to get in touch with.'

'Actually, if you could just drop me back at the casino,
that would be great,' I replied.

Ed glanced at me carefully.

'I have a friend there that I need to see before I go
anywhere else,' I added.

Ed nodded and we set off through the remainder of
Vic Park and down into Burswood. Being in a proper
car again was nauseating. We were moving way too fast
for my brain to process things. Ed seemed to notice my

discomfort. He put on some old Springsteen and slowed down a little. When I glanced across he had his arm on the window and the breeze on his face as if we were on our way to the beach.

In no time at all we were idling in the taxi rank of the casino. I pulled my bag out of the tray and returned to the window.

'Thanks for the lift,' I said.

'Anytime,' replied Ed.

'Where will you go after the south?' I asked.

'Think I'll track back north along the coast. People tend to stay close to the ocean,' he replied.

I nodded and lingered for a moment. There was something I had been putting off asking him and this was my last chance.

'What do you say to the Patrons?' I asked.

'Who?' asked Ed.

'Patrons. The people that aren't Artists,' I replied.

'Ah,' said Ed.

He took a breath and thought it over for a moment.

'I don't know what to say to them, Nox,' he said.

We locked eyes for a moment.

'Luckily I haven't met any yet,' he said.

He flashed a smile. The showman's sparkle in full flight.

'Godspeed, Nox,' said Ed and pulled onto the dusty, abandoned highway. A spark of movement in a sprawling city still life.

'You too,' I replied.

I stood there for a few seconds, then set off upstairs.

For once I felt vital. Not scared or sheltered or insecure. For once I had things I needed to do.

Rachel was mad about the golf cart. Fortunately the cold had almost taken her voice, so she couldn't really yell at me. For a while she tried, despite my explanations, but stopped when I told her I was leaving. I didn't know what to make of her reaction to my meeting with Ed. I explained his theory the best that I could but Rachel scoffed at the idea of leaving her penthouse to trudge back to Carousel. Mostly she just seemed pissed that the Curator was right outside and she didn't get to go down and knock his lights out or something.

It was sad, but not unexpected. I unpacked her shopping and left her be for a while. There were things I needed to sort out before I could take off anyway. Hopefully she would chill by the time I was ready to go.

Back in my suite I spread my things out across the carpet and started packing. Skeleton plans drifted in and out of my subconscious. I had hauled our bikes up from the highway and into the foyer a while back, but they would be rusty now and need greasing. I figured that I might be able to find something I could use in the kitchen. I had to pack light, but it was also winter, so I would need to stay warm at night. Perth could drop to zero on a clear night. What I really needed were some thermals and waterproofing. There were stores for this in the city, but who knows what state they would be in.

Then there was the issue of food. I had been living pretty well in the casino, mainly thanks to Rachel's secret stash. Being on the road again would be a reality check. There were still some cans in the kitchen. Random stuff like beetroot slices and chestnuts. I could also take a stack of chocolate and nuts from the mini-bars. Water was the toughest thing. It would weigh me down like crazy, but it might take some time to find more in the city – especially if it had been populated for a while now.

My feelings towards the city were ambivalent. Tommy had made it sound unstable and dangerous. A rambling place full of Loots, falling buildings and broken gas lines. But Georgia's descriptions of the Collective were all warm and golden. She spoke of vegetable gardens, outdoor cinema and concerts by the fire. A futuristic Artist utopia. For some reason I had trouble buying this. Even more so when she sidestepped my questions about why she left. Ed hadn't been to the Collective for a while now but I didn't think he would have sent me there if he knew it was bad idea. Plus he knew people there – like the photographer that had mentioned Taylor and Lizzy.

Taylor and Lizzy were alive.

I had never truly thought otherwise. But Ed's confirmation sent a jolt deep down to the numbness that had started enveloping my core. I still had no idea what had happened during the fire. Where Lizzy and Chess had got to. And why Taylor had never returned once she found them. I felt angry and needed answers to these things, but was also afraid of what they might reveal. In Carousel I had created deep-seated anxieties that channelled right into this stuff. A life in the penthouses alongside Rachel offered a buffer to these insecurities. But meeting Ed had confirmed that this could never be permanent. Irrespective of whether his theory on the Prix de Rome was true, there was no sheltering from this new world. It was changing too fast. Pivoting dramatically and spitting off into new directions. The survivors had to manoeuvre and adapt. And I was one of them.

Yet something about Ed's theory rang true. A city full of Artists held captive to create works in the ultimate Residency. Perth seemed the perfect place for this. Already one of the most isolated cities on the planet. Severed from the world by ocean upon ocean, desert upon desert. This took the isolation to a disturbing new level. And, if Taylor and Lizzy's album was any indication, the idea had worked. It was fantastical and ridiculous, but also the perfect explanation to the chaos that surrounded us. The problem was that Artists had finished ahead of time. They were out in the world now. A world that didn't yet know what it was.

22

I headed to bed early that night but couldn't sleep. My
gear lay packed and ready on the floor beside me and an
ominous southerly was blowing in against the balcony.
I had spent a while in the bathroom earlier. Washing
and shaving and trying to assess how I looked. My hair
was long and messy. It had faded in colour during the
summer, while my skin had done the opposite. I was still
lean, but had put on some muscle in the chest and arms
during my stay. Dressed another way I could have been
mistaken for a surfer.

I sat up and hit the light on the barman's watch. It had
been dark for a while now, but was only just after eight.
The broken chatter of TV drifted across from Rachel's
room. Probably *Supernatural* or *True Blood*. Rachel was
big into fantasy.

I felt a growing guilt about leaving her alone at the
casino. It was unfounded and irrational, but I couldn't
shake it. Rachel didn't need me, or anyone else. But
she had saved my arse in the gaming room, and let me

mooch away her diesel in the penthouses, when she didn't have to do either. Now I was taking off to find the Finns and get the hell out of this bizarro reality before it was too late. I felt like I had to try and sell her on Ed's theory at least one more time.

The hallway was dark and draughty. I slipped out into it and traced my way to Rachel's door. Rachel ran the TV loud. I got every line of dialogue as I stood outside and knocked. After my third attempt the door shifted inward.

I stepped inside to find Rachel shuffling back to the couch, eyes still fixed on the TV. I followed her over and took a seat on another sofa. She was engulfed in a sea of snack food, throat lozenges and tissues. A strip heater beamed up at her from the floor, bathing the couch in heat and tanning-salon-orange. She was watching *Supernatural*. It seemed pretty dramatic so I didn't attempt a conversation, instead watching quietly until the credits rolled and she got up to pour herself a drink in the kitchen.

'I'm heading to the city in the morning,' I said. 'I was wondering ... The Finns and I could stop back here on our way through to Carousel.'

'Why?' asked Rachel.

'You could come with us to Carousel. I know it all sounds like bullshit, but it would only take a day or two to check it out,' I replied.

Rachel swallowed some pills and started fishing through her drawers.

'You can cut my hair before you go,' she said.

'Sorry?' I replied.

'My hair, Nox. It needs cutting,' she replied.

She found some scissors and made her way to the bathroom.

'Do you really want me doing that?' I asked.

'What else am I going to do? Book into Salon Express?' she replied.

I trudged through to the bathroom feeling like an idiot for not staying in bed. Rachel was sitting on a chair with her back to the basins.

'You'll need to wash it first,' she said. 'Use a bucket and that yuppy organic stuff.'

I sighed and followed her instructions. Rachel lent back in the chair but the basins were too far back to catch all of the water. I splashed a fair bit of it on the floor. Thankfully the casino's clean towel supply still seemed never-ending. When I was eventually done Rachel turned the chair in a one-eighty to look at the mirror and handed me the scissors.

'Short back and sides?' I joked.

'If you want your balls cut off in your sleep,' she replied.

'Holy shit, Rachel,' I said.

'Take two inches off everything, but don't touch the fringe. I'll do that myself,' said Rachel.

I nodded and got on with it. There were a stack of expensive looking combs on the bench. I picked one out and combed her hair straight. Rachel still had the remnants of an overgrown bob. The top half was her natural light brown while the bottom was the patchy blonde of a dye job she had when we first met.

'Have you heard much of Ed Carrington's music?' I asked, remembering why I had come over in the first place.

'Concentrate,' she snapped.

I exhaled and let it go. Rachel watched me as I gingerly started cutting. After a while she seemed to relax.

'Those twins of yours been waiting for you across the river this whole time?' she asked.

I glanced at her and shrugged, defensively.

'I thought they were nobodies when I saw youse in Carousel,' she said. 'Was out on the balcony one day reading a magazine and there they were next to fucking Kanye.'

'I told you they were in a band. Right before you sleazed onto me in the toilets,' I replied.

'Dream on,' said Rachel.

'You don't remember that?' I asked.

'I remember you barging into the ladies' toilets like you owned the place,' said Rachel.

'Oh my god. It was the men's,' I replied. 'You must have been so trashed.'

Rachel snorted and coughed. I continued trimming.

'How come you took off in the morning?' I asked, having wanted to for ages.

'Used to see another trapped Artist on my way to work. I was getting smokes one day when I heard her singing opera or something,' replied Rachel.

'Where was she?' I asked.

'Sizzler,' she replied.

'Seriously?' I said.

'When she wasn't singing she would bang away at those windows like nobody's business,' said Rachel.

It was one of the most tragic stories I had ever heard.

'When I saw youse were stuck too I knew something was going on. Got the hell out while I could,' said Rachel.

I nodded.

'So I can't talk you into going back there? Even for a day?' I asked.

'A Patron like me? No point,' she replied.

This sent a ripple of panic into my chest. I tried not to let on.

'Got a visitor coming in the spring anyways,' said Rachel.

There was something like a twinkle in her eye.

'Who?' I asked.

'None of your business,' she replied.

I sighed. 'Seriously? Come on, Rachel. You obviously want to tell me.'

'A fisherman. I met him last year,' she replied. 'He has his own boat. Takes it up north in the winter. Comes back down in August with crayfish, prawns. You name it.'

This finally explained her endless stockpile of frozen seafood.

'How did you guys meet?' I asked.

'In the freezer room last year. I helped him unload his catch, then we had drinks in the lounge bar,' replied Rachel.

I smiled at the thought of such a regular event still occurring in this weirdo world. The idea that fate wasn't just working against people like Rachel, but was still running in all kinds of strange ways. That amid all of the pompous talk of Artists and Residencies, there were simple, defining events like a fisherman and a cleaner having a drink in a fancy bar. I was convinced that these things kept the earth spinning more than anything.

It made me think of Georgia somewhere down in Fremantle. Travelling all the way across the world to study her craft. Wandering the abandoned city for more than a year before stumbling across my tiny note.

I realised then that I wasn't just hoping to find the Finns when I set off tomorrow.

'Nice,' I replied. 'Will he stay for a bit?'

'Two months. Said we might head south on the boat for summer,' she replied.

She looked at me, then quickly away. It was the only time I had seen any hint of vulnerability in her.

'That sounds pretty awesome, Rachel,' I replied, genuinely.

I finished trimming the back of her hair.

'Wish I hadn't screwed up your hair,' I joked.

'I will fucken kill you, Nox,' said Rachel. Again, way too serious.

'Relax. Relax,' I replied.

Rachel cackled and coughed.

'You sound way too genuine when you say stuff like that,' I said.

Rachel deadeyed me in a way that said she was well aware of this.

I finished up and waited around while she inspected the job with a series of mirrors. Thankfully it passed and I was allowed to go. Rachel took up her spot on the couch and resumed blasting herself with heat and noise. I stood there watching for a moment.

'Alright. I'm off then,' I said.

'Seeya,' replied Rachel, after a moment.

It was casual and dry, as if we were leaving work at the end of the day. I turned and left the room. My time at Burswood was over.

23

The city had been all but abandoned.

Early in the morning I crossed the river on a bridge overrun by birds. They nested between pillars. Lined the handrail looking west at the gathering weather. Sat atop cars and busses, watching on smugly as I pedalled slowly past. At the end, Adelaide Terrace spread before me, linking the causeway with St Georges Terrace like a giant gateway to the west. I swung onto it and made my way up into the teeth of a funnelling breeze.

The city had the look and feel of a park the day after an epic summer festival. Litter of all kinds fluttered about in the icy breeze. Wrappers, ancient newspapers, pages torn from notebooks and sketchpads. There were the remnants of an electricity in the air. Like a sports arena, heaving one moment, empty the next.

The streets themselves seemed wider than normal, as if the empty buildings were shrinking back into themselves. They had the faint smell of barbeque and rotting plant matter. There was more of the street art I had seen in Victoria Park. Again on walls and buildings, but also on the streets themselves where the images ran on for block after block. I got the feeling that the city would look pretty amazing from above.

Gradually I began to see evidence of the party that had swept through. Windows were open and curtains flapping on the upper floors of ritzy hotels like the Hyatt and Duxton. Bottleshops were decimated but for scatterings of cask wines and liqueurs. The rigid, fortress-like frontage of the Perth Concert Hall had been ignored completely. Its stage and stalls too Old World for the new Artists of Perth. Instead I passed a drum kit standing defiantly, almost Tiananmen-like, in the middle of the road. There were amps and leads scattered around from a long-forgotten gig. The giant foyer of a multinational skyscraper had been broken into and transformed into a gallery, lit during openings by a generator and halogen worklights. I cycled up to the windows and peered in at some of the artwork. It was dim now without the generator on but I could see some striking portraits on the wall adjacent.

A makeshift stage had been erected in a corner of the piazza by Stirling Gardens. It held a stool and a solitary microphone stand, both blown onto their side now. There were chairs and beanbags scattered around. A space for spoken word or poetry maybe.

The Collective was meant to be a few blocks north of where I rode, but I was starting to wonder whether there would be anyone there.

I left the Terrace and cycled up through a series of smaller streets. There were places there that I remembered. A good Chinese takeaway. Music stores I used to wander through on lunchbreaks. A second-level karaoke bar I had visited with Chloe and her workmates one Friday night. She had been nervous and opted out of a bunch of shouty duets, before stunning everyone with a perfect solo rendition of 'Somebody That I Used To Know'. It was tragic and beautiful and I remember thinking that there was way more to Chloe than I had seen during our awkward dates and sleepovers. Two months later we broke up without a single fight and she left town to study in Melbourne.

Subconsciously I was taking a detour that would lead me past the stationery store where I used to work. I turned a familiar corner and slowed to a stop on the sidewalk. There it was across from me. The boring red logo. The early-morning opening hours. Streaks of dirt and silt caked to the windows. I was only two years late for my shift.

The door had been crowbarred open and was drifting with the wind. I walked my bike over and pushed it inside. The shop hadn't been ransacked like some of the others. People had cleared out some of the art supplies and taken just about all of the confectionery, but otherwise it looked the same as I remembered. I took a key from a hidden shelf behind the counter and unlocked the staff room at the back of the store. The smell brought a heavy rush of nostalgia. Breakfast pastries. Deodorised carpet. Instant coffee. My boss Julie's bad perfume. I had never liked working there, but the place was loaded with emotions from my previous life. I sat on the floor and tried my hardest not to choke up at how alone I was now, just like I had been before the Disappearance. There were people all around me at work, at home, out at night. But I had coiled inward dramatically after finishing uni and breaking up with Heather for the second time. The ironic thing was that this whole Residency business had kind of changed that. For the first time in ages I had connected with some people. Then met a girl I could kiss without thinking about somebody else. These things had happened even though I wasn't meant to be here. But then they had slipped away. I couldn't help but think that fate had realised my intrusion and was somehow reneging on its gifts. That if I didn't turn up back at Carousel with something definitive I might be left here forever.

I checked the time on the barman's watch and pulled myself together. I had to keep moving and there was stuff in the store that I could use. Batteries, torches and bug spray. I took the best of each of these, along with a dauntingly thick but lightweight writing pad. Before I left I went back into the office and wrote out a note for my boss.

Hi Julie. On my way in today I decided that it wasn't a great idea for me to work here anymore. Nothing against you (although only giving overtime shifts to juniors to save cash is pretty shit – you know that kid you hired Craig steals from the till yeah?). I just need to focus on my writing for a while. Nox.

Julie hated when you texted her emojis, so I drew a couple next to my name and left the note central on her desk. It was juvenile, but made me feel a bit better about things.

I left the store and rode on northward for a while before I emerged onto the first of two outdoor malls. It was wide, barren and deathly quiet. The type of place that shouted *ZOMBIE APOCALYPSE!* from every vantage. In the distance I saw a weird looking device lying central on the paving. I rolled over to it cautiously. A series of generators surrounded something on a raised platform in the middle. I got off my bike and moved inside the circle of generators. On the platform were clusters of giant strobe lights all pointed up at the sky.

It was the nightly lightshow.

A laptop was hooked up to a lightboard, which in turn ran cords down into each of the lights. There was also a small solar panel nearby that seemed to be powering the laptop, and a line of jerry cans ready to refuel the generators. Aside from topping up the fuel in the generators every so often, the lightshow was effectively self-sufficient. It was weird to think of this collection of devices as the source of the art we had gathered to watch almost nightly in the hills. For some reason I had imagined somebody would be down here orchestrating. I had only ever considered the outcome, not the process.

I took a break and ate some lunch on a nearby bench. My legs felt stiff from the riding and would be aching by this time tomorrow. I also had a headache that wouldn't seem to lift. There was an unnerving silence hanging over every corner of the city. I hadn't expected to find it bustling and full, but this was something else entirely. Almost like a second disappearance.

I finished eating and cycled back east towards the Collective. I remembered City Farm being close to the train lines that wrapped around the back of the city. I rolled down past the second street mall and saw the central station over to my left. There was a lot of construction behind the station and I thought I could see the crane Tommy mentioned.

Before he left, Tommy had told me about a giant construction crane that had blown over during a winter storm. I could see a great steel arm sticking up out of the ground where the base should have been. It was warped and bent back in on itself, a bit like a spring. Behind it was a building with a savage hole running the length of its side where the crane had hit during the storm. Empty offices and break rooms now stood exposed to the weak winter sun.

I rode forward to the edge of the tracks. They were fenced off and littered with crap. It smelt pretty bad down there. The same sweet rotting-apple smell that I had picked up on the Terrace, but bumped up a notch and mixed with old eggs. I followed the tracks back eastward and hoped the air might improve. After a while they swung away and a pocket of smaller offices and parkland stretched out before me. I weaved through until I noticed the dirty white top of a marquee to my left.

It was one of hundreds.

Past the final set of offices, rambling out across a wide open lawn, lay what had to be the Collective. There were marquees everywhere. Some were wide and rigid with steel framework. Others were humble and sagging in the weather. Beyond the tents I could see the brown and green of City Farm by the railway. I got off the bike and walked it over past the first marquee. It had some old couches and tables and pile after pile of paperbacks. The next one looked to be somebody's sleeping quarters. There was a mattress on the floor. A rack full of tops and dresses. Clusters of thirsty looking potted plants. The third was kitted out with video equipment and an editing station. There was a power cord running out of this marquee in the direction of City Farm.

I continued on. Tent after tent. But not an Artist to be found.

The largest of the marquees was central in the Collective and had a raised stage with lighting, amps and a mixing desk. Again there were power cords running away towards the farm. The area in front of this marquee was left clear so that a decent crowd could gather beneath the stage. Lizzy must have been excited by this. Maybe she and Taylor had even played there.

Where the hell were they?

Where was anybody?

Something felt risky about yelling out, so I kept quiet and edged forward to the farm area. By the time I reached the final marquees there were dozens of snaking power cords running across to the overgrown farm.

I steered clear of a grid of portaloos and entered the first of the gardens.

City Farm was a patchwork of edible gardens, cafes and bespoke sustainability projects. There was gravity-fed water storage. Banks of solar panels and wind turbines. Festering stacks of compost. Pens for chickens and who knows what else. I wandered through and took in some of the slightly fresher air. The walkways needed a sweep and most of the plants were overgrown and ratty.

In a converted barn I saw a cafe with an outside menu board reading: *Serving during easterlies – Scrambled Eggs & Basil. Fire-Roasted Cherry Tomatoes on Flatbread. Minted Rainwater Lemonade.* Nothing had a price. The chalk was slighted faded, but didn't look more than a few weeks old. It broke my brain to think of a cafe still being open for business. I had hardly eaten anything and should have been starving, but the headache was sending spikes of nausea down to my stomach and a thin sweat across my forehead. I wondered what it meant – *serving during easterlies.*

I took a break on a wooden bench. The scratch and berk of a chicken drifted through the gardens. Otherwise everything was quiet. The wind strengthened and brought another wave of odour in from the city to the west. My sweating increased. I gagged, then threw up all over the paving.

This went on for a good five minutes. By the end of it I was dizzy and my stomach was heaving.

I lent back and took a shallow breath. There was a banging noise somewhere behind me. I turned to find a woman looking at me from inside the cafe. She was waving at me to come inside.

I pulled myself up and shuffled across to the door. The woman took a couple of steps back from the door. I pushed it inwards and stepped cautiously inside.

'Hello,' I said meekly.

'What are you doing here?' she demanded.

I did a double-take. The woman was Hollywood actress Cara Winters.

'Trying to find my friends,' I replied.

Cara looked at me carefully. I felt dizzy and swayed forward.

'You better come downstairs,' she said.

She moved across the room to where a doorway opened onto a small concrete staircase. I steadied myself on the walls and followed her down to a basement where I slumped onto a bench and held my head.

'Do you have any Panadol?' I asked.

'Nope. It won't help with the gas anyway,' she replied.

'What gas?' I asked.

Cara stared down at me like a teacher in a classroom.

'Did you only just complete your Residency?' she asked.

'No, it was a while ago. I was living in the hills. Then the casino,' I replied.

The air in the basement was stale, but clean. The thump in my temples started to subside and I sat back and looked around.

The room was somewhere between a speakeasy and a microbrewery. There were communal tables adorned with candles and scattered glassware. One of the walls was entirely covered in shelving. These shelves held liquor of all kinds. It was a strange collection, by the looks of it just whatever people happened to bring in from the closest store. The far end of the basement housed a complicated brewing setup. Pipes, vats and plumbing. It was hard to tell if they were dormant or still being used. There were also a couple of doors leading away to what looked like some living quarters. On a low concrete ceiling the lights were on and a fan was gently circulating the air.

'Your friends aren't here. The gas drove everyone out of the city. Most Artists have gone west to the beaches,' said Cara.

My heart sank.

'When did this happen?' I asked.

'It was gradual until winter arrived and the westerlies blew in. Now the gas sweeps across us everyday. The headaches are too much. And the nausea,' replied Cara, nodding at me.

'Somebody told me my friends were here,' I said.

'I doubt it. Who are they?' she asked.

'Taylor and Lizzy Finn,' I replied.

There was a flicker of recognition in Cara.

'Lizzy was here for our final show. That was well over a month ago now. Last I heard she left for the airport,' said Cara.

'The airport?' I repeated.

'There's a community there. It's small, but some of the Artists like it,' she replied.

'What about Taylor?' I asked.

Cara studied me once more. As if we were in some method acting class and she was trying to uncover my motivation.

'Are you in their band?' she asked.

'No. I had a Residency with them. In a shopping centre,' I replied.

'A dual Residency?' she asked.

'Yeah I guess. There were actually four of us,' I replied.

'Taylor and Lizzy didn't mention a dual Residency,' said Cara.

I'd been wiped from their minds. Brilliant.

'So you met Taylor?' I asked.

'I remember her being here briefly. After Lizzy arrived she left with a painter,' said Cara.

'Holy shit,' I whispered.

Cara began flicking through some notes that were spread out across one of the tables. Her interest in the topic was waning.

'How come you haven't left the city?' I asked.

'I am to present my soliloquy here,' she replied.

'For the Prix de Rome?' I asked.

Cara looked up.

'Who told you about the Prix de Rome?' she snapped.

'Ed Carrington,' I replied.

She seemed sceptical.

'When was it that he told you?' she asked.

'Just a few days ago. I ran into him at a bar,' I replied.

Cara looked to be running a complex inner monologue.

'Did everyone here know about the Prix de Rome?' I asked.

Cara glanced at me, almost surprised, and shook her head. I couldn't get a handle on her demeanour. She either had a bunch of secrets, or maybe this was just how a real celebrity acted around a nobody like me. Whatever the case, the job of finding the Finns and racing them back to Carousel suddenly felt monumental.

I stood up and tested out my balance. I didn't feel great but I had to get moving.

'The wind won't turn back east until dawn tomorrow,' said Cara.

I stopped and looked at her.

'Right, okay,' I replied.

I lingered, unsure of what to do as Cara seemed to have resumed work on her soliloquy.

'There is coffee in the cafe upstairs,' she said, preoccupied.

Coffee was the last thing I felt like, but I was about to head up there regardless when I had a thought.

'Is there somewhere here I could write for a while?' I asked.

'There are studios through that door,' she replied, and nodded to a wooden door by the brewing equipment.

'Great. Thanks,' I replied.

I headed across the room and was almost through the door when Cara looked up from her work.

'Sorry. Do I know of you? What is it that you write?' she asked.

24

Cara set me up at a studio and made me some ginger tea to calm the lurching in my stomach. I had been unable to dodge her questions about who I was (nobody) and what I wrote (pretty much nothing). Her gaze was piercing and didn't let up until she had all of the information she required. So I spilled and told her I was just starting out. And that I hadn't really written anything since we had left Carousel. And even that had been pretty insignificant.

She seemed oddly interested in the details of the writing I had done in Carousel. How many short stories had I completed in total? Was it a collection or were they separate? Were they edited or just drafts? She even asked me some questions about Taylor and Lizzy's album, as if to confirm what she knew already. Eventually she stopped, almost abruptly, and left me to return to whatever it was she was working on.

The studio was small, but not stuffy. A vent ran across the top of one wall, just above ground level outside. I stood up and sniffed cautiously at the air drifting inside.

Thankfully it seemed okay. The room consisted of a simple wooden desk. A high-back office chair – probably swindled from a nearby business. Some notepads and pens, and a powerboard in case you were lucky enough to have an operational laptop. Otherwise it was cool and empty.

I had been anxious to get writing again ever since my meeting with Ed. My time at the casino felt like a giant, bathrobe-wearing hiatus. Now things were moving again I felt a great pressure to be writing. Ed's theory said that I was to be judged on the work I had created in Carousel alone. But Ed didn't know how I arrived at Carousel. How I conned a pathway to survival. I still hoped to be transported back with Taylor and Lizzy and all of the other Artists, but I felt that I needed to return to Carousel with more than just the short stories buried down in my backpack. Somehow I had to justify my selection by writing more. Writing bigger. And now, with the Finns spread out across the city, I felt as though I was racing the clock on both art and geography.

I shoved aside my swirling mass of thoughts and anxieties and started filling the new notepad with descriptions of the city. It was what I had started doing when we left the hills. Writing third-person prose about the world now. I guess kind of focusing in on its contradiction. How a world with only Artists was beautiful and simple. There was silence and reflection and pockets of gobsmacking art bursting through where you least expected it. But it was also lonely and decrepit. Like the people left were separate to the environment. They lived in it and looked at it and made art about it, but they didn't inhabit its walls and spaces. Of all the people I had met, Rachel was the only one who seemed to have integrated into the new world. Everyone else was still drifting. Focused on bigger things. A lot of artists are nomadic and transitory by nature, and that hadn't changed here.

The pages filled one by one and it felt good to be writing again. After what I considered to be a decent session I got up and stretched and left the room in search of something to eat. Cara was pacing the basement, mouthing words from one of her notepads.

'Hi,' I said.

She continued pacing while I stood awkwardly in the centre of the room.

'Are you breaking for dinner already?' she asked, eventually.

'Um. No. I'm just finished, I guess,' I replied.

She dipped her head and studied me from above her glasses.

'The whole manuscript?' she asked.

'No,' I replied.

'There's no TV here, Nox. If you're still alive and breathing, you might as well be in there writing,' she said.

I looked at my shoes and felt like a seven-year-old.

'Behind that counter are some nuts and dried fruit from the gardens. And there's more tea in the pot by the sink. You're welcome to take whatever you choose back to the studio,' said Cara.

'Alright, great. Thanks,' I replied.

I walked over to the counter and loaded a bowl with as much food as it would take. Cara seemed oblivious. Preoccupied with her pretentious soliloquy. Back in the study I sat down and quietly fumed over her preachy schoolteacher attitude. *There's no TV here, Nox.* What the fuck.

The food tasted good, but I would have preferred something fresh from the gardens. I cleaned out the bowl and washed it down with more tea. Then I looked around and considered sleeping. There was nowhere obvious to do this but the floor, which was concrete, so I sat at the desk and listened for sounds of Cara leaving. I could still hear the occasional flick of a page and clink of her teacup.

Surely I couldn't keep writing. I had already put down way more than my usual amount. I read back over it and made some amendments. The final paragraph ended abruptly so I played around and drew it out with a few more sentences so it finished properly. Then I grudgingly started on another paragraph.

Five hours later I had filled up a third of the notepad.

I stepped away from the desk and looked at the pad as if it was a foreign object. It looked back at me, plump and real. It was as intense a writing experience as I had ever had. Out of my wordy descriptions of place had emerged a character and a narrative. Not somebody I knew or had met, but someone I had invented. A character with backstory, flaws and a motivation that felt interesting. Like I wanted to know more. It also felt as though, if I kept writing, I would know more. I felt a chill and wondered whether this was what it felt like to actually be writing a novel.

I packed the notepad securely into my bag and emerged to find Cara drinking wine and listening to music on an iPod. She pulled off her headphones at my arrival.

'Nox! Pour a glass. I was just about to make us some dinner,' said Cara.

She swept past me and moved behind the counter. I poured myself some wine from the bottle that was open on her table.

'It's shiraz from the great southern,' said Cara.

I nodded and took a sniff even though I had already gulped some down. Cara looked at me expectantly.

'It's good,' I said.

'Western Australia has such stunning wine. It's more than terroir. It's ... personality,' said Cara. 'But you're from here. So you know this already.'

'To be honest we mostly drink cask wine where I live,' I replied.

Cara boomed with laughter.

'What am I saying. You're a young Artist. It's your right of passage, no?' she said.

I smiled and nodded. Her transformation from earlier was crazy. She was still intense, but now in a magnetic, life-of-the-party kind of way. Her hair swept theatrically from one side of her face to the other. When she spoke her eyes locked in and dazzled as if each sentence was a gemstone of gossip for my ears only. The room was big and there were just the two of us, yet Cara radiated into every corner.

'Actually, I was wondering if you could do me a giant favour and head out to the garden for a couple of ingredients?' she asked.

'Will the air be okay out there?' I asked.

'You know, I was up in the cafe earlier and the wind has dropped right down. It looks like we'll have one of those calm and gorgeous winter nights,' said Cara.

'What do you need?' I asked, still not keen on the idea.

'Just a bit of everything,' she said.

She handed me a large basket and flashed another red-carpet smile. I headed upstairs and out through the cafe. It was night and the garden radiated with the soft hum of insects. There was a faint waft of gas in the air, but nothing like the morning. The garden paths were lit by a series of solar lights rising up out of the ground. I followed these around, filling the basket with whatever I could make out in the murky light. The plants were heavy with produce and it wasn't long before I had run out of room.

Back at the cafe I felt a sudden urge to grab my bike and get the hell out of there. It seemed irrational and would be dangerous given the gas and darkness. But something wasn't right about Cara down in that basement. I shrugged off the feeling and headed back inside. There was no way I was leaving without my writing anyway.

Cara gasped theatrically at the selection in the basket as I returned.

'Wonderful, Nox! There is a plate on the table to get us started,' she said.

I wandered over to find an awesome selection of preserved vegetables on offer in all kinds of kooky jars. I found my appetite and crammed a bunch of it into my mouth while Cara started unpacking the basket. When I glanced across, the fresh food had disappeared and she was busy picking out another bottle of wine from the shelves.

'Now ... You and I are going to drink this pinot noir and you're going to tell me what it was like to grow up in this wondrous city,' she said.

'Sure,' I replied, trying to sound enthused.

Cara catwalked over and sat down opposite me. She poured wine for both of us and took a long and lingering taste.

'So tell me,' she said. 'Was it all ... Christmas at the

beach. Children dancing in the shore break. Summer nights camped in backyards with stolen beers and truth or dare. Fooling around in cinemas with girls from other schools. Never during my movies of course!' she added, with a devilish smile.

I swallowed my food and tried hard not to choke.

'Or maybe you're a winter soul,' said Cara, leaning back to look at me from another angle.

'Reading fantasy late into the night while the rain lashed your window. Trips to the country with friends to find bookstores and brew mulled wine over the fire. Maybe there was just one girl. But a special one,' she winked and whispered.

I had no idea how to respond to any of this.

'Kind of both, I guess,' I replied.

'Really?' asked Cara, seemingly intrigued.

'We moved to the hills when I was in high school. It's a long way from the beach. But the bush up there is cool,' I replied.

'Isn't it! And the lights! You know, at night, it's a match for anywhere in LA up there,' said Cara.

I nodded and downed the rest of my glass.

'And when did you know that you just had to be a writer?' she asked.

'Wow, that's tough,' I replied.

Cara hovered, theatrically.

'I studied some literature at uni. I actually wasn't really that good at it. But I remember after I graduated,

I still found myself doing the readings, even though I didn't have to anymore. I guess that was when I knew I had a connection to it,' I said. 'Does that make sense?'

'It makes beautiful sense, Nox,' said Cara. 'Our callings can be aloof and mysterious, but they always call.'

I nodded and pretended to look around the room. It was super intense and weird sitting there opposite such a giant celebrity.

'And here you are now. One of the chosen Artists. In the running for the new Prix de Rome,' she purred.

'Do you think there will be an actual winner?' I asked.

'Why not?' she replied wistfully. 'Ed would never agree. But what an accolade to take back to the world.'

'Don't you already have like two Oscars and a Golden Globe,' I said.

Cara stopped and her eyes froze onto mine. She stood up and leaned slowly toward me.

'I. Want. Everything,' she whispered, just inches from my nose.

Then she broke into laugher and sauntered into the kitchen area. I sat back and exhaled.

'You have attitude, Nox. That's a good thing,' said Cara. 'Now for some real food.'

We ate our way through a stack of amazing produce from the basket I had gathered. Cara was liberal with the supplies. She seemed ravenous and was convinced beyond any doubt that the Residencies were ending soon. *What is left here should be enjoyed. It should nurture us in our final stages of our journey.* I wasn't arguing.

I grilled her for gossip on big Hollywood stars, and found out a few things, but Cara's stories were whimsical and often morphed into morality tales before they could deliver anything juicy. I also tried to eke out more information on Taylor and Lizzy. Knowing for certain that they had been here made me even more confused and angry as to why they hadn't come back to the casino. That Taylor had arrived here first made some sense to me. Maybe she was still looking for Lizzy, and instead she found her painter. And if Lizzy arrived later to find them here together, it would have been ugly. I had seen how those two could fight. But to separate in this world was so definitive. There was every chance it would mean forever.

Cara wasn't the type to soak up a great deal of information on others. On Taylor she had almost nothing. Just that she and the painter were inseparable. I felt happy hearing this, despite everything. Taylor had taken such a lonely journey in Carousel. She deserved love as much as anyone left in this world.

From what I could gather, Lizzy had stayed a lot longer. Cara said she was a regular on the tented stage. One of the bigger names left playing during the final weeks of the Collective. I asked Cara if she left for the airport alone, or whether there were others for the journey. She wasn't certain. The population of the Collective had always fluctuated and the exodus had been chaotic. I hoped she had been with some others. My memories of the Bulls were still vivid and I had to chase away images of her running for her life with a rabid pack behind her.

I did find out that Chess was still with her. Cara mentioned the conjecture on his arrival. There was an unspoken 'no dogs' rule in the Collective due to the overall fear of their presence in the suburbs. Lizzy had been staunch and protective and Chess had eventually found his way into the hearts of the other Artists. In the end he was fed well all about the Collective and patted for luck when many Artists left for the coast. Chess wasn't the bravest of dogs, but it still made me feel better knowing Lizzy had him by her side.

Of Georgia and Tommy, Cara had nothing to tell. She was maybe the biggest Artist of any still in Perth. A real-life gossip-mag celebrity. Even in a small crowd the faces of others were inclined to blur.

Later we sat by candlelight with tea and some fancy artisanal chocolates. Cara twirled one around in her fingers, placed it on her tongue and sighed.

'So Nox. Tell me. In the morning, when the sun rises and the wind turns to the east, where will you go? North to the airport? Or west to the beaches?' asked Cara, as if she were some evil queen spinning a riddle.

'The airport,' I replied without hesitation.

'To find Lizzy Finn,' said Cara.

I nodded pensively and immediately felt myself sobering.

'It will be dangerous. Bulls roam the tarmacs these days,' said Cara.

'Do you know where the Artists are living?' I asked.

Cara shook her head solemnly.

'Only whispers and gossip. Nothing that will guide your search,' she replied.

Great, I thought.

'Look for somewhere bright. If there are painters there they will need the light and air to work,' said Cara.

It made as much sense as anything she had said. I slid my tea aside and felt increasingly edgy. Backtracking to the airport would take time. Then I would need to dodge the Bulls and find Lizzy amid hundreds of potential lodgings. It was daunting, but finding Taylor could take even longer. The beaches of Perth stretched north and south for miles and I had nothing to go on. It could take Lizzy and I more than a month just to search the obvious houses.

Then there was Georgia somewhere down in Fremantle. The face I couldn't shake from my mind. My thoughts of her were full of regret, but she also spoke to me of the future more than anything in this world. For some reason Georgia made it possible to think of the world continuing as it once was. I could see us together in this place. And suddenly it felt like there might be a path back there. Georgia hadn't mentioned the Prix de Rome. It's possible she knew nothing about it. But meeting her made me believe in it more than Ed or Cara or anybody. I needed to find Georgia just as much as I needed to find the Finns.

25

The air was clear in the morning as Cara had promised. I awoke in an empty basement and walked cautiously upstairs to find the cafe awash with sunlight. Outside the air was fresh and freezing. I shivered across to my bike and checked over the brakes and tyres. Cara was nowhere to be seen.

I returned to the basement, packed up my things and double-checked that I had the writing pad. Cara had been awake when I crashed the night before, but there was no sign of her now. I lingered around for a few minutes and considered checking the other studios, but thought better of it. I was about to leave when I noticed the basket was sitting back up on the counter. It was empty but for a note inside. In big, extravagant handwriting it read: *Nox, would you be a doll and fill this again before you leave? I am swamped with work as always. CW.*

I read it over and felt like an idiot for not realising sooner. Cara couldn't leave the cafe. The world's greatest actress still hadn't completed her Residency.

The whole thing made me feel weird and jittery. I grabbed the basket and raced back up to the cafe. The door opened for me without issue. I stood outside and stared back at it. How could a creaky old door have control over somebody like Cara Winters? Sometimes this place was truly messed up.

I filled the basket until I could barely lift it off the ground, then hauled it back inside. Cara still hadn't surfaced. I wanted to wish her luck or something, but felt too edgy to wait around much longer. Eventually, I loaded up and rode out of there.

The airport was north of the Collective, but also on the other side of the river. Rather than backtrack all the way through the city and cross over the bird bridge, I decided to stick to the west side until I was further north. This meant riding through some inner-city suburbs before eventually crossing the river on a highway that I remembered being up that way somewhere.

I had passed through Mount Lawley and most of Maylands when a cold front came through. Initially I just kept riding. It was blustery, but the rain was still spitting and broken. The streets and sidewalks were scattered with debris from last winter and the new front was adding to this. A few times I had to abandon a street altogether for fear of popping my tyres on the sticks and branches. The highway would be clearer – if I could just reach it before the weather got any worse.

A flurry of wind and small hailstones sent me scampering for cover under the porch of a house by the river. I sat out there for a while to see if it would pass and I could keep on riding. The sky was dripping with swampy grey clouds and the rain kept coming. I started shivering and reluctantly broke into the house for shelter.

It was cold inside, and close to pitch-black. I changed out of the wet clothes under torchlight and eventually found the linen cupboard. Moths bombed out of the darkness and slapped into my face and neck. I jumped and swore and fought hard not to freak out completely. Being in other peoples' houses was the worst.

There were couches in a living room down the back of the house. I dumped my stuff on one and wrapped myself in a blanket on the other. Whistles of wind circled about the house and the rain outside became even heavier. It was frustrating, but I was travelling during the heart of winter. If I kept going in this weather I risked crashing the bike or getting sick, and neither was worth it. Instead I lit some candles and continued on with the writing from the night before. Cara's imprisonment was still fresh in my mind.

The storm ran right through the night and kept on for most of the following morning. During that time I had written, slept, eaten, repacked my bag; even found an old street directory to check that I hadn't invented the highway ahead of me. At the smallest hint of blue sky I loaded up and continued north. The barman's watch reminded me that I had already chewed through almost a week since meeting Ed in the hotel. Soon there would be just seven left to get us back to Carousel.

After a few hours riding I spotted the highway. The houses had thinned and the streets widened. Tracking east–west was a four-lane path through the suburbs. I detoured to an entrance-ramp and climbed up onto the debris-free bitumen. It was exposed and windy out there, but other than a couple of stalled freight trucks it was clear and empty. I picked up some speed and crossed back over the river as the sun sank fast behind me. Airport signs popped up almost immediately. *Domestic. International. Long Term. Short Term. Qantas Club.* The domestic terminal was nearest to where I was entering so I decided to head that way first.

Before I got too close I stopped and took some insect spray out of my backpack. This entrance was much more built up than the Bull-infested bushland the Finns and I had stumbled across in the summer. It was reassuring to a point but, really, the Bulls could be anywhere now and I wouldn't be outrunning them with all of the gear I was carrying.

There were more cars at the airport than I had seen anywhere since the Disappearance. Bay upon bay of dirty, abandoned vehicles. Fuel gone bad in their tanks. Batteries deader than dead. Parking debits spiralling into the thousands. Like casinos, airports could be populated at any time of the day or night. This was particularly the case in Perth, where flocks of miners flew in and out on weekly rosters to sites in the desert. As the sun had peaked that morning two long years ago, the airport had been frozen mid-stride.

I slowed down and rolled quietly under the cover of the terminal. A curved glass awning ran the length of the building. Beneath this was a walkway and scatterings of lonely, abandoned luggage. I weaved past them, looking for a way inside. Further along I found an electronic door that was propped open on a suitcase, which had been passing through with its owner at the time of the Disappearance. The doors must have triggered shut when the power cut. I leaned over the suitcase and peered inside.

The long and static spread of an empty check-in foyer. Blank departure screens. Vacant help desks. The flutter of some birds nesting in the ceiling. It didn't look inhabited, but this was just the entrance and I knew a much larger area existed at the rear of the building.

I lifted my bike and bag awkwardly in over the suitcase, then squeezed through myself.

'Hello?' I said in a half shout.

Nothing came in reply. The space felt giant and imposing. Luggage was strewn everywhere. Carry-on bags toppled forward where their owners once walked. Suitcases upright and ready at check-in counters.

A cluster of matching bags in a semicircle where a family had gathered.

I walked the bike along the length of the terminal until I reached the sparser arrivals area. There was nothing to be found. I needed to head up to the shops and lounges on the second level, but this meant leaving my bike behind. I wheeled it over to a Hertz island and hid it behind the counter.

Backtracking, I found a security check at the end of the departures area. I stepped over some queuing ropes and trudged up the escalators that led to the departure gates. I surfaced into a hall of tourist stores and bathrooms. There weren't any windows, but it was definitely lighter up there.

I passed some more stores, resisting the urge to detour in for some fresh shoes and clothes. Eventually I reached an intersection and the source of the light. An atrium connected the hallway to others heading off to departure gates and eateries. It had a frosted glass ceiling that was pulling in the last of the afternoon sun and radiating it outward. The place had a lot of food outlets and it didn't smell so great. I circled around and headed for the departure gates, keen for a look at the tarmac.

It was almost dusk outside. A Virgin jet stood ready and waiting by a gangway. I stepped up to the window and looked at it closely. The tops of the wings had a slightly brown tinge that, from a distance, looked like dirt or dust. Otherwise it still looked ready to board.

At gates five and six I found a jet in the process of refuelling, and another that had begun to taxi away for take-off when the pilots and passengers disappeared. Now it hovered nervously, neither part of the city, nor gone from it. Past this, the empty tarmac spread away into the murky daylight.

Nothing seemed to have been touched in the entire terminal and it was starting to freak me out. Maybe Cara was wrong about an Artist community being here. Or maybe there used to be Artists here, but somehow they had left. I just assumed that Lizzy had come to the airport to hang out. But maybe it was more than that. Maybe she had come here to find a way home.

'Hello?' I yelled. 'Lizzy?'

Nothing.

I took off my bag and paced over to a newsagent. I grabbed a water and riffled through the chocolate bars for something that was close to code. When I turned back around I noticed that a Lufthansa jet was coming in to land on one of the far runways. I wandered over and watched it for a moment or two before my brain did a backflip.

'What the hell,' I whispered.

The jet was just about to touch down. The familiar growling of the engines filtered in through the glass.

I looked around the room for somebody to share my shock, but I was still alone.

The tyres touched down with a squeak and the

spoilers came up. The fucking thing had landed.

I rubbed my forehead. I was getting bizarro inner flashes from my first big overseas trip. I had gone on Contiki in Europe, then stopped in Vietnam, Cambodia and Laos. I saw a snow-covered landscape from the window of a plane. A cobbled square with the statue of a man on horseback. Dusk light across a messy, sleeping dormitory. Backpacks shuffling in a line through forest. Each image was vivid and arresting.

Then I saw myself touching down in Europe at the start of the trip. Leaving Perth I had acted all cool and worldly. Unfazed by the journey ahead. But stepping out of the airport into that frigid, bustling air brought a dread I had no answer for. I wandered, overwhelmed and aimless, until an old guy helped me find a shuttle. Then spent the ride freaking out about all of the people I was about to meet. How they would be young and cool and have stories that I didn't.

I shook off these random memories and forced myself to think. What should I do? Go out there? Who the hell could be arriving on a plane? And what about the Bulls?

The jet slowed and neared the end of the runway. In the last of the daylight I watched as it started taxying my way, before it disappeared, in an instant, into nothing at all.

I blinked, wondering if I had just lost it in the dark. But I hadn't. The plane was gone.

Suddenly something caught my eye at the other end of the tarmac. There were lights coming out of the international terminal. A whole bunch of them. They were torches.

26

'Your first time at the Auroraport and you saw a full landing. That's pretty amazing, man.'

I was talking to a shortish girl wearing overalls and a head torch. There were others behind her that I couldn't make out in the darkness.

'Where did that plane go?' I asked, still breathless from my dash across the tarmac.

'It was an aurora,' she replied, as if it were obvious.

'I don't get it. I heard its engines and everything,' I said.

'I know. It was beautiful, wasn't it,' she replied.

I looked past her to the others. They were looking up at the sky and soaking in the air as if there had just been a thunderstorm. There were lights scattered across the upper levels of the terminal behind them.

'Are you guys part of the airport community?' I asked.

'Never heard it called that before,' replied a guy I couldn't really see.

Some of them were drifting back inside now. It was

all but dark and the wind was freezing out there on the tarmac.

Something touched my leg and I jumped backwards.

'Whoa. Easy,' said the girl. 'The ions are intense hey,' she added, drifting her hands through imaginary water.

'Something touched my leg,' I replied.

I felt it again and reached down to find a dog nuzzling me.

'Chessboard?' I said.

'Nox?' said a voice out of the darkness.

I looked up to a torch shining right into my face.

'Lizzy?' I said.

'Holy fucking hell,' said Lizzy.

Lizzy shot out of the darkness and leapt at me with a giant bear hug.

'Hey,' I said.

She buried her head into my chest.

'Way to blind me,' I said.

Eventually Lizzy sniffed and surfaced to look at me properly. Chess was hovering by her side.

'What are you doing here?' she asked.

'What are *you* doing here?' I replied, a little sharply.

'I don't know. We had to leave the Collective. It seemed kinda obvious to come here,' she replied.

'Why didn't you come back to the casino?' I asked.

'I did. Rachel said there was nobody there,' she replied.

'Wait. You saw Rachel?' I asked.

'Yeah. So random. She is totally living in that place,' said Lizzy.

'I know. I was living next door to her,' I said.

'No way!' said Lizzy.

'When was this?' I asked.

'Like six weeks ago. Me and Chess stopped in there on our way here,' said Lizzy. 'We were snooping around the lobby when Chess started barking and Rachel turns up in her fucking bathrobe. No hello or anything, she was just like, "You can't have a dog in here." Like it really matters.'

I was rubbing my head, trying to grasp the idea that Rachel has done this purposefully.

'I was waiting there for months,' I said.

'She totally blanked when I asked about you,' said Lizzy.

'Why would she do that?' I asked.

'Rachel is a total weirdo, Nox. You know that. She probably wanted to play house with you in there forever,' said Lizzy.

'Didn't you see my note?' I asked.

'Your note? No. We didn't see any notes,' replied Lizzy.

It didn't make sense. Nothing did anymore. I felt dizzy and took a few breaths. Lizzy looked at me and welled up again.

'I'm so sorry, Nox,' she said. 'When you weren't in the city we just figured you must have gone home to check on your house or find Tommy or something. Taylor said she screamed that casino down before heading back out to look for me.'

'I got lost in the gaming room. I went in there to find water and my torch cut out. By the time Rachel found me Taylor had been and gone,' I said.

Lizzy put a hand on my shoulder.

'Do you know where she is?' I asked, suddenly remembering what I was doing there.

'No idea. The beach, somewhere,' said Lizzy.

She sounded casual but I could see the simmer behind her eyes.

'We need to find her,' I said.

'Why?' asked Lizzy.

'So we can get back to Carousel before September second,' I said.

'Why would we go back to Carousel, Nox?' asked Lizzy.

'Because I met the Curator,' I replied.

She looked at me carefully.

Before I could continue there was a shout from behind us. 'Bulls!'

'Shit,' said Lizzy. 'Come on. This place is crawling with those fucking dogs. We need to get inside, stat.'

She pulled me and Chess back towards the terminal. Others were doing the same. I looked over my shoulder at the dark spread of the tarmac.

'What did she mean, Auroraport?' I asked.

'The planes aren't real. They're just images from

our past lives. The atmosphere is all crazy out here. Sometimes particles from the past can ripple through. Kind of like an aurora,' said Lizzy.

She was picking up speed and I had to run to keep up with her.

'But that plane was from Germany,' I replied.

'Doesn't matter. They're not flashbacks. They're memories,' said Lizzy. 'Like what we saw in Carousel.'

'Have you seen the Air Canada plane again?' I asked.

Lizzy didn't answer. People were disappearing into the darkness of a building in front of us. We were the last ones to reach it. Lizzy glanced behind us, then led us around a corner to a door that was propped open with a traffic cone. She pulled it open and kicked away the cone. Chess and I moved inside. As the door shut I heard the scrape of claws on the concrete outside.

27

The Auroraport community was more of a gathering than a party. A few dozen random Artists taking refuge in the plush, upper-level lounges of the international terminal. They lazed around, worked on their art and gazed out the windows at the mysterious aurora jets. Most of them had come from the Collective like Lizzy. The leaking gas had slowly driven Artists to all corners of the city. The airport terminals offered food stores, shelter and a whole bunch of convenience items such as eye masks, paperbacks and mouthwash. It wasn't the worst place to spend the winter.

There were also those who had been in the terminal for a long time now. Lizzy introduced me to a photographer named Kirk who had lived there since completing his Residency at an airport hotel just weeks after the Disappearance. Kirk had spent almost two years photographing the aurora jets and working in a darkroom he had built in a room designed for drug searches. Others had joined him in the months that followed. They had been drawn to the airport by sightings, rumours and the far-flung possibility of escape. Some had stayed, captivated by the phenomenon and fuelled with inspiration for their art. As well as Kirk's photography, Lizzy showed me giant abstracts painted onto the walls of the lounges and a room full of sound recording gear and editing equipment where two engineers had been capturing audio of the aurora jets and turning them into epic scapes.

Lizzy and Chess had reached the Auroraport from the south a bit over a month ago. She told me how they had arrived at sunset and camped out in a nearby hotel, watching for signs of the Bulls.

They were easy to find.

With dusk the meaty frames surfaced in ragged clusters along the fringes of the airport. Moonlight bouncing off their dirty white coats. The empty streets and bushland echoing every snarl and wheeze. They seemed to have an uneasy truce with each other. Food was scarce now and it was better to hunt things like cats and kangaroos as a pack. That first night Lizzy had heard them chase and corner something in one of the car parks. She shivered when she told me of the noises she heard next.

At the height of the following day she and Chess made their dash into the terminal.

'I got here at dusk,' I said, disturbed by her story.

'You were lucky,' replied Lizzy.

We were siting in a corner of the Qantas lounge that Lizzy had made into her room. It had the long sweep of a cushioned bench for a bed. Two armchairs – one for reading, another for Chess. There was an acoustic guitar and some notepads by the dining table between them. The whole area was partitioned off from the rest of the lounge with the temporary construction barriers that were once used to hide the extension work in the growing airport.

I looked around at her place, then out at the long stretch of the lounge. Its transformation was drastic.

'When I was in the domestic terminal, it seemed like nobody had been in there since the Disappearance,' I said.

'Because it's not sealed. The Bulls can get in there,' she replied.

'Holy shit,' I said.

Lizzy nodded.

'Lucky for you they get spooked by the aurora jets,' said Lizzy. 'Sometimes that's how we know one is about to happen. The Bulls start to whimper, or suddenly there's none of them around.'

'Wow,' I replied.

'You know we hadn't seen a jet for nearly two weeks before you got here? Bulls have been massing from all over,' said Lizzy.

'But we can get past them, yeah?' I asked.

Lizzy looked at me closely.

'I think you better tell me about this Curator business,' she said.

I nodded and thought about where I should start.

'I was doing a food run in Victoria Park. It's east of the casino. Kind of on the way to Carousel,' I began.

Lizzy fixed onto me and listened as I recounted my meeting with Ed at the hotel. I tried to take it slowly and give her a good sense of the guy. When I finished she sat back and opened a packet of M&M's. She picked out the blue ones and thought the whole thing over.

'I know it sounds mental. But I just have a feeling he might be right. I really think we should go back there and see,' I added.

Lizzy glanced at me.

'If you think about it, everything kind of adds up. How those taxis dropped us at Carousel. How we could only get out of there once we finished our projects. How every other Residency we've seen has had power and food and art supplies. It just seems too engineered for it not to have an end point, don't you think? Two years gives Artists time to create something big. Something they might not have done otherwise. It's what residencies are meant for.'

I was rambling now and Lizzy put her hand up for me to stop.

'Nox. It's cool,' she said. 'We can go back to Carousel.'

'Serious?' I asked.

Lizzy nodded.

'I know Ed. We were on a bill together a few years back. If anybody could figure out what was behind all this it would be him.'

'Okay great. Thank you,' I said.

'But we'll have to wait for another aurora jet to get past the Bulls. It's too risky otherwise,' she added.

'When do you think the next one will arrive?' I asked.

'I don't know. Nobody does,' replied Lizzy. 'Kirk says there are usually more jets towards the end of winter than the start. So hopefully it will be soon.'

I checked the date on the barman's watch for the thousandth time.

'Do you have any idea where Taylor might be?' I asked.

Lizzy shook her head.

'We had a pretty big fight. All I know is that she was heading to the coast with Sophie,' she replied.

'Is Sophie the painter from Carousel?' I asked.

Lizzy nodded.

'I can't believe she found her,' I said.

'So Tommy told you about the painter in the city too?'

I looked at her and nodded, sheepishly.

'You two suck,' said Lizzy.

She took a handful of M&M's and tossed the remainder of the packet on the table.

'Sorry, Lizzy. I guess I just didn't want to rat on her or

something,' I said. 'I'm sure that wasn't her only reason for wanting to go to the city.'

'Why wouldn't she tell me? Did she think I didn't want them to get together or something? It's so mental,' said Lizzy.

I didn't have an answer. Lizzy stopped chewing and we both sat in silence for a while.

'I just can't get it out of my head,' said Lizzy.

'What?' I asked.

'When I arrived in the city. After two days locked away in some repulsive toilet block. Then a bunch more racing around trying to find you guys in a total panic. I finally stumbled into the Collective and there was Taylor having brunch with her girlfriend. New jeans. New haircut. She was even wearing makeup. Fucking makeup!' said Lizzy.

I watched her and listened.

'I know she had been looking for us. And that she had only arrived just a day before me with the same smoke inhalation and everything. But seeing her so relaxed and happy like that. Knowing that this was why she wanted to leave the hills. Nothing to do with you or me or the Curator,' said Lizzy.

She stared out the window.

'I couldn't speak to her,' she added.

'For how long?' I asked.

'A while,' said Lizzy. 'Until just before she left.'

'What did you say?' I asked.

'She apologised. Again. Then screamed at me to grow up. I screamed back. I wanted to tell her I forgave her. Or that there was nothing to forgive or whatever. But she called me jealous. So I stormed the fuck out of there, went straight up onto the stage and started playing our new album.'

Lizzy took a breath.

'We made this pact way back when we were kids. That we would never perform a Taylor & Lizzy song for a crowd unless both of us were playing. Even if it's just some backup vocals or a shaker or something. It always had to involve the two of us. That way our partnership would never be in question. The music would always need both of us,' said Lizzy.

I could almost see Taylor's face looking up at the stage as her sister launched into the album. Eyes wide and resolute. Skin bristling as a crowd began to gather.

'They left that afternoon,' said Lizzy.

'I'm sorry, Lizzy,' I said.

She blinked and looked at me.

'Do you think we will find her in time?'

'Of course,' I replied.

I don't think either of us felt confident. But at least we were back together.

That night we stayed up late and planned our path to the ocean.

28

Lizzy and I were packed and ready, but the aurora jets just wouldn't come.

Instead a series of wicked cold fronts blew in from the west, reminding us that winter still held a grip over the city. The temperature in the terminal dropped and the Artists shuffled about beneath coats and Qantas blankets. There was a relaxed, ski-lodge vibe to the place. The days were long and quiet and you didn't see much of anyone as people worked away on their art. But at night candles and voices would spring up throughout the lounge as people welcomed others into their faux lodgings to share food and chat over bottles of duty free.

Lizzy seemed at home there, as she did wherever she happened to be. But I also noticed things about her that I hadn't seen in Carousel. She could talk to just about anyone without even trying. Artists weren't necessarily the best communicators. I had been to a stack of gigs where singers would finish songs full of rhyme and eloquence, then struggle to string a sentence together as they thanked the crowd. But Lizzy had it down. She was disarming and found a way through to even the most stilted and awkward of Artists in the terminal. With Lizzy they relaxed and became unusually responsive. I wasn't sure if it was part of her celebrity, or the opposite of this. Either way it seemed like she had been here with these people for years, not weeks.

There was one girl – a musician too, I think – that Lizzy seemed to spend more time with than the others. She looked slightly older than Lizzy, and kind of familiar. When I asked Lizzy about her, she shrugged in a way that made me think there might have been something going on between them. But it seemed at arm's length and I noticed that Lizzy still kept a photo of her girlfriend Erica as the desktop background on her laptop. I considered telling her about Georgia at this time, but copped out and kept it to myself.

My presence in the lounge seemed like it was no big deal. People were friendly enough, particularly when they noticed that I knew Lizzy, but mostly they continued with their routines and I kept to myself. I felt preoccupied, and we would be leaving at the first sign of a jet anyway. I found quiet corners and pushed on with the writing I had started at the Collective. The scope of the story felt pretty intimidating. It was interesting and the words came without too much of a fight. But there was no doubting now that what I was writing was a novel. I couldn't help but think that maybe this could be my ticket home once we got back to Carousel. This scared the hell out of me and I tried not to think about it.

But the waiting was tough. I got bouts of panic over the time we were losing. We would be into August soon and Lizzy had as much of an idea of where Taylor might be as I did. I checked over our bikes and backpacks, and hovered at the windows while Chess looked on anxiously. Lizzy put up with this for a while, but eventually snapped and told me I had to chill. Later that day she took me shopping for clothes to kill some time.

Beneath the lounges was a corridor lined with the regular airport shopping outlets. Lizzy seemed familiar with the place and led us over to a surf store and Country Road outlet. She started browsing and building a pile of stuff for me to try on. The stores were stocking mostly spring lines at the time of the Disappearance, so the selection wasn't great. In Country Road Lizzy found me some jeans and a few t-shirts that were okay. Then we moved over to the surf shop to look around for jackets.

'Do you think I should tell everyone here about the Curator?' I asked.

'I did already,' replied Lizzy.

I looked up from the jackets.

'What did you tell them?'

'Pretty much what you said to me. And that we would be leaving during the next aurora,' she replied.

'Did they say anything?' I asked.

'Different things. A couple of people had heard about it already,' said Lizzy.

'Do you think many of them will go back to their Residencies?' I asked.

Lizzy thought it over.

'It's hard to say. I believe you because we have history. But people talk a lot of crap these days. Especially at the Collective. That place was like junior high,' said Lizzy.

'What if it's true and they miss the deadline?' I asked.

Lizzy shrugged despondently.

'Did Ed mention anything about that?' she asked.

I shook my head. 'I don't think he knows.'

I felt a growing weight on my shoulders. The Artists at the terminal seemed like genuinely good people. I hated the idea that they might miss their portals and be stranded here forever.

Lizzy seemed to notice my stressing.

'I'll talk to them again tonight. Maybe I can convince a few more,' she said.

'Thanks,' I replied.

We shifted along to another rack of jackets.

'How about this?' I asked, holding up a terrible denim fur combo.

Lizzy smiled.

'That's actually pretty cool,' she said.

'Serious?' I asked.

'No, Nox,' she replied, deadpan.

I put it away and we kept looking.

'Although it does kind of go with that new watch of yours,' said Lizzy.

'This watch totally saved my life in that casino,' I replied.

'Serious?' asked Lizzy.

I showed her the light.

'Oh neat,' she replied, sarcastically.

'It's weird how people seem to like you here?' I joked. 'Do you think it will change once they get to know you properly?'

Lizzy feigned some laughter and shifted to another rack.

'What was it like living next to Rachel?' she asked.

'It was actually fine. I mean, she is a total bogan, but behind all the bourbons and the swearing, she's a good person. I was a bit of a mess when she found me in that gaming room.'

Lizzy nodded.

'She didn't find her kids or anything?' she asked.

'Nope,' I replied.

'Did you tell her about the Curator?' she asked.

I nodded.

'She didn't care?' asked Lizzy.

'She has a guy that visits her in the spring,' I replied.

'Shut up,' said Lizzy.

'Serious. He's a fisherman. They hooked up last year and made plans to meet up once he's back from his fishing or whatever,' I replied.

Lizzy was wide-eyed in amazement.

'This fucking city,' she whispered and shook her head. I laughed a little.

'Hey did you know Cara Winters is still stuck in her Residency at the Collective?' I asked.

Lizzy nodded. 'It's tragic. She's going crazy in there.'

'Ed said that's what used to happen sometimes. In the original competition,' I replied.

'Art has a messed-up relationship with sanity,' said Lizzy.

I looked at her and tried to understand what she meant. She held up a navy parka with red chequered lining.

'Here. Try this,' she said.

I pulled it on and looked at my reflection in one of the mirrors. Lizzy stood in the foreground and nodded.

'Come on. You can help me find a camera next door. I want to get some photos of this place before we leave,' said Lizzy.

We found some bags and packed away the clothes to take back upstairs.

'Hey I've been meaning to ask you something about the auroras,' I said.

Lizzy glanced at me.

'When that jet landed I got this weird slideshow of memories. Stuff I remember happening, but I hadn't thought of for ages. Kind of like my mind had discovered a missing roll of film somewhere,' I said.

'Did you fly with Lufthansa sometime in the past?' she asked.

'My first trip to Europe. I took a Contiki tour, then trekked through some of Asia,' I replied.

'Was that stuff in the slideshow?' she asked.

'Yeah,' I replied.

'Kirk says that's how it works. If it's your aurora jet you get a rush of memories surrounding it,' said Lizzy.

My aurora jet.

I mulled over the slideshow some more.

'The last thing I saw was my shuttle ride to the Contiki hotel. I was freaking out,' I said.

'How come?' asked Lizzy

'I don't know, really,' I replied.

Lizzy nodded and pondered this for a moment.

'Did that happen to you in Carousel, with the Air Canada jet?' I asked.

'Kinda. Mine was about our mum,' she replied.

I waited to see if she would elaborate, but the topic seemed somehow raw. Lizzy picked up the bags and looked around for the camera store.

'How many others have you had since you arrived?' I asked.

'None so far,' said Lizzy and left me for the foyer.

I hovered behind and watched her lonely figure drifting past the haunting, empty stores.

29

Chess woke us late into the night. He let out a shrill and solitary bark, then began to whimper. I was ripped from a dream and sat upright on Lizzy's couch.

'Easy, Chessy. What's up?' whispered Lizzy somewhere behind me.

I looked around and noticed a couple of candles being lit in neighbouring enclosures. Chess continued to whimper. But he looked more excited than distressed.

'Nox. Is your bag ready?' asked Lizzy.

'Yeah,' I replied.

'Get dressed. There could be a jet coming,' she said.

I stood up and felt around for my torch. More lights popped up along the lounge. The murmur of voices accompanied them. Lizzy sat and pulled on her boots beside me. Her pupils glimmered with a flicker of moonlight from the tarmac.

'If there's an aurora we need to move fast. Some of them only last for a few seconds and the Bulls are less spooked at night,' she said.

'Which way do we go?' I asked.

'Just follow me once we're on the bikes. Stick to open areas. That way if they see us we can outrun them,' said Lizzy.

She stood up and pulled on her backpack. I followed and we torched our way out of the enclosure. We weaved through some tables and rounded the empty buffet area. Chess had quietened, happy to be on the move.

As we approached the edge of the lounge I noticed the silhouettes of other Artists already at the windows. They stood in small clusters, peering out at the sky and tarmac. Some of them were shouldering bags like Lizzy and I. Kirk was there with his tripod and camera. He didn't have a bag.

We found a place by the glass and looked out into the abyss. The moon was hidden by a thick bank of clouds to the west. A hazy glow filtered down onto the tarmac, offering a whisper of light from the reflective paint, but nothing more. A shadow with a backpack shifted across to Lizzy. They spoke for a moment and hugged briefly, before the person slipped back into the darkness.

The lounge was deathly quiet. My eyes flickered from sky to runway.

'There it is!' whispered Lizzy.

I saw a flash of light to my left before my vision filled with a swimming mass of memories. Danni and I as kids on a plane. A youngish and dorky version of our parents sitting across from us. Mum's reassuring smile as the plane descended. Dad pointing for us to look out the window. The warmth of our clammy faces pressed together as we peered out. The tiny dots of more houses than I could have ever imagined.

'Nox?'

I waited to see more.

'Nox!'

Lizzy shook my shoulder.

'Nox, let's go,' she said.

I caught a glimpse of the flashing hulk of a Qantas jet coming in to land before I spun around and ran for the bikes. People with bags were moving all around us. Lizzy had convinced a whole bunch of them. The Auroraport community were heading back to their Residencies.

We raced down a bank of static escalators to where I had stashed our bikes. This was ground floor but I had no idea which of the doors Lizzy planned to exit. Rather than wheeling the bike, she climbed aboard and pedalled off through the foyer. There was luggage to dodge, but not as much as the domestic terminal. We weaved in and out, one hand on the bike, the other holding a torch. I could make out the chequered back of Chess slinking along beside us.

Lizzy stopped and swung her torch sideways. A series of electronic sliding doors glinted back. They looked secure. She shifted her light to the next set of doors. These had a crowbar resting on the floor beside them.

We rode over and Lizzy looked outside cautiously.

There were taxis. Shuttle busses. A car park. No Bulls that we could see.

Lizzy got off and I held her bike while she used the crowbar to lever the doors apart. They opened without fuss and we wheeled out into the chilly winter air. Together we pushed the door back in place. There were flashes of light bouncing around the terminal inside. Kirk was still taking shots of the jet from the windows above. He was sticking around. Maybe forever.

I followed Lizzy along roads and walkways as we made our way out of the set-down zone. The noise of the aurora jet was fading fast. I tried hard to stay focused. The hit of memories had left me feeling vague and milky. The parked cars were next and we wanted to avoid these if we could. Lizzy fanned out and linked up to a walkway that seemed to circle the car bays. We followed this along and shone our lights around for an exit sign. My torch hit on one, but it was across a car bay.

'Lizzy,' I whispered.

She stopped and I circled the sign. We hesitated and Chess looked up at us nervously. I caught distant flickers of torchlight to the east and west of us where other Artists had split up to avoid the Bulls and were also making their escape. It was only a hundred metres or so to the sign, then we would be in the clear. Lizzy pulled her bike up and over a kerb and set off into the cars.

We crisscrossed through the rows of sleeping vehicles as fast as we could in the darkness. Each row stole our view of the exit and we had to pause more than once to keep our direction. Nearing the end I rolled over an exit arrow on the bitumen. I called for Lizzy to stop. She whipped around and looked at me. I showed her the arrow with my torch. She backtracked and we were about to head out through the final turn when Chess yelped behind us.

He was frozen like a statue at the rear of a car. There were Bulls crowded beneath the vehicle. At least three. Maybe more. Sheltering there until the aurora jet had passed. Until now.

Chess yelped again and actually took a step towards them.

'Chessy, no,' whispered Lizzy.

He hesitated and glanced sideways at her. One of the Bulls snarled in the darkness. Claws scraped across bitumen. The Bulls came bombing out towards us.

Chess leapt backward and skittered away from them. We took off for the exit. My bike felt hulkish and slow beneath me. I pushed hard at the pedals and finally gained some speed when a Bull bit my back tyre and I flew over the handlebars.

I barely missed Lizzy and Chess ahead of me and landed with a thump at their side. Everything was black and I figured I had knocked myself out until a sweep of torchlight hovered on my face. Then I heard Chess barking and a long spraying sound.

Abruptly there was something next to me. I focused

and made out the squashed and ugly face of a pit bull. It was no more than a foot away.

'Shit,' I groaned.

The Bull looked at me and twitched, but didn't shift. It was struggling to breathe.

'Get on my bike, Nox!' said Lizzy.

I struggled to my feet under the weight of my backpack. Lizzy and Chess were between me and the other Bulls. They were starting to recover from the bug spray.

Lizzy's bike was sprawled across the road alongside her backpack. I picked it up and climbed on. Lizzy ignored her backpack and slid onto the seat behind me. I tried to pedal but there wasn't enough room for both of us and she slipped off the back.

'Take off your backpack,' said Lizzy.

I unclipped the front strap and Lizzy ripped it off. Something triggered in my head.

'Don't leave it!' I said.

'Why?' yelled Lizzy.

One of the Bulls was heading straight for us. Lizzy looked at me for an answer but I couldn't find the words.

She hurled the bag at the Bull and jumped back on the bike. I pedalled us forward to where Chess was waiting by a parking gate. We swerved around it and out onto an open road. The Bull was right behind us.

'The gears, Nox!' yelled Lizzy.

I changed up and we gathered some speed. Ahead of

us was a roundabout and some roads heading out of the airport. I swung us east, back towards the highway I had arrived on. Chess whipped along beside us.

'Can you see them?' I yelled to Lizzy.

She turned back.

'No,' she replied.

'Do you still have your album?' I asked.

'Yeah,' said Lizzy, tapping a pocket on her jacket.

I took a breath and slowed a little. The airport buildings had thinned beside us and the highway lay just ahead. I had found Lizzy Finn and we were heading for the ocean. It should have been a great moment. But all I could think about was my bag lying back there in the car park. And my first ever novel, unfinished inside.

30

We rode through the night like the ghosts of another world. Shaken and cold. Nothing to our name but a rusty bike and a shivering border collie. The highway took us east for a time, then swung north and plunged like a river through sleeping, windblown suburbs. To stop and shelter would be to find an exit and take our chances amid those dark and barren streets. So we kept riding and eventually watched the sunrise over the charcoaled hills of the horizon.

Later into the morning Lizzy spotted a petrol station at an intersection to the west of us. We took the next exit and stopped for some water and stale trail mix. There were no other stores around so we rested just briefly, then returned to the highway. I let Lizzy pedal for a while as the aches from my fall began to register. My shoulder had taken the worst of it and was numb until I lifted my arm and felt razors of pain shooting down to my elbow. I was grazed and bloody at my knees and had a stinging scratch somewhere on my forehead.

It rained and we sheltered by the side of a freight truck, then off the highway at a primary school. Lizzy found the nurse's room and bandaged me up as well as she could. There was a dry coat in there that was her size, but ugly as all hell. I watched her weighing up whether to swap it for the damp ski jacket she was wearing. We left without it when the rain seemed to lighten.

That night we spent buried by blankets in a furniture store. The next in a caravan on display at an expo. We found new bikes and scatterings of food and continued northward without much discussion. We were on the main freeway now. It traced the coastline for miles in either direction. Lizzy had questioned my desire to keep heading north. We were already a long way past the city and, in all likelihood, Taylor would be somewhere to the south of us now. But we couldn't be sure, and once we hit the coast we would have to choose to search either north or south. My thinking from our first discussion at the Auroraport was to start out a long way north, then feel confident of finding her somewhere on our journey southwards.

When it felt as though the freeway was nearing its northern end, we took an exit and turned to the west. It was suddenly hilly and green and, for a while, the sun broke away from the clouds. We coasted the downhills slackly and edged meekly over each of the rises. Our bodies needed proper food and rest. Chess included. Eventually the parklands dropped away and we made out the blocky lines of a shopping complex up ahead.

Lizzy pulled up and looked at me. I shrugged, not knowing much about the place. We cycled over cautiously and snooped around. A Donut King had been smashed into at the front, but otherwise the complex looked relatively untouched. It was no Carousel, but the place still gave me the shivers.

With the last of our strength we levered the unlocked doors of a 7-Eleven and spent the next hour in a sugar coma on the floor inside.

Eventually Lizzy sat up and tried to shake off her stupor.

'That was intense,' she said. 'The riding, that is. Although I don't think I've eaten that many Skittles before either.'

I stretched out my arm.

'How is your shoulder?' she asked.

'Fine. Just bruised I think.'

'And your knees?' she asked.

I shrugged like they were no big deal.

'Keep an eye on them, Nox. If they get infected we're screwed,' said Lizzy.

I nodded. Lizzy looked at me carefully.

'I'm sorry about your bag,' she said.

'It's cool. You got that Bull pretty good,' I replied.

'You still have your short stories, yeah?' she said, momentarily alarmed.

I nodded but couldn't get rid of her gaze.

'But you lost some other stuff?' she asked.

'A novel,' I replied.

'Oh shit. Wow. I'm so sorry, Nox. That sucks big-time,' said Lizzy. 'Was it finished? I mean, could you start over?'

'I don't know. There probably isn't time now anyway,' I replied.

I stood up and tried to forget about what this meant and focus on what was in front of us.

'We should try to find some actual food. And some dry clothes,' I said.

Lizzy stayed seated while I searched the shelves.

'So I lied about having our album,' she said.

I stopped and stared at her.

'It's back there in my bag,' said Lizzy.

I sighed and shook my head. We were both screwed.

'Sorry. But you would have wanted to go back for it,' she said. 'It was too risky with the jet gone.'

I didn't say anything.

'Taylor has a copy anyhow,' said Lizzy.

'What if we can't find her?' I asked.

'Then I guess I'm not going home,' said Lizzy.

I looked down and shifted some dust about with my dirty All Stars. My plans were unravelling one by one.

Lizzy pulled herself up so that I would look at her.

'It's all of us or nothing, Nox. That's how I roll on all of this,' she said.

I took a breath.

'Then I need to tell you about Georgia,' I said.

'Yeah, you do,' said Lizzy.

She smiled and shoved me as if we were standing by her high school locker. I held back a smile myself.

'She's an actress from Ohio. We met at the casino and hung out for a week or so before she left for Fremantle,' I said.

'Was this before you met the Curator or after?' asked Lizzy.

'Before. She doesn't know about the Prix de Rome,' I replied.

'So we need to find her and tell her?' said Lizzy.

'If we have time,' I replied.

'Where is Fremantle again?' she asked.

'It's the major port. A fair way south of here,' I replied.

'So we find Taylor and Sophie, head to Fremantle for Georgia, get her and Sophie back to their Residencies, then race the hell back to Carousel,' said Lizzy.

I nodded. It was a simple plan but still chocked full of secrets and holes.

'Great. And while we ride you can tell me all about your new girlfriend,' said Lizzy.

She turned and left the shop in a way that suggested there would be no arguments.

We searched the exterior stores for clothing and eventually found a Kathmandu.

'I never thought I would be so pumped to find a trekking store,' said Lizzy.

We kicked in the door and spent a while gearing up for the journey ahead. It was kind of fun and took my mind off our situation. We left our old clothes in a dirty pile and lined ourselves in the best thermals and windbreakers on offer. Then we found amazing, bouncy socks and actual trekking boots. Lizzy chose her stuff carefully and actually surfaced from the change rooms looking pretty cool. She wore a thigh-length olive windbreaker over some fitted hiking pants and an awesome pair of purple trekking boots. My outfit was less put together but I did find a beanie to hide my greasy matted hair.

We loaded up a couple of new backpacks with spare clothes, torches and sleeping bags and left feeling a million times better about the journey ahead. There was a Coles on the corner of the building. Like most of the place, it hadn't been touched since the Disappearance. We covered our noses against the smell and pushed our way inside. It was jet black and echoed with the skitter of rats. Chess looked like he was going to pop an excitement fuse, so we moved fast. Cans, water, batteries, dog biscuits, disinfectant, Lizzy's favourite shampoo and conditioner. The backpacks were quickly full.

Back on the bikes we resumed our journey to the west. An hour into the ride Lizzy slowed and started sniffing at the air.

'What is that?' she asked.

A wash of cool, briny air had swamped over the suburb.

'It's the ocean. We must be close now,' I replied.

Lizzy and Chess powered ahead of me. For a moment I lost them as the road turned and dipped away. As I followed, a dramatic sweep of Indian Ocean came into view. It spread left and right in a long line against the rigid coast. The water was deep navy in the onshore wind and slits of whitewater popped with luminescence. There was a harbour to our right. I couldn't remember the name of it, but the boat owners wouldn't be happy. A bunch of yachts had been blown into a corner of the marina by a winter storm. They clanked about in a tangled mess of old Perth money.

Lizzy had pulled up at a walkway overlooking a swimming beach. I joined her and we looked down at Chess carving mad loops across the sand.

'This air is so fresh it's kind of making me queasy,' said Lizzy.

'I guess we've been sucking in smoke and gas for so long now that our lungs aren't used to it,' I said.

I looked south and weighed up our next move. House upon house clung to the dunes overlooking every inch of the coastline. The medium distance was hazed over, but I knew that it would continue like this all the way to Fremantle and beyond. Lizzy and I hadn't spoken about how we planned to find Taylor, mainly because there was nothing to say. She and Sophie could be anywhere. I was quietly hoping for some kind of Finn twin telepathy. Maybe Lizzy was, too.

31

It took us a while to discover that the nights held our best hope. During daylight we could call out, search houses, look for footsteps on beaches. But in darkness, if we were lucky, the Artists would reveal themselves.

Lizzy spotted the first lights as we trudged back up from another empty beach at dusk. It was different to the disco flicker of the city lightshow. These lights were warm and static. Lizzy stopped and pointed out a house set into the hill across from us. One of the windows stood out from the others. There were candles burning inside.

We bolted up there and banged on the door like a couple of manic trick-or-treaters. The door was opened by a middle-aged lady holding a can of pepper spray. Our conversation was awkward and underwhelming. She knew nothing of a musician and painter living nearby. Lizzy took the reins and told her about the Prix de Rome. The lady listened carefully and eventually she thanked us. But I worried whether we had lost too much credibility upon arrival for her to take our story seriously. We left disappointed, but with a new plan for finding Taylor and Sophie.

We sheltered away and slept through the mornings, and stayed up searching late into the nights. Before long we discovered that the coastline was scattered with Artists from all over the city. Most of them greeted us with surprise and open arms, hustling our shivering bodies inside to warm beside fires and share in each other's stories. Lizzy recognised some and was a stranger to others. We told them of the Curator and stressed the need to get moving back to their Residencies. Sometimes we stayed for a few hours to share a meal, but mostly we kept searching. There were just weeks to go now and so much still to do.

The atmosphere changed when we reached Scarborough. The place was decimated and teeming with Loots. The towering Rendezvous Hotel had been overrun. Now it pulsed with torchlight and garbled shouting. Shadows darted in and out of balconies, keeping watch on the pillaged streets below. Some of the Artists we met had warned us of a crystal meth epidemic in Scarborough and the signs were all over. Streets glinting with glass, trash and urine. Stores that were busted open and vandalised, but still had shelves full of food. Walls of harrowing artwork that had been redone, over and over, in manic attempts at perfection. Lizzy kicked away some rocks from under her boot, before cringing and realising that some of them were teeth.

We skirted around the hotel and stuck to the cover of a cycleway in the dunes. It was overgrown with saltbush and my skin prickled at the thought of a meth-head playwright hiding somewhere ahead.

Around midnight the wind picked up and it started to rain. It was light at first, then heavy and almost sideways with the westerly. Lizzy glanced at me but neither of us wanted to stop until we were clear of the suburb. So we rode on into the weather.

We probably could have moved faster on foot. On the bikes the wind pinned us down and swayed us sideways. Occasionally the path would rise or the bushes thin and I would catch a vista of wild ocean over our shoulder. Each time it looked the same. It was as if we were pedalling exercise bikes at a gym.

I looked back at the Rendezvous. It was fading, but still tall and ominous against the shifting sky. A pair of nautical searchlights cut frantic lines through the blackened suburb. They scanned the windblown beach behind us. Blocks of beachside apartments to our left. Then, alarmingly, swept across the cycleway ahead of us.

Lizzy and I braked in unison and looked back at the building.

'Crystal Loots,' whispered Lizzy.

The searchlights continued to jitter around us.

'We have to keep moving. Get out of their range,' I replied.

Lizzy was about to reply when one of the lights swept

past her face and stuck. There was a muffled shriek of glee from somewhere in the tower. I watched from the front row as Lizzy's eyes ran a gamut of emotion, then landed, grudgingly, on fear.

'Come on!' I yelled.

We took off along the path. The light clung to Lizzy's back like a tracer. Before long the second light found my back.

'We gotta get off this path!' yelled Lizzy.

It was impossible to see more than a few metres in front of us. We turned off the cycleway regardless and splashed down onto a car park. It was big and wide and the lights kept on us. At the far side we pulled the bikes up onto the slushy lawn of a playground. Beyond this were some buildings. A school maybe. I steered us towards them and the lights followed frantically. We turned a corner and hid behind a building. The lights lost us, but hovered nearby, waiting for our next move.

We took a winding path through the school until we eventually found ourselves in a different car park. I looked back to see if the lights had managed to follow. They were still hunting through the school.

'Should we keep going?' I asked Lizzy.

She was drenched and slumped down over her handlebars.

'I vote we hide out in that bus,' she replied.

I followed her gaze to a regular looking school bus parked alongside the school's gymnasium.

We hid our bikes under the bus, then struggled in through a window. Chess followed, clearing the jump easily after a dozen false starts. The bus was a bit musty, but otherwise not so bad. I turned around while Lizzy stripped off and pulled on some dry clothes. I was just finished doing the same when a distant beam of torchlight swept past the windows.

We hit the floor.

There were voices outside. Muffled and broken, but close by. In the school maybe.

My stomach tightened. The light flickered past again.

We lay wide-eyed and motionless as the voices moved closer. Chess's ears traced them from the front of the bus to the side. I slowly reached for the bug spray in my bag.

Lizzy stopped me. She gestured to her ear.

I listened for the voices. They sounded strangely similar. I realised they were all coming from one person. It was the nonsensical babble of a solitary addict. Something about milkshake flavours and the Liberal party. Gradually they started to fade.

Lizzy and I stayed curled up on the floor long after they were gone. We were exhausted, but too wired with adrenaline for sleep.

'Have you seen Crystal Loots before?' I whispered, eventually.

'Yeah. Sometimes they would sneak into the Collective to steal clothes or whatever. But there were a lot of us there to scare them off,' said Lizzy. 'Not like out here.'

'One of them stole my golf buggy while I was shopping in Vic Park,' I said.

Lizzy smirked in the darkness across from me.

'He needed a car to take to the hills. To find the Curator,' I said.

'Didn't you find Ed, like, right after that?' asked Lizzy.

'He was drinking a beer a few streets away,' I replied.

Lizzy shook her head. 'What hope do they have in this place? No family. No cops. No rehab programs.'

I sighed and nodded. She was right. It was a sad state of affairs.

We listened to the rain on the roof for a while. Being in the school bus felt safe and nostalgic. As if we'd handed the controls to somebody else for a while. I was drifting off to sleep when Lizzy turned and finally asked me about the aurora.

'What did you see during that second aurora?' she asked.

I sat up slightly. 'Oh. It was my first time on a plane. We were on a family holiday to Adelaide. Ages ago when me and Danni were just kids,' I said.

Lizzy nodded and waited for me to continue. I felt pretty awkward about the whole thing.

'It didn't last long. I just saw us on the plane. Then the view from our window,' I said.

'What was the view?' asked Lizzy.

'Just houses. We were coming in to land back in

Perth. Dad said that if we looked hard enough we might
be able to see our house,' I replied.

'Could you?' asked Lizzy.

I shook my head and smiled.

'There were thousands of them,' I replied.

'Did you remember how you felt?' asked Lizzy.

I thought about it as Chess snored softly in the aisle
between us.

'I felt like everything was big and intimidating. Before
that I think I felt like our house was the whole world.
But looking out the window I realised that it was just
one tiny dot amid a million other tiny dots. Like it was
nothing at all, but also, kind of, everything we had.'

Thinking about it brought up a heavy dose of
emotion. Lizzy seemed to notice this and stopped with
the questions. She nestled down beneath the seat and we
listened to the rain some more.

'What was your mum doing during the Carousel
aurora?' I whispered.

Lizzy was silent and, for a moment, I thought she was
asleep.

'She was standing at an airport,' said Lizzy.

'Where abouts?' I asked.

'I don't know,' said Lizzy.

'You don't remember?' I asked.

'The vision was so short. It was impossible to tell,' said
Lizzy.

I remembered back to that day under the dome. How

Lizzy was standing with a big smile and tears spilling from her eyes.

'Do you think she was on her way somewhere?' I asked.

'I just saw her in a terminal. I couldn't tell if she was going somewhere, or waiting for someone. But there was this expression on her face. It was as if something had shifted in her world. Something that wouldn't be the same ever again,' said Lizzy. 'Then she heard something and turned away.'

'What was it?' I asked, sitting upright.

'I don't know,' she replied. 'The aurora stopped.'

Lizzy rolled over and used a jumper for a pillow. I lingered for a moment, trying to find something to say. But I couldn't. There was every chance now that Lizzy would never see another.

After a long, fractured sleep through the day, I stirred just in time to catch the sun setting on a broken sky to the west. Lizzy was up, nervously humming some Feist and checking over our bikes.

'Hey,' she said.

'Hey,' I replied.

'There aren't any more houses over that hill,' she said, nodding out the window.

'What's there instead?' I asked.

'I was going to ask you,' she replied.

I couldn't think of anything and shrugged

apologetically. Lizzy was pensive and we packed up quickly.

After a short ride the land began to rise, before the houses and cycle paths ended abruptly with fenced-off bushland. I realised then that we had reached the army barracks. For the regular apocalyptic survivor this would be good news. Safety, weapons, maybe a fallout bunker or something. For us it just meant a big detour inland before we could resume our search of the coast.

Sometime around eight we bridged the hill and rolled down into the coastal havens of Swanbourne and Cottesloe. There was a heartening scatter of lights amid the Norfolk pines. Lizzy turned and smiled, then beelined for the closest one. It was a grand looking wood and stone place with an old boat named *Doris* out the front.

Lizzy knocked and before long a burnt-out old rocker came to the door.

'Evening,' he said.

'Hey,' replied Lizzy.

'What are you trading?' he asked.

Lizzy paused and we glanced at each other.

'Oh, sorry. Nothing actually,' said Lizzy. 'We're trying to find my sister. Taylor Finn.'

The guy looked at Lizzy strangely.

'Musician from Canada. Hangs around with a painter. Looks a lot like you?' he asked.

'Yes!' Lizzy and I replied in unison.

'Yeah I've met her,' he said.

'Do you know where she is?' asked Lizzy.

The guy shook his head.

'Most people that are still around are up here in one of these houses,' he replied. 'But there's no phone book, you know.'

Lizzy and I hovered momentarily.

'Look for lights at night. And solar panels in the day,' he added.

'Thanks,' replied Lizzy. 'We also wanted to pass on a message from the Curator.'

The guy looked immediately sceptical. Lizzy shuffled back to give me the floor. I tried to think of a way to sell it to him, but came up blank. Lizzy nudged me, so I just told him straight.

'Ed thinks there might be a chance we could get home if we go back to our Residencies exactly two years after the Disappearance,' I said.

'With the art we created there,' added Lizzy.

The guy looked at us, then down at Chessboard.

'What date is that?' he asked.

'September second,' I replied.

'Ed Carrington said this?' he asked.

I nodded. Lizzy started backing down the driveway.

'Sorry. We gotta go,' she said.

The guy nodded. He seemed to be thinking it over at least. I waved and turned to join Lizzy. We raced on to the next house.

It was a frustrating night. Most of the houses we checked had Artists that had either met or heard of Taylor Finn. Some of them even mistook Lizzy for her, with welcoming smiles and talk of things we didn't know about. But none of them knew where we could find her. The Artist population was nomadic and fragmented. People would shift on a whim for better food, water or solar panels. None of the residents doubted that Taylor and Sophie were here somewhere. But none could offer anything concrete.

So, one after the other, I delivered my spiel about the Prix de Rome and we continued through the suburb. The lights started to drop away as the night dragged on. It was late and people were going to bed, maybe even with plans to leave for their Residencies upon hearing our news. Eventually the suburb was blacked out entirely.

Lizzy slumped down at a bus stop and ruffled Chess despondently.

'Where the hell are they?' she said.

I sat down too. My legs were burning from all of the hills.

'We'll look again when it's light. Shout the whole suburb down if we have to,' I replied.

Lizzy sighed and nodded.

'Does that awesome watch of yours tell you the date too?' she asked.

I nodded.

'We're into August now aren't we?' she asked.

'Yeah,' I replied.

Lizzy exhaled and trudged over to the large, sombre looking mansion across from us. Chess glanced at me with something akin to worry and trailed after her. Lizzy was diminutive and beaten down, but also probably the toughest person I had ever met. I hoped this would hold out until we found Taylor and made it back to Carousel.

32

That night I remembered something as I slept. I woke early with just a breath of it still in my mind. Lizzy was asleep at the other end of the couch. I shuffled past her and found my way out of the house we had commandeered. The sky was arctic blue and dazzling morning sunlight twinkled down through the Norfolks. I squinted for a moment, then set off for the beach.

Cottesloe was neat and largely untouched by the Disappearance. I emerged from the houses and cafes to where the iconic surf club stood with its pastel walls and arches. Behind it the ocean fizzed with a clean winter swell. I stood on a bank of knee-high lawn and scanned the beach below. It was pristine and empty but for a bobbing array of abandoned kayaks by the groyne. I hesitated for a moment. To the south of this groyne was a long sweep of coast leading down towards Fremantle. Lines of gentle tumbling waves fanned out across each of the curving beaches. On the second of these, by a snaky pathway through the dunes, lay a pair of towels on the sand.

I saw them in the water from halfway across the beach. They were sitting on their boards and chatting as blips of swell shifted beneath their dangling legs. Taylor's hair looked longer and tasselled about her face in salty clusters. Sophie was blonde and seemed tall from where I stood. She was laughing while Taylor's hands drifted about in conversation. They seemed at home with one another.

We'll find a house right out front of the best beach. Wire up some solar panels. Grow a garden. Teach ourselves how to surf.

Taylor said this to me in a crappy apartment on the night of the fires. I had asked her about whether she could ever imagine just accepting things and settling down. About one day finding a place in this new world. Looking at them out in the surf I realised then that she had done exactly that.

A set rolled through and the pair of them paddled for a wave. Sophie missed it. Taylor slid down the face and stood upright for a moment, before tumbling into the whitewash. When she emerged she was staring straight at me.

I waved like an idiot and walked towards her. She stood in the shore break and continued to stare. Behind her Sophie had seen me now too.

'Hey,' I yelled.

Taylor kicked off her leg-rope and trudged awkwardly towards me. She stopped a few metres away. Sophie hovered in the background.

'Nox,' said Taylor.

'Hi. Nice wave,' I replied.

'Where were you?' she asked.

For a moment I was confused.

'I looked everywhere for you in that place,' she added.

'Oh. Yeah sorry. I got lost in a gaming room and couldn't get out,' I replied.

'Why were you in a gaming room?' she asked.

'Looking for water,' I replied.

'And why couldn't you get out?' she asked.

'My torch stopped working. It's pitch-black in those rooms without power,' I replied.

'Did you see my note?' asked Taylor.

I nodded. 'I waited there for you guys to come back.'

I was a bit taken aback by her barrage of questions.

Taylor took a breath and wiped her nose. It was hard to tell if she was crying or just wet from surf.

'I mean, I wanted to go back. We just figured you must have left and I didn't know where else to look for you. Then me and Lizzy had a massive fight and I had to get away from that fucking Collective,' she said.

I stood there listening. Taylor seemed suddenly overcome with emotion.

'I'm sorry, Nox,' she said, looking away. She was definitely crying now. Sophie put a hand on her shoulder and gave me a friendly smile. She was tall and athletic looking. Her hair was the cropped blonde of an eighties exercise model.

'It's cool, Taylor. I'm fine. I actually remembered what you said about the beach house and teaching ourselves to surf one day,' I said.

Taylor smiled and laughed a little.

'We have the best house here, Nox. There are like hundreds of plants and vegetables. And an art studio. And rainwater. And so much solar power. Sophie wired up a hot-water system last week,' said Taylor in a flurry that wasn't really like her at all.

Sophie and I shared a slightly awkward smile.

'Hi,' she said.

'Hi,' I replied.

'Will you stay for a while?' asked Taylor.

'No,' I replied.

Taylor's expression dropped.

'It sounds awesome, but we have to leave,' I said. 'All of us.'

The two of them looked at me. Water dripped from their vital, pensive faces.

'Why?' asked Taylor.

'I found the Curator. He told me what's going on here. And when it's going to end,' I replied.

'When is it going to end?' asked Sophie.

'Soon. Just a few weeks from now,' I replied.

'What's going to happen, Nox?' asked Taylor.

'The Curator thinks that a portal is going to open. Actually, lots of portals – one for each Residency. He says that if we all get back to our Residencies in time, and we take the art we created there, the portals might take us home,' I replied.

Taylor and Sophie shared a glance. The three of us stood in silence as the ocean foamed at our ankles.

'Is that fucking Chessboard?' asked Taylor.

I turned and saw the darting black and white coat ripping along the sand towards us. I couldn't help but smile at his beaming, toothy grin.

'Yep,' I replied.

A figure emerged from the dunes behind him.

'And Lizzy,' I added.

33

Sophie and I hung out for most of the day while Taylor
and Lizzy did their best to reconcile.

Sophie was indeed a painter – still lifes, mostly – who
hailed from Melbourne. I found out that she was actually
in Perth on a residency at the time of the Disappearance.
Her story was so meta that my brain physically twitched
inside of my skull. I guess she was slightly awkward
looking. Just in the way a tall model could be when you
saw them for the first time in real life. But I felt at ease
around her right away. Sophie was earnest, but didn't
take herself too seriously and had a way of finishing each
word to the very last syllable that was pretty endearing.

She showed me around the house they had made into
their home. It wasn't the plushest place we had seen.
Actually it was old and rambling. The original house
was made of stone with a pitched iron roof and wooden
floorboards. It had extensions jutting out all over. At the
front was a dusty winter sunroom and porch. The north
side had a long deck with chairs that peered out over the

ocean, but were hidden from the road by an overgrown hedge of rosemary. The extension on the south side was only half finished, but scheduled to be some more bedrooms and a bathroom.

The backyard was amazing. There was a massive studio kitted out with pottery gear, textiles and a stack of items gathered together by Sophie and Taylor. A roof of hanging grapevines covered a paved area with tables, chairs and an outdoor stove. Then there were the gardens. Sloping away from the house and terraced by giant pillars from a long-lost fishing jetty. I could see Taylor's touch all over. There was a grid of pipes running from a rainwater tank to irrigate the beds. Fresh seaweed mulch spread around delicate seedlings. Jars lined up and ready to preserve the last of the winter harvest.

I understood why Taylor and Sophie had chosen the place. With the stone and the gardens and the ocean, it had a permanent feel that was immediately reassuring given what was happening all around us. It wasn't going to be easy for them to leave.

'In the afternoon we generally hang out in the sunroom at the front. It's warm there, even when the weather is bad,' said Sophie.

We were sitting down in the garden, while Taylor and Lizzy had been having it out inside.

'It's an awesome place,' I replied.

The voices of the Finns softened and Sophie glanced over her shoulder.

'Does Lizzy seem okay to you?' she asked.

'She's edgier than normal, I think. Generally Lizzy just brushes stuff off. What will be will be, you know?' I replied.

She nodded. I considered plunging into the whole aurora jet business. Sophie was a good person and I felt like I could tell her most things. But all of that stuff still felt so dense and confusing. I was only just getting a handle on it myself.

'Lizzy hasn't had a lot of things go her way since we got here. I think she's just over it now. She's ready to go home,' I added.

Sophie nodded and looked out over the garden. I hoped that she didn't feel implicated in anything I had said. That wasn't my intention. Plus I don't think Lizzy felt that way anyhow.

'Taylor has so much guilt about you guys. And about Rocky,' she said.

'Really?' I asked, surprised.

'Yeah. I don't know if she realises, but she thrashes about like crazy when she sleeps. And whenever something nice happens, like we watch a great sunset, or something new pops up in the garden, or she likes something that I paint, Taylor can't stop herself from crying. It's awful,' said Sophie.

'Wow,' I replied. 'What a mess.'

Sophie smiled through a couple of tears.

'It's beautiful here though,' she added, shaking her head.

I thought about it and looked down over the garden to the abandoned train tracks and beyond.

'I have to ask, were you seriously hoping to go shopping that day at Carousel?' I asked.

Sophie laughed and rolled her eyes.

'Taylor grills me about this constantly,' she said.

I smiled.

'I had actually only just finished my Residency and had no idea that it was Boxing Day. Carousel was the closest shopping centre and I badly needed some supplies. So I thought I would try my luck,' she replied. 'To be honest, the place was so creepy and abandoned that I was kind of glad the door didn't open.'

'It totally was,' I replied.

There were footsteps behind us and Taylor emerged from inside. She wandered over to us and messed up my hair.

'There's some lunch inside for you, Nox. I would make a move before Lizzy destroys the lot of it,' said Taylor.

I was pretty sure she just needed to talk with Sophie, but I was starving anyway, so I headed inside and found Lizzy by the kitchen bench. She was eating an orange and staring off into space while Chess slept off his beach adventures on the floor.

'Hey,' I said.

She smiled in reply. There was an array of fresh fruit and vegetables ready to eat on the counter.

'Everything cool?' I asked.

'Yeah. We'll sleep here tonight and leave for Fremantle in the morning,' she replied.

The thought of seeing Georgia again sent a ripple of nausea through my stomach. I tried to ignore it and started on the lunch.

'We'll need to leave ourselves enough time to get back to Carousel,' said Lizzy, cautiously.

We shared a glance. I knew what she was saying.

34

I had wiped the idea of leaving with the others from my mind. It was easier that way. I still had the short stories from Carousel, and I guess none of us really knew what would happen on September second. Not even Ed. But deep down I knew I was different to the other Artists. Maybe not a Patron like Rocky or Rachel. But not a sheltered Artist either. For a while, writing the novel had made the bridge seem narrow. I had started to think that maybe it was all just a matter of timing, as Tommy had suggested way back in the hills. But not anymore. I realised now, without a doubt, that I could have left Carousel at any time. That my presence in this world was an accident, not fate.

It should have made me low, but instead I felt a lightness and clarity. My only concern now was finding Georgia and getting her and my friends back to their Residencies. Art had been a burden ever since I had lumped at Carousel. It had hovered over every moment, reminding me that writing was primary, while living came second. I felt guilt when I wasn't writing, and struggle when I was. The rare days when I managed to wipe it from my mind had felt like the final moments of a dreamy summer holiday. Sweet and warm, but with the lingering dread of school the next morning. If this was the life of an Artist, they could keep it.

I decided that after September second I would return to the beach house. Chess could come with me. He would miss Lizzy, but be happy by the ocean. Maybe one day we would meet some other Patrons somewhere and together we could build a weirdo life together by the sea. While the others were outside I took out my short stories and stashed them in a cabinet in the study. When the time was right I would take them out and read over what I had written in Carousel. Remind myself of Rocky and the Finns, and all that had happened while we were stuck in there. The whole thing was way overloaded with emotion and I tried not to dwell on it too much. Plus we had things to do.

Our bikes were grindy and rusted from our journey from the Auroraport. There would be newer ones around if we decided to look for them, but we were short on time and these bikes had been good to us. So we greased them up and checked over the brakes and tyres. Sophie seemed to be into this stuff. She also rigged up a pedal-powered light to each of the handlebars and found a set of walkie-talkies, setting them to charge via the solar panels. They didn't have the greatest range, but the casino debacle proved how screwed we were without them.

Sophie's artwork from her Residency was a small still life of an abandoned family breakfast. She had been living rent-free with a host family in their big riverside house as part of her real-world residency. When she drifted downstairs on the morning of the Disappearance, the chatty breakfast she had become accustomed to was replaced by silent, creepy limbo. It reminded me of a documentary I had seen about nine-eleven. An engineering team were going through some of the neighbouring buildings that had escaped the destruction. They had waited weeks, or maybe even months, before being able to get inside. I remember them describing how, when the first plane hit, people working there had dropped everything and run. One engineer spoke of an abandoned breakfast meeting where plates of pastries and fruit lay frozen in time beside pots of coffee on a table caked with ominous grey dust.

Sophie told me that she knew immediately upon seeing the breakfast that morning that something big had happened.

Taylor had framed the painting and hung it central in the sunroom. I helped Sophie take it down, then watched her roll it casually into a mailing tube and stuff it into her bag. We harvested what we could from the gardens and packed it up to take with us. Lizzy and I each took long and amazing hot showers in the outdoor wash area. My mood brightened when I saw that the wooden shower door was gnomed by a faded old dude from the garden. The rainwater felt silky and magical against my dry and dusty skin. Afterwards Taylor trimmed my hair, helped bandage my knees and gasped at the crazy rainbow bruise that had surfaced across my shoulder.

'That fucking airport,' she had said and I wondered how much she knew about Lizzy and the auroras.

Before we knew it a fat yellow sun was plunging into the ocean out the kitchen window. We finished up and gathered at a table for dinner. Taylor heated some homemade tomato sauce they had bottled and we ate it with pasta, mushrooms and a garden salad. She and Sophie watched on in amusement as Lizzy and I shovelled it down like animals. After dinner we sat by the fire playing Scrabble and drinking Sophie's mulled wine as sheets of drizzle washed over the windows to the west. Taylor and Lizzy rediscovered the chatty ping-pong banter that had filled their bedrooms growing up and later charmed their crowds between songs. I felt warm and a part of things and my thoughts drifted to Rocky and Carousel, for once with nostalgia rather than sadness.

Next came fruit and pots of melted white chocolate. Then fingers of single-malt whisky and liqueurs. Then rambling and hilarious ghost stories and retrospective birthdays toasting. Then a pot of tea that nobody touched because we were already asleep. Then just darkness and our thoughts, and a hangover that, for once, might be worth it.

35

We blew into Fremantle on an icy northern wind. One bridge was still intact, the other busted apart by a floating cargo liner. A city-bound train stood rigid and ready at the station. Doors still open. Something furry darting inside as we rode past. The heritage streets were wide and empty like a western. Alfresco furniture clinked and clattered outside cafes and restaurants. Where tables were missing we found them across the street, hurled up with their umbrellas by giant gusts of winter wind.

There were no signs of Bulls that we could make out. Instead the port town had been overrun by birds. Seagulls perched hawkish and dirty on hotel balconies. Flocks of river birds thundered across from the Swan to fill the sky with shifting patterns of silver and black. Tiny wrens bombed down from rafters to circle us before disappearing back into hidden nooks. Chess skipped along at our feet, fighting every instinct to bark, chase and scatter them all.

We drifted the main streets with no real plan of how we might find Georgia, or anyone else for that matter. The stores we passed were mostly intact or already open at the time of the Disappearance. Nothing we saw suggested that the town had been heavily inhabited like the city and elsewhere. Eventually Lizzy pulled up between the old market building and football stadium. At a roundabout a statue of a famous footballer had been caked in white by the birds. Lizzy circled the guy and looked around, then rolled over to join the rest of us.

'So, what's the plan?' she asked.

Our search had landed inevitably on my shoulders.

'She was hoping to meet up with some Artists that were living in the west end of town. There are these big old Victorian houses down there,' I said.

'Doesn't sound creepy at all,' said Taylor.

'Which way is that from here?' asked Lizzy, keen to keep moving.

Sophie found west and pointed it out for us.

We set off and bumped down a road littered with Norfolk pine needles. This led to a park and then onto the fishing boat harbour. We walked our bikes across the thick spongy grass and out onto the decks and promenades of the marina. The air was thick with salt and the remnants of long-forgotten fishing hauls. Most of the boats we could see were still tethered neatly to their moorings. Beyond them, though, we glimpsed another giant cargo liner that had gently run aground, this time on a southern swimming beach. Past the breweries and seafood restaurants was a maritime museum and the start of the Victorian buildings.

This was old Fremantle. Towering facades of decorative brickwork and grand late-Georgian entrances. I think most of the buildings were part of a university now, but maybe there were other inhabitants too. These were the type of streets you could walk often without ever knowing what lay inside each door.

Lizzy yelled a hello and we listened as it bounced around the concrete.

Nothing came in reply.

We passed a couple of cafes and a restaurant where the doors stood ajar and the shelves were emptied inside.

'There's gotta be somebody around here somewhere,' said Taylor.

She looked up at the buildings. Most had three storeys and likely dozens of rooms inside. There was a thud from somewhere behind her. Lizzy was kicking at one of the large arching doors. Taylor sighed. It was weird to see them reversing roles from Carousel.

Sophie and I moved over to help her.

The door was heavy and wouldn't flinch for any of us.

'Wouldn't you leave it open if you were living here?' asked Taylor.

The three of us stopped and looked at her.

'Think about it. You probably wouldn't have a key to begin with and even if you did it's not like you can go to Walmart to make copies for your friends. If I really wanted to live in one of these weirdo Tim Burton mansions, and I managed to find a way inside, I would be leaving the front door open rather than running down fifty levels whenever I got a visitor,' said Taylor.

'Depends on the visitor, I guess,' I replied.

'Yeah, but this place is way deserted compared to, like, anywhere else we have seen,' said Taylor.

'Okay. Do you guys want to check the doors over that side of the road while me and Nox try this side?' suggested Lizzy.

'Sure,' answered Sophie for her.

We set off riding door to door like posties. Nothing opened on the first street, but halfway along the second Lizzy and I heard a screech and turned to see Taylor and Sophie peering inside the doorway of a tall grey building titled *Humanities*.

'It wasn't locked?' asked Lizzy as we joined them in the doorway.

'Nope,' said Taylor, knowingly.

I stepped past them and looked around at the shadowy space.

There wasn't much to the entrance. Just a dusty reception area and a large wooden staircase heading up to the second and third levels.

Sophie leaned over the reception desk.

'Look. Torches,' she said.

She picked up a regular looking torch and tested it

out. The light came on first go.

'For the trip up the stairs?' I suggested.

'Hello?' yelled Lizzy, abruptly.

The three of us jumped and Taylor glared at her. There was no answer. We rested our bikes by the staircase and took out our own torches.

'Switch your radios on, too,' said Taylor.

We fumbled around and clipped them to our pockets and belts. I glanced at Taylor and saw the anxiety that had swiftly consumed her face. She had lost us once already and wasn't planning on having it happen again.

The stairs creaked beneath us but weren't layered with dust like others I had seen. On the first level we found tutorial rooms, some toilets and a long room at the back of the building that was strangely empty.

'What's the deal in here?' asked Lizzy.

We torched around the dim space, finding nothing but floorboards.

'Did you say that Georgia was an actress, Nox?' asked Sophie.

'Yeah,' I replied.

The three of us looked at Sophie.

'Don't you think this looks like a drama space,' said Sophie. 'You know, like for workshops and rehearsals.'

'Oh yeah. It totally does,' said Taylor.

I was starting to freak out at the idea that Georgia could actually be there somewhere. What the hell was I going to say to her? When I replayed the invitation to join her in Fremantle it felt blasé and casual. Not the trigger for some dramatic reunion.

Lizzy led us up the second flight. There were more classrooms and a line of offices for academics. One side of the building had been altered some time ago to form a small lecture theatre. The whiteboard at the front was scrawled with text about some type of theatre movement. The writing was faded, but from how long ago we couldn't tell. The staircase to the final floor had a sign reading *Staff Only*. We headed up there and finally found where the Artists had been living.

What was once a lunch area and meeting room had been transformed into a kind of bohemian sleepout. There were mattresses on the floors and a pile of sheet and blanket sets. Couches circled tables full of candles and books. There was a kitchenette with some portable gas cookers and a scattering of canned food. Clothing racks lined with an assortment of men's and ladies' jackets, pants and jumpers. We quietly wandered the abandoned space until Taylor spotted a fourth staircase. It was smaller than the other three and led us out onto a gusty rooftop terrace.

There was nobody out there either. Crusty deckchairs and beer bottles full of cigarette butts spoke of distant summer parties. A few buckets and funnels were strewn about in an attempt to catch water, but otherwise it seemed as though the terrace had been left alone since the season turned. It was a pity, given the panoramic view it offered over the harbour, park and patchwork rooftops of old Fremantle.

We shivered up there for a few moments, then headed back inside.

'What do you think?' Lizzy asked me.

'It looks like what she described to me at the casino,' I replied.

Lizzy nodded, but didn't seem convinced. I wasn't either really.

Taylor and Sophie were digging around the kitchen.

'It doesn't seem like anyone has been here for at least a day or two,' said Sophie.

'Do you think they went to find food?' said Taylor.

'Maybe,' replied Sophie. 'There's not a lot left here.'

I hung in the middle of the room as the others did their best to pretend that we weren't in a rush. I wished that I could sense Georgia's presence or find a telltale piece of jewellery that would confirm her history there.

'Wait. Do you see a diary anywhere?' I asked, rummaging through the tables.

The others joined me.

'What does it look like?' asked Sophie.

'Just a regular diary. But it's from last year,' I replied.

The four of us dug around for the best part of half an hour. We found a random collection of paperbacks, and a couple of notepads, but no diaries. Eventually I gave up so that the others would feel okay to do the same.

We lingered up there for a moment. Nobody really

knew what to say. We could search some of the other buildings, but I think we all knew that we had already found what we were looking for. Maybe we had just been too late.

Taylor seemed to pick up on the silent panic building in my chest.

'Oh well. Let's wait here for a bit. See if anybody comes back,' she said.

She looked at the others for support. Sophie's came easily; Lizzy's took a moment longer.

36

We had just over a week to get back to Carousel. It seemed like more than enough time, but waiting up in that building had all of us on edge.

Lizzy felt it the worst. She would pace up and down from the rooftop. Grill me for anything on Georgia that I might have forgotten. Take Chess out for impromptu walks that Taylor insisted on joining.

Something had shifted in Lizzy since reuniting with her twin. It was as if she had grown tired of fate. Up until now she had played along with the world as well as anyone. She had made her art. Joined the communities. Bought into the Prix de Rome. Yet the world had given her nothing in return. Just a broken memory of her mother that raised more questions than answers. I got the feeling that now that she had found her sister, Lizzy wanted nothing but to get the hell out of here before something else could happen. And I totally got it.

For Taylor and Sophie the anxiety was less obvious. They were still a bit awkward around each other – or

maybe just around each other in a poky bohemian
sleepout with two other people – but together they also
radiated a calming positivity. Their relationship proved
that good things could happen in this world. They gave
off a John and Yoko type of vibe and I was seriously
grateful for it.

We had been there two nights already and more
than once I had stood staring at the ocean from the
rooftop and all but decided that we should leave. For
all we knew Georgia and whoever else was once here
could have already heard of the Prix de Rome and
be on their way back to their Residencies. But each
time I returned inside to tell the others, Taylor and
Sophie would stop what they were doing and offer such
reassuring and steadfast smiles that I would forget
about it completely.

On the third day I was on the rooftop watching
a swirling breeze shuffle through the Norfolks when
Taylor surfaced alone to join me. She leant back on the
bricks beside me and looked around at the green and
grey patchwork of Fremantle.

'I prefer this to our last rooftop,' she said.

'Totally,' I replied.

I glanced at her. 'Do you think we should leave a note
and get moving?' I asked.

'It's not that far to Carousel, really. And Sophie's
Residency is pretty much on the way. We still have some
time,' replied Taylor.

'Thanks,' I said.

We stared out at the ocean for a while.

'Hey I've been meaning to ask you about your writing,' said Taylor.

'What about it?' I asked, cautiously.

'When we were about to leave the hills you were worried about whether there would be time for it on the road yeah?' she asked.

I nodded.

'So?' she asked.

'I've done a bit of stuff,' I replied.

'Lizzy said you lost some work at the Auroraport?'

I nodded, but didn't elaborate.

'That sucks, Nox. I totally get why you wouldn't want to start over right away,' said Taylor.

It was a weird thing for her to say. I got the familiar sense that once again Taylor Finn knew more about me than I realised.

'Did you guys hear anything about Tommy while you were staying at the beach?' I asked, changing the subject.

'Nope. He'll be okay though. Tommy is a tough little dude,' she replied.

'I hope so.'

I turned and glanced up at the hills. They were hazy and distant, but I could make out a tinge of green amid the grey and black.

'I was thinking of taking something back to Carousel for Rocky,' said Taylor. 'Any ideas?'

'Aside from a sick BMX?' I replied.

'Yeah. Or a Commodore,' joked Taylor.

'I don't know. Rocky had pretty weird taste,' I said.

'I guess we all did when we were his age,' said Taylor. 'Lizzy had a sexy poster of Lisa Kudrow on her wall for most of junior high.'

I laughed and Taylor joined me.

'Seriously?'

She nodded and laughed some more.

'Holy shit. I can't believe I just told you that. Nobody knows about that,' said Taylor.

'It will be pretty safe with me here,' I said and immediately wondered whether I had let on too much about my plans.

Taylor didn't seem to notice.

'I really want to get him a hacky sack, but who knows where we would find one,' said Taylor.

We stood in silence for a while and enjoyed the patchy sunshine.

'Did Ed say whether everyone that was back at a Residency on September second would go home?' she asked.

'You mean Rocky?' I asked.

She nodded.

I shook my head.

'I don't think he has the full picture yet. It sounded like more of a gut feeling. He said to me, this is what I think, not what I know,' I said.

Taylor and I gazed out at the ocean and mulled this over for a while.

A folk singer's intuition.

Without a doubt Ed's was stronger than most. It had probably even given birth to a lot of his great songs. But it wasn't much for an entire city to be pinning its hopes on.

37

That night we were woken by garbled static on Taylor's radio.

I was tired and dopey and needed time to confirm that it wasn't part of my dream. I had been up late writing a note to leave for Georgia. I told her about my meeting with Ed and the Prix de Rome. About how important it was that she got back to her Residency in time, even if the whole thing sounded crazy. At the end of the note I added that I should have gone with her to Fremantle, but I was glad that I didn't because now my friends might be able to get home. I told her I had freaked out when she asked me because being with her felt like part of the future, not the shitty present, or the distant past. Finally I told her that I might not be around after September second, but that it didn't mean I wouldn't be okay.

I had no idea how to sign off so I stupidly drew a smiley face beside my name. The eyes were too close together and it looked weird. I cursed and considered starting over, but couldn't deal with writing all of that stuff again. So I pocketed the note and planned to tell Sophie and the Finns that I was ready to leave when they woke in the morning.

But then Taylor had forgotten to turn off her radio after an evening walk with Lizzy.

'What is that?' said Lizzy from across the room.

Taylor shuffled around in the dark. Sophie's torch came on, then Lizzy's.

'Taylor?' asked Lizzy.

'It's my radio,' she replied.

The noise came again. It was dirty and broken, but it sounded like a human voice.

I sat upright and turned on my torch. Taylor and Sophie were huddled over the radio, listening intently.

'Is there ... in Fremantle? We're ... boat ... the lighthouse. Please ... us.'

The three of them looked at me. The voice was shrill and panicked.

And American.

'It's her,' I said.

Fremantle had lighthouses on each side of the harbour. The south light was close to town and flashed green. The north light was all the way back across the river and pulsed an ominous, distant red. We pulled on shoes, wheeled out our bikes and radioed over and over again. Green or red? Green or red? Green or red?

Finally there was a tiny broken crackle.

'Red.'

The streets were pitch-dark and bristling with wind. Sophie's handlebar lights threw manic beams of blue across roads, buildings and the skulking form of Chess as we raced through the west end grid, then powered toward the working bridge. The radio chatter grew sparse, then stopped altogether as we crossed over the river.

I was working from memory and hoped to hell that I hadn't turned too early as we swung left and cut under the train line. There was ocean ahead of us somewhere. The fizzing rumble of shore break consumed the night air. We passed another railway track and the hulking cubes of shipping containers and warehouses. Abruptly the road stopped and our lights found only dunes ahead of us.

'Which way to the lighthouse?' yelled Taylor.

I was saved from answering by a blip of light to our left. We waited a moment, then it came again.

'Over there,' I replied. 'At the end of this road.'

We fanned out across the road and raced towards the light. The wind was really howling from the west. My guess was that their boat had been blown in against the rocks.

'Hello,' our radios chattered in stereo.

It was clearer now.

'Where is your boat?' I replied.

'Hello! We're against the rocks. Near the lighthouse,' came the reply.

As we closed in on the light, the road jutted out into proper ocean. We were on a groyne with rocks and water on both sides of us now.

We pulled up beside the lighthouse and peered over the edge. It was a nasty drop down to the dark, choppy water.

'Do you see anything?' asked Lizzy.

The four of us were leaning over and torching around.

'There's nothing here,' said Taylor.

Sophie turned around and ran across to the wilder, northern side.

We followed and for a moment were suspended in a great swathe of red light. Five frozen figures of the apocalypse. A second later it was gone. Our pupils coiled outward and we searched the ocean below. I heard voices, then a crackle of radio.

'Here! Down here!'

We swung our torches left and found them.

A steel fishing dingy was pinned against the rocky groyne with a full load of passengers. From where I stood I counted at least six of them. We clambered closer, trying to get above them but the rock jutted out in a way that made it difficult to see them properly. It was a three-metre drop to the boat and climbing up onto the rocks looked impossible. They were large and steep and each new swell covered the lower third in water.

I looked past them to the end of the groyne. It was just a boat length away. The wind that was pinning them against the rocks was also whipping viciously around the end of the groyne. If the boat edged too far towards the end and lost its grip on the rocks, they could be swept south forever.

Another swathe of disco red. I realised that Lizzy was the only one still with me on the rocks. I turned and saw Taylor and Sophie running back towards us with a lifebuoy. It was roped to a metal stand somewhere behind them. They gathered beside us and prepared to throw it down. Taylor took my radio.

'Grab a hold of this buoy and use the rope to pull yourselves up over the rocks. Only one at a time or it could snap,' said Taylor.

There was some chatter in the boat, then somebody radioed through an okay. Sophie flung the buoy to the right of them and let the wind drift it up. The rope went taut beside me. There was some clunking below. Long seconds ticked by. The red light came once. Then again. Finally a figure emerged up and over the rocks.

It was a guy. He was skinny and drenched. We helped him down onto the road, where he sat, hunched and drawn.

'What the hell are you guys doing out there?' said Lizzy.

'Fishing,' said the guy, meekly.

Next came a short girl who was shivering severely. Then an older guy who needed to be pulled up over the final rock. Taylor and Sophie were kneeling beside them on the road, sharing some water we had brought along and both of their jackets. Lizzy and I stood at the rock awaiting the remaining passengers.

The rope had been taut for a while. Just as I was wondering if something had happened the lighthouse drenched us in red and Georgia rose up out of the darkness.

She was stunned by the light and Lizzy and I caught her just as she stumbled forward.

'Hey,' I said.

Her teeth were chattering and her eyes were wide and shaken.

'Nox? Hey. God. I can't ...' said Georgia, her voice suddenly gone.

She teared up and dropped her forehead onto my chest. Lizzy was watching and flashed a smile before turning back to the rope. It was still slack.

'Yo,' radioed Lizzy. 'Who's next?'

She waited, head down against the hammering wind.

There was no reply.

I looked at the rope. It skittered loosely along the rocks. Lizzy turned to me and radioed again.

'Hello?'

She listened for a long and horrible moment.

'We got blown around the rocks,' the reply finally came. 'We're on the other side. Throw the buoy on the other side!'

'Shit,' mouthed Lizzy.

I left Georgia and clambered over to help Lizzy pull in the rope. It was heavy and awkward. Our radios crackled again.

'Throw the ... on ... side!'

Sophie was on the road behind us now. Finally the buoy scraped up over the rocks. We tossed it down to Sophie and she raced it across to the other side of the groyne. Lizzy and I followed while Georgia and the others stood, stunned and horrified.

'I can't see them!' yelled Sophie.

She was atop of the rocks, ready to throw. Lizzy and I shone our torches out into the abyss.

'There!' said Lizzy.

I followed her light and found a silhouette of black to our right. It was already so small. Sophie shifted and hurled the buoy towards them. It caught in the wind and knifed out dramatically into the distance. Rope slithered and slithered beside me. Then stopped. The buoy crashed down into the water.

It was halfway short of the boat.

Lizzy and I stared at each other. There was nothing we could do. Our radios crackled with something we couldn't make out.

The boat was already too far gone.

38

We could only rest the surviving Artists for a day.

Things were getting tight. Just seven sleeps remained until the Artist portals would open. Georgia and Claudia (the short girl from the boat and Georgia's long-lost collaborator from WAAPA) had to get all the way to Mount Lawley. The older guy Henry's Residency was also north of the city. Jake's was closer, just south of Fremantle in the coastal suburb of Coogee, but he was more sickly than anyone and would need time to travel even a short distance. And for us, Carousel was still a long way east. There would be a river and a freeway to cross. And who knows what else we would stumble into on the way.

The four survivors were starving and badly dehydrated. They had drifted out of the port almost four days ago on a harebrained whim. They took fishing rods, oars and some snack food. After a fruitless few hours they realised how hard it was to row the boat against any breeze. When the offshore wind picked up it simply turned them around and blew them out to sea. They had bobbed out there, eating the occasional raw fish and drinking from a tub of stale water until the howling nor'-wester blew them back to shore.

The same shrieking wind that had saved them may have also doomed their friends.

We had discussed heading south to try and find the remaining three. But there was no basis to the plan. The next major port was thirty ks south and there was no guarantee they would land there, or anywhere else for that matter. We hadn't told Georgia and the others, but the wind had shifted back offshore in the morning. Given what we now knew of their supplies, the odds of survival weren't good.

The fishing trip had been a stupid idea. But fuelled with time, hunger and naivety, we couldn't guarantee that we wouldn't have done something similar. This world was asking questions of everybody now and the repercussions were immense. So we comforted them the best we could, then shifted their focus to the road ahead. Georgia and Claudia were on board, Henry too from what we could gather. He didn't talk much and seemed preoccupied, if that were even possible. Jake wasn't convinced by Ed's theory. He was the type of whip-smart hipster kid I had sold sketchpads to a hundred times over in the store. There wasn't time to sway him. In the end everyone had to make their own decision anyway.

Our plan was to leave in the morning and head inland together until we hit the freeway. From there Georgia, Claudia and Henry would take it north, past the city and back to their Residencies. The rest of us would continue along the highway until we hit the river and Sophie's Residency, then make our way further east until we got to Carousel. Jake's plans were vague and shifted by the hour.

We needed some extra bikes and more food, so Sophie and the Finns were out getting this organised. I was in the kitchen making the others eat and drink as much as their bodies would take without hurling. Georgia and I had spoken a little, but mostly she had been sleeping.

As the others lay motionless in post-lunch comas, I watched her jolt awake, then pad over to the kitchen. She was still wearing my jacket from the night before.

We smiled a brief hello. She stood beside me at the counter and looked on as I gathered a pile of cans to take with us in the morning. Her gaze was vacant and I had no idea what to say.

'I'm really sorry about your friends,' I said, careful not to wake the others.

'They weren't really my friends. We were just living together,' she replied.

Georgia seemed detached. Or hardened, maybe. It was happening to everybody.

'Will you come next door while I take a bath?' she asked.

'Sure,' I replied.

There was a warehouse apartment next door that Georgia and the others used for the bathroom sometimes. I followed her up an exterior staircase at the back of the building, then in through a broken window. The bathroom was dusty and cold, but had a large triangular spa bath in the corner. A garden hose snaked through a window into a stock pot atop of a gas burner. Georgia released a clamp at the end of the hose and water began trickling into the pot.

'There is a rainwater tank on the roof,' she said.

I nodded.

She lit the gas and we stood back and waited for the water to warm.

'Your hair looks cool,' said Georgia, suddenly brighter.

'Thanks. Taylor cut it last week,' I replied.

'Those two are super nice,' she said.

'Which two?' I asked.

'Taylor and Lizzy,' said Georgia.

'Oh. Yeah, I guess so,' I replied.

Georgia eyed me curiously.

'No, I mean, they totally are. It's just weird when you hang out with people all the time, I guess you kind of forget,' I replied.

Georgia checked on the water.

'How long did it take before they came back to the casino?' she asked.

'They didn't, actually. I went looking for them after I met Ed,' I replied.

'Oh. Right,' said Georgia.

It was awkward. I wanted her to see that I was okay about them never coming back for me. But in reality I probably wasn't.

'Lizzy came back. But Rachel lied and said I wasn't around,' I added.

Georgia shook her head.

'They left the Collective like everybody else?' she asked.

'Yeah,' I replied.

'You know, I used to get the worst headaches in that place, but I always just figured they were from drinking,' said Georgia.

I smiled and nodded.

'So where did you find them?' asked Georgia.

'Lizzy was at the airport. After I found her we came down the coast looking for Taylor and Sophie. They had a beach house in Cottesloe,' I replied.

Georgia shook her head at the scope of the story.

'We're so lucky you guys were in Fremantle when you were,' she said.

I looked at her and felt embarrassed.

'We actually came here to find you,' I said.

Georgia looked at me for a moment, then turned away and welled up.

'Sorry. I'm such a wreck these days. I get so emotional when I'm not doing any acting,' she said.

'It's fine,' I said.

She was sitting on the edge of the empty bath and crying. I sat down beside her.

'It's not fair, what happened to those Artists in the boat,' she said.

I exhaled and stared at the floor.

'Everything in the world is so fragile now. We're all like fine china or something,' said Georgia.

I passed her some tissues from the basin.

'My mum has these china teacups,' I said. 'She bought them ages ago when she was studying in London. They were always locked away in a cabinet by the hall. But I remember when my grandad started getting really sick, we came home from school one day and suddenly Mum was using one. Not even for anything fancy. Just a cup of water or whatever. So, Danni being Danni, she asked Mum if she could have her orange juice in one. Danni is clumsy as all hell, but I remember Mum just looked at her and said, "Danni, if you or any of your friends ever want to use the china, you just go right ahead."'

Georgia smiled and calmed a little.

'Maybe they're still in your house,' she said, hopefully.

'Maybe,' I replied.

'I wish there was more time so we could go up there together,' said Georgia.

I was suddenly on the edge of bawling myself. Georgia leaned over and kissed me on the temple.

'Thank you for looking for me, Nox,' she said.

I took a breath and squeezed her hand. We sat there together as the water slowly simmered.

'Whoa. What is that?' said Lizzy.

'Henry's sculpture,' replied Taylor.

'Wait. Not *the* sculpture?' said Lizzy.

'Yep,' said Taylor.

Lizzy groaned.

She was standing in the doorway of a warehouse opposite to the Humanities building. Taylor, Sophie and I were already inside looking at the mammoth steel sculpture that Henry had created back in his Residency. It was essentially a series of steel sheaths protruding out from a small central sphere. The interesting thing, or one of the interesting things, was that each sheath was completely unique in its shape, width, direction, lustre – everything – despite originating from identical pieces of steel. Rather than a structured process, Henry had ensured this was random by heating them to bending point then letting them fly like kites from a third-storey window during the biggest storm of winter. Each one was shaped by the shifting wind and air pressure as it dried and hardened. He then attached the sheaths to the central sphere in a complicated and alluring pattern. Taylor said it looked like a hostile zorb ball.

'How did he even get it here?' asked Lizzy.

'I guess that's the good news,' replied Sophie.

'Oh yeah?' said Lizzy.

'Back at his Residency he also built a way of transporting it,' said Sophie.

'Wait till you get a look at this,' said Taylor.

We led Lizzy down to the back of the warehouse where Taylor dramatically opened a roller door. Daylight spilled in over a pair of tandem mountain bikes. They sat a few metres apart from each other and had been connected by welded steel rods, kind of like a catamaran. Similar rods trailed from the rear of each bike to a long wooden platform on wheels. The platform had a special grid of cut-outs to match the shape of Henry's sculpture.

Taylor climbed aboard one of the bikes and looked up at her twin.

'Isn't it the dorkiest thing you have ever seen?' she asked.

'Pretty much,' replied Lizzy. 'Four riders isn't ideal.'

This was what I had been pondering with Taylor and Sophie. There would only be three riders going north once we reached the freeway.

'Apparently it can be ridden with less. Henry says even two people, if the road is good,' replied Sophie.

'Unlikely, given what we've seen so far,' said Taylor.

'The freeway might be okay still,' I said.

Lizzy glanced at me, then back at the giant sculpture behind us.

'Dare I ask what kind of Artist Claudia is?' asked Lizzy.

'She's a director. Theatre mostly,' I replied.

Lizzy thanked the heavens and we turned our attention to loading the platform.

39

We farewelled Jake and left early the next morning. The
roads out of Fremantle were steeper than I remembered.
We quickly discovered that, even with four riders, it was
basically impossible to ride Henry's sculpture up any
significant incline. His spindly old body was frail and
still recovering from the boat ordeal, while Georgia and
Claudia had lost their fitness while hibernating through
the winter. Aside from my shoulder, I was feeling
reasonably fit, as were the Finns and Sophie, but even
our legs couldn't deal with the volume of steel on that
platform.

So we were forced to push it most of the way. This
often took five of us, leaving the remaining two Artists
to pull the other four bikes. Needless to say, it was slow
going. It took us all morning just to get out of the city
centre and onto the flat of the highway where the bizzaro
catamaran could be ridden again.

The passing suburbs were largely desolate. Neat
coastal houses had morphed into tiny urban jungles.

Lawns powering upward like hedges. Trees and shrubs crowding over windows, doors and walls. For a while we rode alongside a golf course where the abandoned buggies of early-morning members still dotted the greens and fairways. There was the sprawling Fremantle cemetery, famous as the resting place of AC/DC frontman Bon Scott. Taylor and Lizzy eyed it regretfully as we cycled past without time to stop. Visiting Bon's headstone had been next on their list after shopping on the morning of the Disappearance.

After an afternoon of steering the awkward structure through an ugly mess of banged-up freight trucks we emerged at a bridge overlooking the freeway. To the south lay grey skies and barren lanes. To the north was the distant and pensive cityscape of Perth. Exhausted, we backtracked and found the closest house that was big enough to shelter us for the night.

Georgia and Claudia collapsed onto a couple of couches. Henry wasn't even able to get that far. He had sat down in a patio to take off his shoes and remained there, gingerly sipping on warm Gatorade as the rest of us unpacked around him. When we were done I convened in the front garden with Sophie and the Finns to figure out what the hell we were going to do.

'Does anyone honestly think these guys have any chance of hauling this thing all the way to the city?' I asked.

'Past the city,' added Sophie.

'Where is Henry's Residency?' asked Taylor.

'It's a technical school in Leederville,' replied Sophie. 'Maybe five kilometres north of the city.'

'They're screwed,' said Lizzy.

'And they are so exposed if they keep moving at that pace. Pit bulls or Loots could circle them before they could do anything about it,' said Sophie.

Taylor was getting anxious about where the discussion was leading.

'I don't see what more any of us can do for him,' she said.

Somehow I knew this moment had been coming. It felt inevitable. Like I'd seen it in a dream.

'Carousel is only a day or so from here on normal bikes,' I said. 'You guys should keep going east and wait for me there. I'll ride with these guys to Leederville, then WAAPA. By that stage I will be east of the city again. On a good bike I can ride south from there to Carousel within a day.'

Taylor looked away. Lizzy took a breath. Chess peered up at us anxiously.

'Okay. But if you run out of time you gotta leave him, Nox. It's no good none of you guys making it back to your Residencies,' said Lizzy.

Taylor stared at her sister in disbelief.

'You think we should split up again?' she asked Lizzy.

'As opposed to all of us hauling that thing to the city? Yeah, I do, Taylor. I'm going home on the second. I can't do any more time in this place,' said Lizzy.

'This is such a shit idea,' said Taylor.

'Yeah well, sometimes shit ideas are all there is,' said Lizzy. 'Actually, most times, in this place.'

'That's a cop-out and you know it, Lizzy,' said Taylor.

'So what do you want to do, huh?' asked Lizzy. 'He has to go with her.' She gestured towards the house.

Sophie and I hovered awkwardly beside them. I glanced at her and she gave me a small, reassuring smile. I liked Sophie. She was wise beyond her years and didn't need to say much to prove it. I realised then that I would probably never see her again after tomorrow.

I edged forward towards Taylor.

'It's cool, Taylor. I've been on the road heaps since the casino. The freeway will take us right alongside the tech school, then it's just another suburb over to WAAPA and I'm on my way,' I said. 'I wouldn't miss being back there with you guys and Rocky for anything.'

Taylor held firm for a long moment, then turned and put a hand on my shoulder. Her gaze was sharp and defiant in the dusky grey light.

'Don't screw around once you get them back there, Nox. Say your goodbyes and get your ass back to Carousel. We'll be waiting for you at that door,' she said.

I nodded and she left for the house without another word to Lizzy.

'I'll pack you up some batteries and torches to take,' said Sophie.

'Thanks,' I replied.

'Keep your radio on, too. You will be out of our range for most of the way, but sometimes those things pick up a signal from miles away. You never know your luck,' said Sophie.

We hugged briefly and she followed Taylor inside.

'Thanks,' I said to Lizzy once we were alone.

'Don't think that I'm not freaking out about this, yeah,' said Lizzy.

She caught my gaze and held it until I nodded.

'I just figured that you would be going with Georgia no matter what we said. I think I knew as soon as we dragged her out of that boat. Henry's god-awful sculpture is kind of irrelevant.'

I smiled and looked at the ground. She was probably right.

'You don't think it's kinda cool?' I asked.

'The sculpture? I don't even know anymore,' said Lizzy.

We stood out there for a few moments longer.

'I'm sorry that aurora wasn't for you,' I said.

Lizzy shrugged and tried a smile. 'Maybe soon I won't need one so bad.'

40

Lizzy and I returned to the house for some food cooked in pots on the family barbeque. Taylor had told the others of our revised plan and a tangible air of anxiety hovered over the evening. I'm sure the northern Artists were relieved to hear of the help, but it also confirmed that there were real doubts about their ability to get back to their Residencies in time. A single day's riding had illustrated just how much their bodies had suffered on that fishing boat. I got the sense they were also still reeling from the rocket-like transformation in their world. Their situation had shifted from aimless to frantic in a matter of hours. Jake hadn't been able to make this transition. Now the others also seemed caught out by its magnitude.

With this in play it was difficult to gauge Georgia's reaction to the plan. As the others fanned out across the house to sleep, we drifted upstairs together and had quiet sex in one of the bedrooms. It went by quickly, but was also affectionate and felt like it was about more than just our bodies. Afterwards we lay up there in the dark, not saying too much. Georgia had an iPhone half full with precious charge and we listened to a couple of her favourite Death Cab for Cutie songs and nestled down beneath the covers.

Later I thought she was asleep when she rolled over to face me in the dark.

'Hey what did you mean by that note you wrote for me?' she asked.

'What note?' I asked.

'The one I found in your jacket. I assume you were going to leave it for me if you didn't find us,' said Georgia.

Amid the drama of the boat and the rescue I had forgotten all about it.

'Oh yeah, sorry. Which part?' I asked.

'It said that you might not be around after September second,' she said.

I took a breath and wondered where to start.

'I'm just not sure if the whole Prix de Rome thing will apply to me,' I said.

'Why?' asked Georgia.

'Because I'm not really an Artist like everybody else here,' I said.

'Nox. You're fine. That's how heaps of us feel. How do you think it was for me and Claudia when we arrived at the Collective? You know Cara Winters was totally living there?'

'Yeah,' I replied, not wanting to go into it.

'You just need to believe in yourself. God. All of us do,' said Georgia.

'Okay,' I replied.

She kissed me lightly and brushed back the front of my hair.

'Sorry I bailed on you at the casino,' said Georgia.

I looked at her, surprised.

'Things were moving pretty quickly there. Sometimes that stuff kinda freaks me out,' she said.

'You're fine,' I replied.

Georgia laughed for just a moment, then closed her eyes.

'Thanks for coming with us,' she whispered.

I held her and this time she did fall asleep. I lay beside her and wondered whether there was any chance she could be right.

In the morning we said our goodbyes on the freeway overpass. Our hugs were brief and void of heavy emotion. In this way we convinced ourselves that our plans were solid and that worry was unwarranted. It felt cold and unnatural, but was probably still the best option. Before we rounded the corner I turned back for a final look at the Finns. They were steadfast and silhouetted on the elevated bitumen. Hands on their hips. Hair kicked up and full of attitude. In another life it could have been a page out of *Rolling Stone*.

Henry had perked up in the morning and seemed to be pedalling okay behind me as we set off. He was a quiet old guy with crazy Einstein hair and skin that had gone past tanned to a deep and oaky brown. Georgia had told us Henry called himself an inventor rather than an artist – if the two things were separable. It felt like a good thing to be helping him and he seemed genuinely grateful. I looked over at our co-riders. Georgia and Claudia were thin and pale, but looked focused on the tasks ahead. First getting Henry and his sculpture back home, then returning to WAAPA to perform the one-woman play that had freed them from their Residency. The giant sculpture glinted and shimmered behind us. From a distance we must have looked like a Christmas sled merged with something out of *Mad Max*. It was hard not to laugh at how ridiculous things had become.

Before long we boarded the first of two bridges and found the lanes mostly clear. There was just the occasional sideways car, but plenty of room to go around them. From here the freeway hugged the river all the way to the city. This was a good thing for us as it meant the road would stay flat until the final bridge. So long as we kept our momentum we should be close to Leederville by the end of the day.

We quickly realised we weren't alone in our quest. Twice we saw the tops of riders hammering down the freeway in the opposite direction. I caught a glimpse of the second one with enough time to see a giant poster tube strapped to her back. At midmorning a lone sailboat cut dramatically across the river back towards Fremantle. Then, as Henry's cramping stopped us to rest beneath an overpass, Claudia spotted the letters *P d P* freshly tagged in a beautiful, exaggerated fashion on the concrete.

'P d P?' I asked, as we sat beside it.

'I think it might stand for Prix de Perth,' said Claudia.

Ed's message was out. It had been passed on, absorbed, and now lay woven into the fabric of this new world. All around us the Artists of Perth were mobilising. We felt excited and anxious in equal measure.

By late afternoon we were moving at a crawl, but had finally reached the long second bridge that joined South Perth to the city and beyond. It rose up, stark and grey like the back of a whale against the late winter sun. Again we stopped to rest. This time all of us were cramping. Henry's sculpture seemed to have retained its strange relationship with the wind. Sometimes it felt as though the sheaths were funnelling each passing gust and propelling us forward faster than we could ever have cycled. Other times it was as if the whole sculpture was designed to catch wind and trap it somewhere inside. The drag on our bikes was intense.

I stretched my shoulder and looked out at the windswept bridge with apprehension. If we couldn't get up the incline, Henry was screwed.

Georgia and Claudia looked wrecked but I was starting to freak out about the daylight remaining.

'Should we have a go at it?' I asked them.

They took a breath and nodded. I looked back at Henry. Slowly and gingerly he climbed back aboard.

We edged painfully away from the wall and started our ascent. The wind was really hammering across the bridge from the west. The sculpture caught a waft of it and kicked us forward enough to gain a bit of momentum with our legs. Steadily we rose away from the shoreline. It was hard not to stop and look around. To our right ferries drifted loose like ice cubes in the fat of the river. Cars banked at distant city exits like faded and forgotten Lego. Beyond them the city bristled with static grey towers, brazen birds circling the buildings like tenants. And, to our left, Kings Park towered over everything. Old World and steadfast in its grandeur.

The next gust caught in the sculpture and hemmed us down against the road. We all but stopped.

I looked across at Georgia and Claudia. They were pedalling the best that they could. We edged forward another metre or so, then were set back again. The majority of the incline still lay ahead of us, yet we couldn't gain even a metre in that wind.

Henry yelled something from behind me. I turned to see him pointing to the left. There was nothing there but empty lanes. I looked at him again. He kept on with the frantic pointing. Georgia and I guided us diagonally to the left and we tried again with the pedalling. It was suddenly easier. Henry's sculpture was back on our side.

We reached the edge of the left lane and came to a stop, having gained ten or so metres forward. Henry pointed back in the other direction. We turned the bikes to face the diagonal and tried again.

It worked. Henry's weirdo sculpture was tacking us across the bridge.

Suddenly we were halfway up. Then three quarters. Then the road flattened beneath us and we realised we were cresting. I looked over at Georgia and she smiled back with relief. The freeway dropped away and swung past the city in front of us. We sat back on our bikes and steered our way past the exits and overpasses. The road banked left and dipped again. I scanned the exit signs. Ahead of us in the swampy daylight was the exit ramp into Leederville.

41

We stayed the night in Leederville with Henry and his sculpture, then left the following morning. Henry was shattered from the journey. We had hauled his sculpture into the lobby of the tech school and set him down on a couch with a pile of sports drinks and trail mix. He stayed there through the night, and rose only slightly to thank us and wave us off in the morning. The guy wasn't in good shape, but he just had to get through the week. Four more nights and his portal would open.

It took us until midday to find new bikes at a store in North Perth. Our legs were sore and crampy and we would have preferred to walk the short distance from Leederville to WAAPA, but a bike was essential for my journey to Carousel, both for speed and safety. Time was short. I would need to rest at WAAPA overnight before tracking south to Carousel. I planned to ride fast through the chequered eastern suburbs. Reach Carousel in a day. There were things I needed to say to Taylor and Lizzy before the portals opened. If I was going to be stuck in some Patron wormhole forever I wanted to be baggage-free.

Claudia led us through the leafy suburban streets. This had been her neighbourhood for a while before the Disappearance. First during her bachelor degree studying film at the adjoining university. Then during her year and a half at WAAPA, immersing herself in the world of theatre. Georgia had told me of Claudia's growing reputation as a blunt and demanding director. How she clashed with the ego-driven acting kids from Sydney and Melbourne who would resist her and resent her, before skulking back when teachers and peers heralded their understated performances. Georgia told me she had been trying to collaborate with Claudia for a whole year before the Disappearance had made it happen.

We arrived at WAAPA by three as the sky clouded over and winter threatened a final stand. I followed Georgia and Claudia inside and watched as they reacquainted themselves with their former home. They moved through a foyer decorated to promote an upcoming production. Down hallways lined with workshop areas and framed headshots of alumni. Past a box office where they had plundered the snacks and drinks more than a year ago now. And finally into a backstage area with change rooms, a shower and, amid the shelves of garish props, a cluster of couches and blankets that had been their home.

Claudia tried out a couple of the hanging lights. They worked first time. She shrugged as if to say, *of course they do*.

'Are you guys cool if I take the first shower?' asked Georgia.

'Yeah, George. Enjoy,' said Claudia.

I gave her a smile and she trudged off into the bathroom. Claudia sat on a couch while I tried to stretch out the rocks in my calves.

'Do you know if we are meant to be performing the play at the time the portals open?' she asked.

'No. Sorry. I'm not sure,' I replied.

Claudia sat there seriously. Perfect posture in spite of her exhaustion.

'Do you believe it?' I asked.

She shrugged, honestly.

'Do you?' she asked.

'Yeah. Definitely,' I replied.

'Because of the Curator?' she asked.

I thought about it and shook my head.

'I mean, I don't think Ed would make it all up. But he never said to me that the portals would definitely happen,' I said.

Claudia waited for me to continue.

'He just said that the art world was at a crossroad. That artists needed a new kind of residency to produce the art of the future,' I said.

'You believe it because of the art you have seen here?' she asked.

I thought about all of the art I had experienced. The darkness and pop of Taylor & Lizzy's new album. The haunting charcoals of Peter Mistry. Kink & Kink and all of their weirdness. Photos Kirk had taken of the memories of jet planes. The hulking windblown sculpture we had hauled all the way from Fremantle.

'Yeah,' I replied. 'That's exactly why.'

Claudia considered this for a moment, then nodded.

'Will you watch us rehearse the play tonight?' she asked.

'That would be awesome,' I replied.

I had showered and changed and now sat nervous in a theatre of empty chairs. Georgia was onstage already. I could just make her out in the darkness. Claudia was somewhere offstage beside her. The set dressing was stark. Just a writing desk and a beaten-up couch. I held my breath and waited. Long and important seconds ticked by.

Claudia struck a light and Georgia's head snapped upright.

'What good is the wind if it does not bring her smell?' she boomed.

My skin rippled. It was electric.

The whole play was, really. A biting, witty exploration of a famous writer beset by insecurity and expectation. Claudia ran it at a dazzling pace and, despite not having rehearsed it for months, Georgia's delivery was fantastic.

With her bouncy hair and accent she came off a bit like a young Laura Linney. When Claudia eventually faded the lights I had completely forgotten that the theatre was empty.

Afterward I found the pair of them hugging and beaming backstage. The bubble I had seen around Taylor and Lizzy with their music now surrounded Georgia and Claudia too. It struck me then that theatre existed for the moment even more so than music. Sure there was writing and rehearsing, and sets and costumes, but in the end it was an hour or two on a stage somewhere, before it disappeared into oblivion. Even for prolific actors or directors, these hours were tiny blips in a lifetime of hustle. For Georgia and Claudia I think that rehearsal had been like waking from a long and fitful slumber.

I congratulated and complimented them both, then drifted away to let them debrief and bask in the moment.

It was quiet and still amid the concrete of the props warehouse. I packed a bag ready for the morning, then lay awake thinking about home. The tiny dot on the ground that I had searched for all those years ago. It was all we had then. And it was all I had now. I realised that I had to go back there after the others had gone. It wouldn't be easy, but I felt like I was ready to deal with whatever it threw up. And I finally felt like I would be ready to write then too. Not for status or acceptance, or to buy my way home. But because it felt like something I could do.

I held onto this and found the strength in it to take me to sleep.

Late into the night Georgia woke me and we tiptoed into a classroom to fool around like teenagers on a school camp. For those few, suspended hours we built a bubble that the world couldn't penetrate. A glimmer of infrared heat in a desert of space and darkness. More than anything I remembered the brush of her hair across my forehead. The echo of her whisper. The flicker in her eyes before each smile.

42

I rode southwards beneath a patchy, broken sky. It was
early and the suburbs were static like paintings in a
lobby. I had a direction and a destination, but hadn't
yet considered my route. Eventually there would be a
bridge, then some roads and a highway. The road back to
Carousel felt sure and inevitable.

I pulled up at a hill on the fringes of Mount Lawley.
I was sweating and shed a couple of layers into my bag.
The weather was shifting and humid. Where I stood was
in sunshine but storm clouds roamed the city just ahead.
There was the blink of lightning and washes of rain
down there too. I finished my water and circled around
towards it.

I was just a suburb away in Northbridge when
lightning struck gas and the entire city erupted.

There was no escalation or warning. Just the hint of
a light in the sky, then a chilling and immense boom.
I veered into a shopfront and cowered from the noise
more than anything. Waves of it saturated the air in a

way I didn't think possible. My eardrums bulged inward. I covered them with my hands and cowered even lower. I felt the heat then too. The street tunnelled with a scorching desert wind. I edged out and peered down its length.

The city was gone. Replaced with a heaving black netherworld. Fizzing red embers danced like insects by a thousand light bulbs. Smoke eked from the darkness and dripped with a sickly yellow. I was both awestruck and terrified.

There were more explosions. First distant, then one that felt right on top of me. I flinched and kicked at the door of the shop where I sheltered. The lock buckled, then snapped. I pushed my bike and bag inside, then rammed the door shut. It dangled loosely on its hinge. I shoved a trolley of dried noodles up against it and a box of something else against that. Through the glass I watched as the street was lost to smoke and embers.

My ears didn't ring, rather delivered everything to my brain on a sloppy delay. The whistle of wind beneath the door. Droning smoke alarms. The rattle of windows at the back of the store as I raced around to seal myself inside.

I was in a leaky Asian mini-mart. There were aisles of dried goods, sauces and spices, a counter by the entrance and a storeroom and kitchenette at the back. The store was untouched and heavy with dust.

I sniffed at the air.

Smoke was drifting inside. I jittered about from front door to back, wondering if I should stay put or get the hell out of there. The plumbing was long gone and the only water I could find was a half row of Mount Franklin in the Coke fridge. I found a rusty old fire extinguisher on a wall in the storeroom and sat by the back door reading the instructions over and over again. The words were shaky and blurred. I was shivering in spite of the warmth outside. I put the extinguisher aside and took a bunch of long, slow breaths. The air didn't taste great, but at least it calmed me a fraction.

From what I could see, the smoke was still thick outside. I would have to stay put for a while. If a fire started I could use the extinguisher and some water bottles to put it out. If these didn't work I could take one of two exits and try my luck outside.

Although it had happened right in front of me I still couldn't process the fact that the city had exploded. Month on month of seeping gas had finally been ignited. If it had happened last summer we would have watched it curiously from the safety of the hills. Or the summer before and we might have shrugged it off as just another noise outside the walls of Carousel. But now, just days out from the portals reopening, it had caught me dangling and exposed. Others too, probably. A blast like that could have easily taken out the freeway or surrounding bridges.

I thought of Sophie and the Finns, screeching to a

halt in the suburbs and staring northward at the carnage. Of Georgia and Claudia who I left just that morning. Wishing they had asked me of my route so they knew how much to worry. And then Cara Winters. Holy shit. She was probably still living in that basement. Was it low enough to withstand an explosion like that? Would she have air to breathe until the portals opened?

Perth was crumbling at the final hurdle and it felt like the proper apocalypse had begun. I realised then that my life after the portals would be as much about physical survival as it would anything else. It was lonely and daunting. Again I saw Luke Skywalker dangling alone in the universe. I slunk down low and held the extinguisher in my arms like a pillow.

I knew it was dark outside when the smoke took a hue of red.

I had sat through the entire day watching the same blanket of grey out the window. A layer of it rested on the ceiling inside now, despite my efforts with a roll of packing tape. Low to the ground it was still fine. But I had little idea of what was happening outside. The city was on fire, I could tell that much. The temperature was well above normal and there was a rumbling noise that was akin to the hills burning. Thankfully it didn't seem like it had jumped the train lines that separated the city from Northbridge. The glow I saw in the smoke now was dull and from the left, rather than all over.

Still, I was stuck. There was no way I could find my way through that level of smoke. Plus I didn't know how far I would need to travel to be clear of it. If there was a breeze outside I could try to head upwind until I found clean air. But, from what I could see, the smoke was fat and static.

I was too wired for sleep but needed something to take my attention from the minutes ticking by on the barman's watch. As well as food, the shelves had some random stuff like cooking utensils, ornaments and party supplies. I dug around and found some receipt books and a pen. I didn't feel like it – at all – but sat down and started rewriting the novel I had begun at the Collective. It felt mechanical and soulless, but kept me busy through the night until eventually I slept.

Waking was disorientating. Hours had passed yet the shop looked the same. Smoke still covered the windows. A red glow still emanated from the city. There should have been daylight, but the sun had been blotted. I stood and stretched, then paced about the store. Right now there was still time to get back to Carousel, but eventually, inevitably, there wouldn't be. For the first time since the casino it seemed possible that I might not see the Finns again.

I grabbed some waters and the writing pad and pushed the thought right out of my mind. Instead I concentrated on the writing. I tried to remember what

I had already written, but also free myself up within the process. The writing had worked before because I found a tone I could pull off and a character that felt honest and real. I focused on rediscovering these things first and foremost.

As the city burnt to stumps and ash beside me, my novel grudgingly came to life. I wrote hunched over on the cold concrete floor. Standing like a cashier at the shopfront counter. On a milk crate with a box of soy sauce for a desk. I took breaks every hour to survey the smoke and find food on the shelves.

Night came, again. Still my view didn't change. I was getting quietly desperate, but the writing was helping. I spiralled eagerly into its oblivion. The pages held warmth and safety, but also control. I set an alarm on the barman's watch and slept for just two hours. When I awoke the date on the watch had changed to September.

'Screw it,' I said.

I packed the notepad safely into my bag, took a long drink of water and got ready to leave. There were disposable face masks in aisle two. I taped two of them together and wrapped them tightly over my mouth and nose. Sophie had given me two torches along with the radio. I strapped them both to the handlebars and switched them on. The radio was on already. So far it hadn't picked anything up, but I clipped it to my belt regardless. Lastly I took a packet of battery-powered party lights from a tub near the counter. They were kitschy and ridiculous, but offered additional light and I couldn't be fussy. I coiled the globes around the frame of the bike and plugged in a battery from the dwindling stash in my bag. Suddenly my bike pulsed like a Christmas tree. I was about to leave when I remembered something I had seen on the shelves.

Hacky sacks. There was a small array of them on a shelf amid the party supplies. I raced back over and picked one out for Rocky. With this packed safely into my bag I pushed my way out of the mini-mart.

The smoke enveloped me almost immediately. It had a sharp, metallic smell that hung in the back of my throat. I walked the bike down and out of the store, then took a moment to assess how much I could see.

Next to nothing.

Just smoke and the giant red glow of the burning city. This would have to be my guide. If I could keep it on my right side I should eventually make it through to the river. There were bridges there that would take me into the suburbs where the smoke might lift or maybe even disappear.

I set off slowly, walking the bike rather than riding. My torches cut a swathe through the immediate smoke, but simply found more and more ahead of it. Without proper sight I ran the front tyre along the side of a kerb to keep my bearings. It was slow and clunky. Often the kerb disappeared into a side street or driveway. Sometimes there were cars in the way. At one point I lost the kerb completely and fanned out until I hit the other side of the road.

As daylight approached I encountered a different problem. The glow of the fires was diminishing with the rising sun. All around me the smoke took on a yellowy orange. I had to squint through stinging eyes to make out the red of the city, until eventually I lost it altogether.

I stopped and stood on the road like a flashing neon loser. Without the city to guide me I was screwed. I turned in a circle and tried to find the red. There were two directions in which the light seemed brighter. One was the city, the other was the sunrise. But I couldn't tell them apart. Heading east towards the sun was what I wanted. That was where the river lay. But if I chose wrong I could end up heading straight for the fire. I lingered for a moment. My head was thumping and it was hard to concentrate. Suddenly I thought I could see a third light from behind me and got totally disorientated.

But it was definitely there. A beam of soft, steady light that was coming towards me. I felt all warm and drowsy – as if I was in some cliché death scene. There was a noise then too. A horn, long and hypnotic. When the light was too bright to keep looking I turned away and waited.

Abruptly the horn stopped. Instead I heard a door open and felt the lights dim down. There was a familiar ute idling in front of me.

'Ed?' I asked.

The door shut and there were footsteps.

'Nox?' said a voice that wasn't Ed's.

'Oh wow, it *is* you. Are you having a disco out here or something?'

A face appeared in front of me. Tanned and boyish. I recognised the smile, but it was made unfamiliar by smoke and a large pair of swimming goggles.

'Tommy?' I asked, confused.

'Oh sorry. Yeah it's me. Just with goggles for the smoke,' said Tommy.

'Isn't that Ed's car?' I asked.

'Man, good call. Yeah he lent it to me yesterday so I could drive up and film the city,' said Tommy.

'You found him?' I asked.

'Oh yeah. It took me forever. But yeah. I found him,' he replied. 'Are you alone out here?'

'Yeah,' I replied.

'Oh man. You should come in the car with me. This smoke will fuck you for sure,' said Tommy.

'I need to get back to Carousel.'

'To your Residency. Of course. It's the same for me. I need some time to edit this footage before tomorrow,' said Tommy.

'So can you take me in the car?' I asked.

'Oh yeah of course, Nox. Man, I would be a major ass to leave you out here alone with your disco bike,' said Tommy.

I choked up with relief and realised how sick I felt from all of the smoke. Tommy loaded my bike and bag into the back and we shut ourselves inside the cab. Then we crossed the river and headed, finally, for Carousel.

43

Tommy and I cruised out of the city as if it were any old day. The blanket of smoke and chaos faded like a dream in our rear-view mirrors. Ahead of us there was sunshine, suburbs and hills tinged with the baby green of spring. We took a highway eastwards and Tommy chatted away about some of his many adventures.

Fighting the bushfires alongside a drummer in the hills. Tracking Ed all the way south to the forests. Discovering a whole community down there and reuniting with Genna and the Aussie couple. Following Ed's trail back north in a golf cart amid the worst of the winter storms. Almost giving up when a ute pulled up beside him at a lonely southern beach. The explosion in the city and his final day of filming.

I could picture Tommy in all of it. The skinny kid with the smile. Out there alone against the elements. Like a figure cut from Tolkien or Hemingway, he was this world's great adventurer.

He asked me a bunch of questions about my own

journey since the hills, and I did my best to answer. At the end of it all Tommy shook his head for a while.

'Oh wow. That's a crazy story, Nox,' he said.

I took a breath and looked at my watch. It was midmorning on the first of September. We would be back at Carousel within the hour.

'Hey Tommy, do you remember our interviews in the hills?' I asked.

'Oh yeah sure,' said Tommy.

'I was wondering if you ever came across the Artist we talked about. A guy named Stuart?' I asked.

Tommy broke into an even bigger smile than normal.

'Man, I can't believe I didn't remember until just now. Stuart is living at this awesome beach house. I spent a night there on my way back to the city. He works on illustrations mostly,' said Tommy.

'Do you think it's the same guy?' I asked.

'That's what I was wondering when I met this guy. So I asked him all kinds of questions about the Disappearance. He said he was at a bus stop, just like you were, when he got picked up. I think that maybe there was a double up with the taxis or something.'

I exhaled. It was a relief to hear that Stuart had made it through. His story had weighed heavily on me for a while now. I liked the idea that he was by the beach somewhere, alone with his art as this whole thing intended. Tommy seemed chuffed to tell me too, but I don't know how much it really changed about my situation. My place in the Residency was still an accident.

'You're going home with us, man,' said Tommy.

'I don't know, Tommy,' I replied. 'I don't really have anything to present.'

'Oh come on. You told me all about your writing. It sounds cool I think,' said Tommy.

'Thanks,' I replied.

I was trying hard to stay positive. A lot of stuff had gone right since I left the casino. I had found the Finns and Georgia. Got them on the way back to their Residencies, along with a bunch of other Artists. And now, thanks to Tommy, I was just minutes away from making it back to Carousel myself. But I couldn't shake the Skywalker vision from my head. And now it came in conjunction with another. I am alone in Carousel. At first I'm fine. Chilled even. I wonder what the Finns are up to and think about some dinner. Then I look down at the barman's watch. The numbers are cold and certain. It's September third and my entire life stretches out before me into nothingness.

Tommy looked at me.

'It's okay to freak out I think,' he said. 'Most of the Artists I have met have freaked out. Some of them big time.'

'You never seem to freak out, Tommy,' I said.

'Oh yeah, sometimes I do. Like when I got all the way to the forests and Ed had already gone. I lost my shit on my bike man. That's why I ended up driving a stupid golf cart,' he said.

I couldn't help but laugh. Tommy joined me and barely missed a stranded bus.

'You know you're driving on the wrong side of the road, yeah?' I asked.

'Yeah but fuck it. In Denmark we drive on the right,' he replied.

I laughed again.

'So you think the Residencies will end tomorrow?' I asked.

'Oh yeah,' he replied.

'How come?' I asked.

'I think because of what happened when I met with Ed,' said Tommy.

'What happened?' I asked.

'The whole time I was looking for Ed I thought he would be like a superhero. Or at least a wizard with some magic or something. But when I finally met him at that beach he was just a normal guy. At first I was kind of bummed. Then I realised that if he was a superhero or a wizard, then all of this would just be bullshit like a comic or a movie,' said Tommy.

I nodded, but wasn't totally sure that I followed.

'When I found out he was just a normal guy who couldn't do magic or anything I thought, oh wow, this is a real situation and anything can happen. That's when I knew the Residencies would end,' said Tommy.

I smiled. Tommy had probably just made better sense of it than anybody.

We swung off the highway and into the suburbs surrounding Carousel. Tommy started fishing around for something on the dashboard.

'I was going to save this for when I drove back into the uni, but I think I want to listen to it now with you,' he said.

I watched as he loaded a CD into Ed's scratched up old player. There was a pause, then the cab filled with a pulsing, kinetic beat. Tommy beamed at me from behind the wheel.

'What is this?' I asked.

'Oh man, this is teenage wasteland!' said Tommy.

'What?' I asked.

'It's "Baba O'Riley" by The Who,' said Tommy, beaming.

He cranked the volume and lowered the windows. The bassline dropped like a giant rumble of thunder. I knew the song. An epic stadium anthem from the seventies. Adopted by generation after generation as an ironic celebration of their youth.

'This is our victory song, Nox!' roared Tommy.

He screamed out into the empty golden streets. I looked at him and laughed and let myself believe it was true. That we had indeed made it through the rollicking teenage wasteland. Together we sang and shouted and swung dramatically across the barren car parks of Carousel.

44

We found Taylor and Lizzy outside of the centre, surrounded by pit bulls.

Their bikes and bags lay in a savaged line along the car park. Sophie and Chessboard were gone. The Finns were alone and backed up against the long, stark wall of Target. Just a solitary can of bug spray stood between them and the wheezing Bulls.

'Oh shit,' said Tommy, stopping the music.

They were still all the way across the car park from us.

'Floor it, Tommy!' I said.

He shifted gears and hurtled us towards them. I watched as Taylor ran out of spray and desperately threw the can at the Bulls. They ignored it and edged closer.

'We're going to be too late,' I whispered.

'Oh shit. Do you hear that noise? I think I busted the engine maybe,' said Tommy.

Something was roaring outside of the cab. It was big and mechanical. Taylor and Lizzy looked up and saw us racing towards them.

Abruptly the Bulls paused, then scattered like tiny, frightened puppies.

Tommy hit the brakes and we shuddered to a stop. The Finns were gazing skyward. I stepped from the car and did the same.

A shimmering white jet was banking through the morning sky. Dappled across its tail was the iconic red maple leaf. The wheels were up as it rose gracefully away from us. We watched in awe until it blinked, then vanished into blue.

The suburb was quiet once more.

I looked at Lizzy. We all looked at Lizzy.

Her head was down and her eyes closed. Taylor put a hand on her shoulder.

'Lizzy?' she whispered.

Lizzy opened her eyes and looked at her sister. She had a smile I hadn't seen for a long time.

'I saw the rest of it,' she said.

'What was she doing? Do you remember it now?' asked Taylor, riveted.

'She was waiting for us after our first tour of the States. Remember? We arrived back at the terminal and for the first time ever there were fans there waiting for us,' said Lizzy.

'Oh yeah! I remember,' said Taylor.

'Mum was there too, but we couldn't see her at first. Then you spotted her hovering behind them with this look on her face. The same one she has when she sees a happy dog with those wheel things for legs,' said Lizzy.

Taylor nodded and blinked away a couple of tears.

'She was freaking out, but so happy for us. Then we yelled her over and she met all the fans,' said Lizzy.

'They ended up being more interested in her than they were in the band,' said Taylor.

They laughed together for the first time in forever. I exhaled and felt a small weight lift from all of us.

The Finns took stock for a moment, before turning to greet us. They looked tired and haggard and, oddly, kind of young.

'Hey Nox. Hey Tommy,' said Taylor.

'Oh hi Taylor. Hi Lizzy,' said Tommy.

This made us all laugh. We shared some hugs, then Taylor stepped back to look me over.

'See, I knew you were awesome all along,' she said.

I smiled and thought back to our chat in the projection room all those months ago.

Lizzy joined her and gave my hair a shake. A shower of ash spilled out.

'Whoa,' said Lizzy.

'Sorry,' I said. 'I got caught out in the smoke again.'

'Are the other guys okay? We were freaking out when the city went up. Taylor wanted to ride her fixie over there with a fire hydrant,' said Lizzy.

Taylor shoved her.

'You did,' said Lizzy.

'They're fine. Back at their Residencies,' I replied.

'I was on my way here when it happened. Then I ran into Tommy.'

Tommy was standing beside me smiling.

'You were just cruising around the city in your car?' asked Taylor.

'Oh no,' laughed Tommy. 'I just borrowed the car to take some footage of the fire.'

'It's Ed Carrington's car,' I added. 'He and Tommy are mates.'

The Finns and I shared a smile.

'Of course they are,' said Taylor.

'Is Sophie okay?' I asked.

'Yeah. We dropped her off yesterday. Before those fucking Bulls started chasing us,' said Taylor.

'Man, they were totally scared by that plane,' said Tommy. 'It was an aurora jet, yeah?'

'Yeah,' replied Taylor.

'Oh wow. Ed told me about those. I wish I could have filmed it,' said Tommy.

I suddenly remembered that Chessboard wasn't with them.

'Where is Chess?' I asked.

Taylor looked at Lizzy and waited to see if she would answer.

'He's fine,' said Taylor, eventually. 'Lizzy let him go last night.'

My heart sank.

'Go where?' I asked.

'Back to wherever he was when all of this happened,' replied Taylor. 'So maybe he can go home like the rest of us.'

This caught me out. I hadn't stopped to consider whether animals such as Chess might be able to get home.

I looked at Lizzy. The goodbye was still raw.

'Was he okay?' I asked her.

Lizzy sniffed and nodded.

'I think he wanted to go. Chess was always so clingy, but ever since we crossed over the freeway he started acting kinda restless and aloof,' said Lizzy.

'Last night he just stopped at an intersection and wouldn't follow us anymore. Something inside him wanted to go south. Eventually we just knelt down and gave him a ruffle. Then he took off into the night like a freakin' dire wolf.'

'So cool,' whispered Tommy.

We all took a breath and looked around at the quiet, brooding centre.

'Should we check this place out?' asked Taylor.

'I think Tommy needs to get going,' I replied.

'Right now?' asked Lizzy.

'Oh yeah. I have to get to uni and back up this footage, then do some editing and meet up with Genna I guess,' said Tommy.

'You're a busy guy, Tommy,' said Taylor.

He nodded and smiled. Taylor and Lizzy gave him a

big hug, one after the other.

'You get back to that library first and foremost, yeah?' said Lizzy. 'No more cruising around looking for adventures.'

Tommy laughed. I hugged him, too.

'Thanks for the lift.'

'Oh man, it was no problem. Do you want your disco bike out of the back?' he asked.

Taylor and Lizzy raised their eyebrows in unison.

'It's cool,' I replied. 'Just the bag.'

Tommy took it from the tray and handed it to me.

'See you back in Perth, Nox,' he said.

I nodded and we shared a look that the Finns probably noticed.

Tommy climbed back into the ute and took off with a big smiling wave. As he pulled out on the highway we heard the beginning of 'Baba O'Riley' bouncing back out into the suburbs.

Carousel had lay dormant and steadfast since our departure. Too far from any concentration of Artists to be ransacked. Too creepy to be entered by anyone travelling solo. Fatefully sheltered from the fires and storms that had chased us across the city. It welcomed us back without fanfare or emotion. I felt nostalgia, but it wasn't akin to the warmness of a childhood bedroom or grandparent's garden. More similar to how I felt seeing my old high school. There were good memories, but also bad ones, and confusing ones, and a whole swirling mixture of others. And time moved slowly there, as it always had in Carousel.

We moved out of our original entrance into the hall between the east end and the west.

'Pretty weird,' said Lizzy.

'Pretty weird,' I nodded.

'Should we go see Rocky?' asked Taylor.

'Definitely,' I replied. 'But I need to talk to you guys about something first.'

'Okay,' said Taylor, pensively.

We took a seat at an island couch and I got a flashback to the first time we met. I had been nervous then, as I was now. The Finns looked at me and waited.

'Okay, so, none of us really know what is going to happen tomorrow, right?' I asked.

The two of them nodded.

'But if the portals do open, and it's only Artists with work that can go through, there's a chance I might not be coming with you,' I said.

'Why?' asked Taylor, immediately.

'I guess there are a couple of reasons. Firstly, the taxi that brought me here was meant for another Artist. An illustrator named Stuart. Tommy has met this guy, and thankfully he made it through okay, but I still bullshitted the driver that morning. It wasn't me he was supposed to be sheltering,' I said.

Lizzy took a breath and thought this over.

'What else?' asked Taylor.

'I don't have any work to present,' I replied.

'What about your short stories?' asked Lizzy.

'They're back at the beach house,' I replied.

Taylor stared at me. Lizzy groaned.

'You forgot them!?' said Taylor.

'No. He left them there,' said Lizzy. 'Didn't you, Nox?'

I nodded. Taylor shot up and stormed across the dusty floor.

'They don't matter, Taylor. Those stories were just some stuff I played around with to kill time. You know that I could have left here at any time. It was the same for Rocky,' I said.

Lizzy was quiet next to me.

'I'm just not an Artist like you guys. I'm not even sure if I want to be anymore,' I said.

'You still don't get it, do you?' said Lizzy, quietly.

Taylor stopped and looked at her sister.

'Get what?' I asked.

'It doesn't matter whether you want to be an Artist or not. You don't get a choice one way or the other. We are what we are, Nox. Some people just decide to fight against it,' said Lizzy.

She was staring at me like only a Finn could.

'You're a writer, Nox. Both of us have seen that. And it's not an easier life, or a cooler life. It's just a life like any other.'

I looked away and felt my conviction fading. I thought

back to those long hours in the mini-mart. When the world was crumbling and writing had somehow sheltered me through.

'You're writing something tonight,' said Taylor. 'I don't care if you want to or not. You can do it for me and Lizzy. And Rocky. And those guys in that boat,' she said.

I took a breath.

'Okay,' I replied.

Eventually Lizzy put a hand on my shoulder.

'We're rooting for you, Nox. We've only ever been rooting for you.'

45

The novel still had a way to go, but I had reconnected with it during my time at the mini-mart and, with one night to go before the end of the Residencies, it was the only thing I could really see myself writing. So there I was, sitting at a table facing the glass-filled east entrance, Rocky's kooky garden beside me, the final day of Perth's bizzaro hiatus fading into darkness above us.

I had showered and eaten and changed into some clothes sourced by Lizzy. Taylor had made me espresso and told me to radio whenever I needed more. The two of them were undoubtedly mad at me, but beneath this I felt their support and belief. I think they knew that my decisions had stopped being driven by fear. There had been other motivations, and maybe some that weren't totally admirable, but the world had thrown a whole bunch of stuff at me, and, for the most part, I felt as though I had responded. I think the Finns were mainly mad at me for not wanting to make it home for myself. Now that I was back at Carousel, and with the deadline looming, I realised that I really, really did.

So I sat there with my receipt books and a notepad and I wrote, and I wrote, and I wrote. It wasn't like a flood or an avalanche, or anything remotely poetic – just a steady flow of sentences and paragraphs. Each one maintaining a tone and building on the last. No tinkering or second-guessing. Just the continual forward momentum of a character negotiating what, to me at least, felt like a complicated and interesting world.

The writing felt like a job, but in a good way. I wasn't waiting for something brilliant to manifest and define me as a true Artist or offer membership to some illusive, imaginary club. I was simply using the skills I had to write the best sentences, paragraphs and chapters that I could. And it felt about as natural as anything I could remember.

Taylor and Lizzy surfaced at different points throughout the night. Taylor kitted out in a fresh hoodie and jeans alongside her trusty and nostalgic All Stars. I hadn't known Taylor before Carousel, but couldn't help but think that she would be returning as a different person. She held a confidence now that seemed greater than her stage presence or celebrity. For Taylor this surfaced now in her calm and in her silence. I think that meeting Sophie may have been a part of this. Their relationship had enabled her to solidify who she was, and also who she wasn't. As I watched her quietly tending to Rocky's garden in the early hours of the morning I realised that Taylor Finn had been as fragile as anyone to have lived in this mammoth concrete oasis.

Lizzy was a coiled bundle of hope and excitement. For two years I had been in awe of her patience and acceptance. Nobody had played ball in this world like Lizzy Finn. But now, swapping from black jeans to blue, then back again, she was like a jittery kid waiting to cash in her savings. The aurora jet that saved them from the Bulls had also reminded Lizzy of her love for her former life. Lizzy was the indie rock star at the peak of her relevance. She had the whip-smart girlfriend, the cool mum, the warehouse apartment and the calendar full of travel. Two years away from these things in the apocalyptic vacuum of Perth had been akin to a lifetime. Now Lizzy buzzed like a teenager who knew their secret list of hopes and dreams had somehow already manifested, and that each hour was steadily ticking them closer.

But these very same hours were dragging me towards a lonely abyss.

I had written a lot. More than I thought possible, really. But above me now, where I refused to look, was the violet glow of morning.

I raced onwards, while Taylor and Lizzy hovered nervously in my periphery. The Disappearance happened two years ago at six fifty-two am. Suddenly the numbers on my lucky barman's watch read six forty.

I finished the paragraph and the chapter, and sat back

to take stock. The Finns watched me intently as the sun peeked its rays across the floor. I took a long, steadying breath.

The novel wasn't finished.

I was close, but all out of time.

'Nox?' asked Taylor.

I looked at her. Then Lizzy. I shook my head.

Lizzy bombed towards me.

'Pack it up. Bring it with you anyhow,' she said.

I hesitated as Lizzy grabbed my backpack and zipped it open. Together we piled the notepads and books into my backpack. Taylor teetered behind us with tears in her eyes.

'Get the bikes!' said Lizzy.

Taylor spun around and wheeled over the three new mountain bikes that had stood ready through the night. I shouldered the backpack and we climbed aboard. Rocky's garden sat tranquil and awesome beside us. His new hacky sack resting neatly within the foliage. The three of us stole a final look at it, then raced down the hall for the door that marked our arrival.

46

We stood outside on a narrow concrete walkway. The morning was cold, but bright with sunshine. Taylor's hair tickled past my forehead. Lizzy's breathing was fast and shallow in my ear. All of our eyes were on the barman's watch.

Eventually, inevitably, the one turned into a two.

A breeze touched our faces. It was warm and nostalgic. As if everyone we ever knew had just brushed past us.

For a moment nobody moved. Then Lizzy lifted her head and looked around at the walkway. Taylor and I followed.

Nothing had changed.

We glanced at each other, then pulled on the door into Carousel. It opened without issue and we stepped back inside.

Lizzy led us down the small corridor and out into the hall. It was silent and empty. Abandoned stores lined the walkway as far as we could see. Familiar islands blipped up selling juices and mobile phone covers. Barren couches sat ready for tired shoppers and staff on their lunch break. But nowhere were there people.

I noticed Lizzy's shoulders slump just a fraction. 'We should have been inside. Not out on that walkway,' she whispered.

'Wait,' said Taylor. 'Look at the shelves.'

I followed her gaze to the island beside us. The fridge was neatly stocked with waters and soft drinks. The counter lined with jars of fresh cookies.

'Holy crap. The stores are closed, too,' said Lizzy. 'Aren't they!?'

She was right. The shops beside us were closed over with transparent rollers. I turned and looked down the length of the hall. It was the same all the way along. Carousel had been wide open when we arrived, not closed like it was now.

'Do you have your album?' I asked.

Taylor reached into her pocket and pulled out a small red USB stick.

'Check your bag,' said Lizzy.

I pulled it off and unzipped the front. My messy pile of unfinished book lay inside.

'It's still there,' I replied.

'Oh my god,' said Lizzy, hopping excitedly.

'Wait. Shouldn't there be people in here? Security or something?' asked Taylor.

'Let's go to the dome,' said Lizzy.

We raced down the glossy halls of our weird old home. Past Myer and Dymocks and JB Hi-Fi, and a dozen other places where we had spent so many days. We slowed as the corridor opened up before us. Crystal morning light radiated out from the dome ahead. It was ethereal and almost beautiful, the way it funnelled down and spread throughout the centre. The open dome meant that the outside world would always be a part of Carousel. It had seemed stupid for as long as I had known about it, but standing there with the Finns it suddenly made simple, perfect sense.

I looked at the Finns beside me and felt as grateful with the world as I had ever done. Taylor turned my way and was about to say something when a voice broke in.

'What are you doing in here?'

We jumped and turned to see a middle-aged security guard walking towards us.

None of us said anything right away.

'Hey?' said the guy.

'Hey, yeah sorry, we were just about to leave,' said Lizzy.

The guy looked us over in a way that wasn't super reassuring.

'What's in your bag?' he asked me.

'Nothing. Just some notepads,' I replied.

He grunted and unclipped his radio.

'You can wait here for the police,' he said.

'Whoa, it's cool man,' said Taylor. 'We just came inside by mistake.'

'Sure,' he said.

It was pretty condescending. He lifted up his radio again.

'What a dick,' said Lizzy.

'What did you say?' asked the guy, stepping forward.

It wasn't exactly the welcome home we had dreamt about.

'She said you were a dick, arsehole.'

The four of us turned around to the source of the noise. Rachel was standing across the hall with a cleaning bucket and a face full of attitude.

'Holy shit,' whispered Taylor.

The security guard looked at her disdainfully.

'They came in through the back door, which you fuckwits left open again after your smoko last night,' said Rachel.

The guard hesitated. There was a noticeable shift in his demeanour.

'You wanna radio that through?' asked Rachel. 'Go on. Tell them how the whole place has been open for half the night.'

'Whatever,' he replied, eventually.

The guard wandered past us and pretended like all of a sudden he didn't give a crap. Rachel glared after him until he was lost from view.

The Finns were wide-eyed beside me. Lizzy mouthed *what the hell!* Taylor shrugged.

'Hey Rachel,' I said.

She looked us over.

'Carrington was right, eh,' she grunted.

'I didn't think you were coming back?' I asked.

'I wasn't. Just ran outta shampoo,' she replied.

'Did you just make a joke, Rachel?' asked Taylor.

'Typical Artists. Think you're the only ones in the world with ideas,' replied Rachel.

Taylor and Lizzy broke into laughter.

'What about your fisherman?' I asked.

'Didn't show,' she replied.

'Shit. I'm sorry, Rachel,' I said.

'He's a man. What do you expect,' she replied.

I looked at her and tried to gauge her reaction to all that had happened over the past two years. As usual Rachel was either unreadable or unaffected. Or both.

She took a folded-up gossip magazine out of her sweater. It was open to a page where the Finns were pictured next to Kanye at some awards ceremony. She shoved it at a confused looking Taylor and Lizzy, along with a pen.

'Make sure it's neat. Nobody's going to bid on some primary school scribble,' said Rachel.

Taylor and Lizzy were on the edge of hysterics, but played along without a fuss. Rachel inspected the signatures and stuffed the magazine back in her jacket.

She picked up her bucket and headed back over to the toilets.

'I would clear out of here if I was you. They're not all

as stupid as that last guy,' she said over her shoulder.

'Okay. Thanks Rachel,' said Lizzy.

She disappeared into the toilets. The three of us were alone once again.

'I mean, the lady just redefines weird, doesn't she,' said Taylor.

Lizzy sighed and nodded. I was still trying to figure out what had just happened.

Rachel's presence in Carousel meant that Patrons had made it back also. I was stoked for her. She had kids here and I never totally bought into her happiness at the casino. Rachel deserved a shot at her old life as much as anyone. But it also meant that the writing in my bag hadn't been what had saved me. It finally confirmed what I had suspected from the start. That people like Taylor and Lizzy, and all the other Artists I had met along the way, were different to me.

For a moment the gravity of this felt like it might swallow me completely.

Then I felt the weight of the backpack on my shoulders. And I remembered that it was heavy with words that I had written. I was confident that if I sat down and tried hard enough, I would be able to write more of these words. Maybe this didn't qualify me as an Artist right away. Maybe it never would. But suddenly it felt like something that could be a part of my life. I had always thought of living and creating art as separate endeavours. But if my time in the Prix de Perth had proven anything it was that the two were irrevocably linked. Art alone wasn't enough to sustain the world, that was clear. But life without art seemed equally impossible. I thought of Taylor and Lizzy funnelling their grief over Rocky into a brand new album. Of three lonely souls taking solace in a nightly lightshow over the city. A cleaner dealing with the loss of her children thanks to fantasy TV. A film student surviving peril after peril with only his camera to guide him. And of those days in the mini-mart when the world had closed over and I had nothing but my writing.

Suddenly all of the stuff that had been freaking me out for so long kind of drifted away. So long as I could write, I felt like I could live. And nothing else seemed to matter.

When I came to, Taylor and Lizzy were both looking at me.

'You okay?' asked Taylor, seriously.

I nodded.

Lizzy put a hand on my shoulder and gave it a squeeze.

'Can we get out of this place?' I asked.

'Totally,' replied Lizzy.

The three of us cut across the dome and made our way to the front doors. Lizzy took the handle and pushed it open dramatically. Taylor and I smiled and followed her out onto the walkway. We stopped and looked back through the glass at the quiet, empty centre. Beside the door were a neatly packaged stack of flyers. They looked out of place. Not the type of thing you would expect to see left at the front entrance of a shopping centre.

Taylor reached down and took one. Lizzy watched her curiously.

'What is it?' she asked.

Taylor held it up to us. In a simple, elegant font were the letters:

P

d

P

Beneath this it read *An Exhibition*. There was a venue and a date and everything.

'Is that what I think it is?' asked Lizzy.

Taylor nodded with a pretty wry smile. 'Wow. This place,' she sighed.

'Do you think we will be able to play the album?' asked Lizzy.

There was a hint of doubt in her gaze. As if she still wasn't sure if Taylor would want to.

'Are you kidding? We're going to rock the hell outta that thing,' replied Taylor.

Lizzy beamed and skipped over to the car park. Taylor held onto the flyer and we followed her out to the front of the building. A wash of strange noises filled the air around us. The hum of early-morning traffic. The beep and whirr of industry. The chatter of voices from a nearby park.

I could hear something else, too. A kind of clapping noise from somewhere behind us. I turned and looked back at the towering hulk of Carousel. In the distance a silhouette shifted against the pastel white walls. A kid was flipping a skateboard around a ramp outside Target. I stood and watched him for a moment. He was tall and a little stooped, but the kid had some moves.

'Holy hell,' whispered Lizzy Finn beside me.